STICKY VALVES

BOOK ONE OF THE SADDLEWORTH
VAMPIRE SERIES

Sticky Valves by Angela Blythe
Book 1 of the Saddleworth Vampire Series.

First Edition.

Please contact me for details of future books at www.angelablythe.com

Published by Willow Publishers.

Cover Illustration and Design Copyright © 2017 by Dark Grail
https://www.etsy.com/uk/shop/DarkGrail

Editing by A.S.Blythe

This is a work of fiction. Names, characters, places, and incidents either are the products of the author's imagination or are used fictitiously. Any resemblance to actual persons, living or dead, businesses, companies, events, or locales is entirely coincidental.

Contents

Sticky Valves

1 - The Chase

He needed to run and run fast. He didn't know in what direction or for how long, but he needed to run.

They say that in times of emergency the body sometimes allows people to do acts of superhuman strength and he hoped that it was going to be true for him. After ten days locked in a cellar with no food and barely any water, he wasn't in the best condition to be doing this and if he was truthful he never was much for athletic activity but he needed to run as fast and as far as possible.

His feet were sore, his shins cut by branches and shrubs, but he had to put this all out of his mind. That thing would be on his trail soon if he wasn't already behind him and, if he was caught, he was in no doubt that he would be dead this time.

Why the hell had this happened to him? What had he done to deserve this? Just a night out with the lads, a few too many beers and he woke up in that cellar.

The noises in that house...the coppery smell of blood and rotten things. Hours and hours in the dark and then...then...*he* would come down, and just spend hours watching him. Walking round and round him in the dark. He didn't attack, or speak, or touch him. And there were no breathing sounds, only sounds of dry lips being licked with a rasping tongue. Then he would go, silently, up the stairs. And shortly after the noises would start again. Women, men, children. Muffled voices, laughing. Screaming. Heavy noises on the floorboards above him. His laughing. Then silence.

He was enjoying the chase. This particle of meat, of sustenance intrigued him. He didn't know why, but it gave him immense pleasure to smell the fear of this man. To taunt him in the dark, then observe him. With a watering mouth he would go down to the cellar, and watch him getting thinner and thinner. He never was a fan of fatty blood. This game, this exercise will give it the flavour of adrenaline and oh, how he loved that. Did this man really think he had escaped? No one got the better of him. If he escaped it was what *he* had planned.

The hunter was thrilled to have discovered this wonderful area. These particular villages. Isolated, northern settlements, whether on the moors, or nestled in valleys, were bathed in fresh air, warm sunshine and cool rain. The people, mainly interbreeding with the other villagers, had produced the sweetest meat, the most exquisite blood he had ever tasted. He would herd them like cows. Some would be breeders. Most would be feeders. Gone were the times he would have to feed on dirty tasteless humans. Like eating dog food, to a human.

The monster continued to track the man. Sometimes he would be behind him. Sometimes in front. This was so easy. He had decided he was going to slit the man behind the knees, one at a time. Put his mouth over the lovely hole and suck on the nectar. The sucky hole, his favourite. He would then put his long fingers inside the cut, wiggle it open a bit more. Then he would get his tongue deep inside the flesh. Nothing was going to deny him this.

He ran on, his lungs burned. He was going to get away. There was no sign of his captor. He thought he saw a light to his left through the trees. It was a distance away, but it looked like car headlights. He must be near a road. He had done it. He was going to get away. He strove on, dug deep and ran even faster.

'Simon, if you sing that bloody song one more time I am going to stick that microphone where the sun does not shine'. The bus roared with laughter and applause at Barry's statement. One rendition of the Queen hit *We are the Champions'* was probably acceptable, but after doing it five times, it would wear down even the most ardent Queen fan.

Simon put the microphone down to even more applause than he got for his singing, and found his way back to his place on the bus. The peace and quiet was not to last long though, grabbing the newly released mic, Gary launched into one of his usual speeches.

'Ladies, Gentlemen and members of the committee'. More roars from the captive audience.

'We are again victorious in the march of Friarmere Bands quest for glory. The winners of the Eckington Brass Trophy for best overall band, best march and best soloist.'

'Don't forget a cheque for a Thousand Pounds,' interrupted Ernie Cooper from the back of the bus.

'Aye, if we don't all drink it first Ernie,' replied Simon.

'Anyway I think it's only fitting that to celebrate our landmark victory we should all raise a glass or a can and sing the Friarmere Band Song.' Most people, knowing that the 'Friarmere Band Song' only actually consisted of singing the word Friarmere repeatedly to some football based chant could only raise a half-hearted cheer. This could actually be worse than listening to *We are the Champions.*

Simon got back out of his seat with his hands in the air to dance around to the Friarmere song. He was trying to pull some of the lady players out of their seats to dance with him, but was having no takers.

Ernie Cooper looked out of the window with a heavier heart than most, he loved 'banding' and had been part of a Brass Band for most of his life. He actually couldn't remember a time in his sixty five years when he wasn't involved in a local band in some form or another, but at times like this he wished he was home with his feet up and watching a film. Even travelling back on the train would have been better than being trapped on a bus with forty, mostly drunk people, whose ideal form of entertainment seemed to be something akin to bear baiting in the middle ages. It wasn't their fault he thought to himself, he wasn't much for popular entertainment and his wife always reminded him that in *Planes, Trains and Automobiles* he was more the Steve Martin character singing *Three Coins in a Fountain* whilst everyone else was wishing he would shut up and sing the theme to the *Flintstones.*

Still it had been a good contest and the band had won convincingly and in the end that was what it was all about. All the weeks of practice, tantrums and heartache had paid off and they had another trophy for the cabinet and some more money in the funds.

I'm nearly at the road. I'm safe. He ran faster. He couldn't miss his chance.

'Jesus what was that?' Said the coach driver, undoing his seat belt and activating the hazard warning lights on the coach's dashboard.

'Simon? Simon?' Lynn Cooper was up out of her seat and moving towards Simon who was now a crumpled mass in the foot well of the coach.

'Is he ok?' He said looking at Simon

'I don't know,' Lynn replied. 'He certainly has had a bad knock.'

Ernie got up and grabbed the mic.

'Right everyone calm down, it looks like we have hit something'

'Was it an animal? Oh god what if it's a deer?' Sue said.

'We don't know, I am going out to look now and I need everyone to stay calm and stay in the bus. I don't need any more accidents.'

'Ernie! I am coming with you, I am the only one here with traffic management experience.'

Ernie looked at Michael Thompson and had to stop himself shaking his head. Of all the people on the bus he was the last person he needed getting in the way and unfortunately the last person who would listen to him either.

'What traffic management experience? You've never been a policeman or even a Special Constable.'

'No, but I was a steward for three years on the Yorkshire Show, I have directed more traffic round more obstacles than anyone on this bus and that includes our resident policeman Keith. And before you say anything, Keith has passed out, he couldn't direct anything at the moment.'

'Look we haven't seen a car for the last ten minutes, I don't think we need anyone to bother with traffic management. Lets just see what we hit and then get moving.'

'It's the empty roads you need more management for Ernie. Empty road means more speed, lack of concentration next thing you know, BANG! We've got a Ford Fiesta welded onto the back of the bus.'

'And I suppose you standing in the middle of the road waving your hands about like an idiot will stop that will it?'

Ernie looked at Thompson, he knew that nothing short of a cricket bat would stop him getting off the coach and parading around directing traffic like he was on duty outside Buckingham Palace. How he could cope with this man being on the committee for another nine months was beyond him. Thompson had an opinion about everything, had done everything and was one of those people who never stopped trying to tell you about it. Sadly though the truth was that Michael Thompson had done nothing with his life, still lived at home with his younger brother and with all the recent closures in his factory was looking at redundancy at forty and spending the rest of his life claiming benefit. If there was a picture in the National Art Gallery entitled 'Loser,' Michael Thompson's face would be staring out at you.

'Ok, ok but don't wander off and if something hits you, we aren't picking you up, you stay where you land.'

'Charming,' muttered Thompson as he moved past Ernie and tried to get a handle on the situation, that he was sure only he could manage. As he got off the bus he looked up and down the road. Total darkness not even a glimpse of a set of headlights. Ernie was right, there were no cars likely to come here at this time of night. Still he was off the bus now and it was time to take charge, maybe this was the moment that he would be hailed as a hero, the man that saved the day.

He turned right and went around to the front of the bus where the driver was examining the headlights and the panels, cursing loudly.

'All ok?' He asked.

'Jesus!' The bus driver exclaimed. 'You nearly gave me a heart attack. What the hell does it look like? I've got a smashed headlight and indicator, lots of blood and a dented panel. My heart rate is going through the roof and I need a cigarette and a stiff drink.'

'Anything I can do?' Thompson asked.

Before the bus driver could respond Ernie came to join them.

'I thought you were directing traffic?' He said to Thompson.

'Directing Traffic? On this road?' The bus driver sounded irritated and close to the edge, his voice rising to quite a high pitch by the time he got to *'road'*.

'Nothing to direct at the moment,' Thompson responded.

'Look, just go and position yourself somewhere just in case or get back on the bus. I don't want to be here any longer than we have to be, Simon might need to be in hospital.'

'But....'

'Just do it Michael. Do something useful or get out of the way.'

Michael stared at Ernie for a moment. One day he thought, one day I will be Chairman then what will you do? You've only got nine months then you are up for the vote and I am going to win that vote, I'll make you clean the instruments and arrange the uniforms. I'll get my own conductor or maybe I'll conduct the band myself, nothing will stop Friarmere when I am Chairman. In fact I will call myself President of the Band. He turned and walked back around the bus, consoling himself with his new plan, never thinking that every single person on that bus would rather vote for anyone but him in any coming election. But again Michael Thompson never let reality come between him and a plan.

After ten minutes of searching Ernie and the bus driver could see no sign of what they had hit.

'If it was a sheep I'll bloody kill that Farmer Kipling,' said the Driver

'He lets them buggers roam all over the bloody place and you can never trace them back to him, he never marks them.'

Ernie looked at the marks on the bus.

'Bloody big sheep then to have hit the bus up here? Has Kipling got many six foot sheep?'

'Bounce.'

'What?'

'Bounce, hit something like that and it can bounce, comes back at you much higher.'

'Bollocks, so now Kipling has been breeding rubber sheep has he?'

'Look its true, remember John Gardner?'

'The biker who died a while back?'

'Yeah, he came over the moors one night on one of those wide handle custom jobs. Wasn't going all that fast from what they can tell, hit a sheep and was found next morning dead, bike halfway down the moor covered in sheep shit and him dead on the road with a dead sheep on his chest. Bounce, dead sheep knocked him off his bike on the rebound. Well known round these parts.'

'Sounds like a load of old sheep shit to me. So what do we do now, don't want to be here much longer especially if whatever we hit is still bouncing.'

'I reckon we get going?'

Ernie climbed back onto the bus.

'How's Simon?' He asked Lynn.

'Better, he's still a bit groggy and he won't be singing for the rest of the night but I don't think it's serious.'

'Wont be singing? Every cloud. It's true what they say.'

He picked up the mic.

'Right everyone, we are finally on our way. We have looked everywhere and can find no sign of anything we could have hit. We strongly believe that the animal, whatever it was, has gone further into the woods and to be frank I am not going anywhere near there in the dark. The driver is going to call this into the police as soon as we get back and we have left a marker so we can find this location again if we have to.'

'Isn't he going to get cold?' Asked Tony.

'Isn't who going to get cold?'

'Thompson, I take it he is the marker?'

'Isn't he on the bus?'

'No, not seen him since he left to do his Traffic Management'

Ernie put his head in his hands, Thompson bloody Thompson. I should just drive off he thought. A bouncing sheep might kill him if I'm lucky. He slowly lifted he head from his hands and got off the coach again.

'Michael!' No response.

'Michael Bloody Thompson you have 5 seconds to get on this bus or we are leaving you here.' No response.

Ernie got his phone out, he hoped he had a signal out here. The hills often had a tendency to play havoc with mobile reception, at least that's what the mobile companies told him. He pressed the wake button and the screen glowed into life. Scrolling through his contacts to the letter T and then to a contact labelled *Tosser,* he pressed the call button.

Putting the phone to his ear, he could hear it ringing. After five rings someone answered. Well it was more like heavy breathing than an answer

'Michael?' More breathing, if a little quicker.

'Michael its Ernie, where the hell are you?'

'In the woods.' It was Thompson but he sounded breathless.

'What the hell are you doing in the woods? You are supposed to be directing non-existent traffic on the bloody road!'

'I saw something, no, I thought I saw something.'

'What? An animal? Was it something we hit?'

'It was nothing, I'm coming back,' the call ended.

Five minutes later, Thompson appeared at the edge of the woods. Frankly he looked like he had been dragged through them backwards, he wasn't a snappy dresser but it was fair to say he was looking pretty rough by the time he reached the coach.

'What the hell happened to you?' Said Ernie.

Thompson didn't look at him, he kept his head down. 'I told you I saw something.'

The monster had dragged the body off the road. Some idiot had followed them but he had dealt with that situation. This wasn't how he had planned it. This wasn't how he had planned it at all. He watched them talking. Fools. They had ruined his game and now they would pay. Or play. He laughed quietly. Tomorrow, he would move them onto his chessboard. This is where his plan would really start. His plan to conquer this land of blood cows. They had put themselves into the game really, and would all live to regret this night. Or die regretting it, that option sounded better. He watched the bus as it drove off. The board on the back said 'Friarmere Band' and had a phone number underneath.

He then squatted over the man who lay on his front, and sunk his teeth into the back of the neck. He began to feed.

2 - Friarmere

Late October in Saddleworth. A collection of scattered villages that skirt round the edge of the Pennines. Arguments still rage on whether they are in Yorkshire or Lancashire. Red or white rose.

The air is clean and cool, the trees are golden and red, and their leaves will drop any day now. Saddleworth lies in a valley 7 miles long. Cut out by the River Tame, long before man came to walk the land. He has been around a long, long time too. Stone Age Man was here, Roman roads run through, even a church that started its life in the 1200's. Many ghosts walk its fields, its hills, and its buildings. This area is so old it is mentioned in the Domesday Book.

Farms sit on the hillsides of this valley. The meadows are lush and well watered from the many days of rain. The rugged moorlands at the top of the hills are far too inhospitable to sustain animals and crops. Vast and desolate, one should always stick to the footpaths. Rocky, with thick clumps of heather and peat, these hills are often covered in fog. They will always be watching over this valley, as if to say, one day we will claim you back into our wilderness.

Old walls, parts of which have crumbled to a litter of stones, show where ancient boundaries lie. Sometimes an aged milestone can still be read, but usually to a place that no longer exists.

Within these areas are small collections of trees, hidden paths, caves, and ancient dry riverbeds. Plenty of places to hide.

It was during the Industrial Revolution that Saddleworth's economy and population really grew. The woolen mills and later cotton mills meant that this area sustained its workers well. Giant seething black buildings, with tall chimneys became the centre of these villages. And as these mills grew in size, so did the amount of small dwellings clustered around them. The great buildings yawned in the morning, sucking all the workers in with its first breath and then, in the late afternoon, tired and ready for a few hours rest it disgorged them back out on to the streets. The railway and the Huddersfield canal cut through this valley taking goods east, over the Pennines into Yorkshire or west, into Manchester and on to Liverpool.

The houses traditionally are built in grey stone, the same as many in Yorkshire. These workers houses run along the valley within these villages. Roads came and more houses were built. Modern larger homes with better facilities. They spread upwards from the arteries of this community, up the hills, claiming their right to live in the fields and meadows and trees.

With the decline of the textile industry, the vast mills lay empty and hollow. Some to be demolished, some to be converted. Over time the filth and grime of the mill years, the smoke and stains, have been cleansed from the buildings. But they are not forgotten.

The modern Saddleworth's industry is its heritage and culture. The tourism industry is booming. The original little grey houses, now have brightly painted doors and window boxes. Those old dirty streets sparkle, with new coffee shops, a museum and gift shops. Boutiques and delicatessens, a quaint post office. They have it all. Pubs with real ale and open fires, a civic hall, which hosts many famous names. There is a cricket club, a golf club and a rugby club. So many festivals, Brass Band, Morris Men, Canal, Folk, Music. Always a reason to visit here. Thousands of people descend on Saddleworth on 'Whit Friday' to watch the Church Processions of Witness. Waving colourful banners, and each with its own brass band to herald it on its way.

The centre of this community, the largest of the villages, is Friarmere. Named after the Black Friars that lived in the Grange that sits high and dark on the hill above the village. The highest mountainous Pennines border the north and south of this village. A deep quarry cut into the side of the north face. Many dark deeds have been done here. To the east, the great viaduct, which has the canal boats underneath it, cuts the village off from its neighbour there, and to the west a long road that runs along the side of the old railway line.

Friarmere holds the communities only bank and village police station. A high school and a beautiful primary school in the hills, with fantastic views. It is on a bus route, with buses between Manchester and Huddersfield every ten minutes. The houses aren't cheap and all have sloped gardens, being hillside dwellings.

The old Friar's Grange sits and broods above Friarmere. Huge and cut off from the rest of the village by a wall and large metal gates. For years a chain and padlock have been around the two gates. No one likes to walk past there. Not as it is usually in anyone's general direction of walking. It is out of the way and down a small dirt road. Dandelions and thistles push in from the sides, making the route even narrower. It is a haven and sanctuary for insects, wasps and mice. The house is the only thing at the end of the road and, as it is been empty as far as anyone can remember, it is largely forgotten. Another reason that no one likes to walk down there is that it backs on to the old graveyard. Again, a metal locked gate is on the back wall of the Grange. But here it is just a small, arched, person sized gate, with ornate curves. A short cut to the old church. The house dates back to about the 17th Century. A look in either gate would find tall grass and weeds that block the view. The house can be seen from a distance, rising above the walls in the centre of the ocean of grass. The closer one gets, the less there is to see.

The only person that is aware of the Grange on a daily basis is Christine. Christine's house is half way down that small dirt track and not many people visit Christine either. She has alienated most of Friarmere with her behaviour in the past. Overbearing, money grabbing and cutthroat, she owes money to more people that can squeeze in her kitchen. Christine became quite excited about six months ago when a 'For Sale' sign went up at the Grange. She would have been interested herself if she had got the money and the inclination to renovate. The house she lived in desperately needed it, everything was rickety and old, low ceilings and lots of small rooms. But she told any visitor that came that it was 'period' and that saved her from doing any work to it. She did however, like the prestige that owning 'The Grange' would give her, so was quite annoyed when she saw one day, about a year ago, that it had indeed been sold.

Often on long dark nights, especially during the winter, she thought she saw dull light in the windows. Moving from one to another. It's my imagination. I must be tired. It's definitely not the Black Friars walking round that old house, looking for someone to haunt, she thought. She took a look from her window towards The Grange for any signs of the new owners whenever she walked past it. She was determined that if she couldn't own it, she was going to make sure she *made a connection* with the new owners and spend as much time there as possible. There could be good business deals to be done.

About a month ago, about ten pm, she saw a removal trucks' lights going past her house down the track to the The Grange. She thought, at this time of night, a visit from their new neighbour would be unwelcome, so she would wait until about ten in the morning. Christine went to bed, drifting off to the most wonderful dreams of owning The Grange. She awoke the following day, covered in sweat and panting. Somewhere through the night, this had turned into a nightmare. It was nine o'clock. She got up, dressed in her most impressive outfit and did her hair. After putting on an extra layer of bright red lipstick, she set off down the track. Christine held a business card with her personal number, in her hand. Swinging her hips to the left and right, she worked her wiggle dress. Along with her high heels, she thought she looked thinner and sexier than ever today. She regretted it instantly as she walked on the rough and uneven ground, turning her ankles every thirty seconds. When she got to the bottom, she was disappointed to see the chains round the gates again and the truck nowhere to be seen. She shouted and rattled the gates. No response at all. If she didn't know any better she would think it was still empty, apart from the rats that is. She decided this would have to wait for another day, or later today. Rain had been forecast for later and she didn't want to come down here in her wellies. As she walked back and was slightly up the hill, she felt like she was being watched. Eyes burned into her back.

She looked quickly back at the house. All the windows still looked empty, with no curtains. She started walking again, and immediately had the same sensation. The eyes watching her were on the roof. The vampire had scaled the outside walls, flat on his stomach, he moved from side to side defying gravity as he crawled like a lizard. He lay low, flush against the tiles. The eyes were red and the mouth open, hungry and sensing. She shivered and hurried home.

3 - Band

'Settle down everyone, lets have some bloody quiet. I can't hear myself piggin' think in 'ere!' Barry yelled.

Ernie shook his head. Barry was *in one* tonight. The rest of the band had better mind their p's and q's. This was the first practice back after the contest at the weekend and their unfortunate collision with a bouncing sheep. On Mondays, Susan and himself had to collect subs and the hundred club, which brought in the main income for the band. He liked Susan and was extremely pleased when she had been voted on the Committee as Secretary. Susan had been coming to every band meeting anyway as her husband, Tony, played trombone, her son Bob, played percussion and so did her best friend, Laura. Ernie thought that the best committee members were the ones that weren't players as they could give a lot more of their time and it also left the players to just concentrate on what they did best - playing.

Barry was shouting again, but it must have been in a lighthearted way as everyone burst out laughing. It usually was directed at a particular baritone player named Stephen who was constantly putting his foot in it or generally daydreaming about girls. Andy shouted something back from the horn section and laughter erupted again. Andy was as sharp as a knife, but a little too cutting sometimes. Stephen was slow on the uptake sometimes and it was a general joke in the bandroom on a daily basis. But when the chips were down everyone looked after everyone else and they were a family.

Susan looked up from her mountain of paperwork. *Why is it that I am always fully concentrating when something funny is said and I miss it*, she thought. She looked over to Bob who was texting his friend Adam, as usual. Sue gave him the angry eyes and mouthed the words *put it away* hoping Barry hadn't seen it. Tony looked towards her and mouthed 'what'. She gestured towards Bob and acted texting on a mobile with her fingers and shook her head. Tony was a legend. Longish hair, beard and cowboy boots. He wasn't your typical *bander*. Wherever Friarmere band turned up, people would be looking for Tony in particular to have a beer with. She looked back down at her paperwork, and started filling in competition forms again. From experience, she glanced back up at Bob and he was texting again but not looking at her. She leant forward and poked Laura in the arm with the end of her pen.

'Tell him to stop it, Laura.' Laura moved forward and picked up a timpani stick, hitting Bob gently on the knee with it.

'Concentrate,' she said. Sue wished she had more success with one word, but those hopes had long gone.

Friarmere Band had lots to do tonight. With Armistice Day, concerts and Christmas not to far away, there was plenty to practice. They warmed up with a hymn, and then got down to work.

There was a good mix of pieces tonight. Slow mournful pieces and hymns for Armistice plus 'Land of Hope and Glory' for a lunchtime concert they had after the service. They would also include some good old favourites that people could sing along too, wartime songs. Lili Marlene, White Cliffs of Dover and Roll out the Barrel. These needed no practice and they would get out the music out on the day. Just for that day.

They then went on to a few faster numbers to entertain at concerts. 'Lightwalk', which was a Salvation Army number and 'I've Got Rhythm'. Shaun, their drum kit player was very fast and well beyond the standard of this band, but he enjoyed the laughs they had, it was local and also his dad Geoff, played here. Which meant he got a lift.

Bob played timpani super loud to the next one, a version of 'Bohemian Rhapsody' and that was how Barry liked it. Bob was the little star in making, and Barry gave him lots to do. He would often move from timpani, to xylophone to glockenspiel in about twelve bars. And as time went on, with the music Barry picked, he was doing it more often than not.

Ernie put the kettle on in the back room where Freddie, the music librarian, was housed. This was cup of tea number three, for the committee tonight. Usually on cup of tea number three, the biscuit barrel was passed around too. Susan washed the cups, dried them and then sat back down. Bob made her a gesture towards her that meant he wanted her to make him a 'hot blackcurrant'. Kids? Who would have them?

The band continued to play on. Barry, the Musical Director, was a Master of his Craft. He had a rich pedigree of success with his previous bands and Friarmere were lucky to have him. They hoped he would stay until he retired, which was a long time, as they had never won so many competitions or had rose through the banding sections so quickly. Brass bands play in sections, like football leagues. Friarmere were in the fourth section when Barry had taken them on but now were in the second section after winning again and again at their area contest at Blackpool each spring.

They played 'Goldcrest', the first part of Little Suite for Brass and Concert Prelude. They started on 'Fingals Cave'. Finally they practiced a few Christmas numbers. In general, like the sing-alongs on Armistice Day, they played Christmas Carols from their books at the concert and on outside carolling jobs without practice. But they always did the greatest and largest Christmas Concert in the village. Always at the Civic Centre, this was a joint concert with the local primary school. The music teacher there would have the children practice lots of new Christmas based songs and carols from about October onwards. She would then send the music to Friarmere Band so they could play along with the choir. Now most people would think that a brass band could drown out a school choir. But not this choir. Three quarters of all pupils were members of the choir. So it was a marvellous musical night. Solo items, from both camps and many joint items, plus carols for the audience to sing along to.

At ten o'clock, Barry stopped.

'We'll call it a night, there, folks. Ernie wants a word though.'

Ernie walked to the front of band. He waited a short while until there was quiet. He had noticed he managed to achieve this quicker by sighing very loudly whilst checking his small piece of paper, full of notes. 'Just a bit of housekeeping everyone and news. Could everyone bring their subs up to date, if possible? If anyone is going to the club, could you use the small room as they have got a cricket function going on in the big one? Also we have had a ten-piece band job booked for this weekend. Sorry to land it on you like that.'

Everyone groaned. They liked plenty of notice for band jobs. A few people said 'oh Ernie,' and 'well, I can't do it'. When the noise had calmed down a bit, Ernie started with the list, 'Alright, who's going on the top seat?'

'What night is it at the weekend, Ernie?' Asked one of the cornet players, Maurice.

'Saturday night. Bonfire night, it is. eight 'while' ten. I'll sweeten the pot as well to you all, and say he is paying us big bucks and is throwing in a buffet for you players.'

'And beer?' Maurice asks.

'I was told wine, and plenty of it. The person who has booked it has a vineyard somewhere abroad,' Ernie replied.

'Count me in,' said Maurice.

'Alright. Sophie?' Sophie was the principal cornet and would automatically have the top chair if she wanted to do the concert. Maurice was her 'bumper up'. Her number two.

'No, Ernie. I've already got tickets for a big bonfire and a few of the others are coming as well.'

'I know what you mean, I am supposed to be taking the grandkids to one as their Mum is working that night at the hospital. You'll be on the top chair then, Maurice. Anyone else, before I have to tell this guy that I can't do it'

'I'll go.' A few people said. Conversation was getting quite loud now and the promise of free food and especially free wine had changed a lot of the players' minds.

Ernie started to write the names down, 'ok, I've got two cornets, a euph, a bass, a bari...er... a trom...er what about persecution?' This term for percussion had started when Barry had arrived and stuck.

'I'll do it,' Woody said, 'as long as I can get leathered. So I'll need a lift, there and back.'

'I'll give yer a lift, Woody,' said Michael Thompson. 'I might as well go and do the committee stuff, pick up the cheque and the likes if our Stephen is going on bari anyway.'

Ernie wrote Woody next to percussion and Michael's name at the bottom of the list. 'Woody, if you are getting leathered, as you say, can you make sure you don't start until after you have played?' He looked over his glasses to Woody, who briefly nodded his head, whilst fiddling with his stick bag. 'Right, tenor horn. Andy?'

'I'm not doing it, Ernie. I always do it. Someone hasn't taken their turn on the ten piece all year.'

'I don't want to do it either,' said Vicky.

'What Andy says is right, Vicky. He does it every time and you can't expect Pat to do it all either, she's seventy.'

'Thanks Ernie,' Pat said sarcastically. 'Vicky, you can just do it. You aren't behind the door at Christmas when you are having your free meal and Malibu all night.' Pat winked at the rest of band. She was a feisty old bird.

'Fine!' Vicky snapped.

'I just need another cornet.'

'Liz will do it,' Andy volunteers.

'I thought we were going out, Andy.'

'No, we can't afford it this week. We would only be stopping in, watching rubbish.'

'By rubbish, you mean all the stuff I like. Well I'm recording it and I'll watch it when I get in.'

'Not if Match of the Day is on, you won't.' Andy replied. Liz sighed.

'What is this concert anyway, Ernie? What are we playing?'

'From what I can gather, you can play what you like. It's a house warming party combined with a Bonfire Party. There's you, and a disco and food and fireworks. Should be a good night. A lot of bigwigs have been invited and people local to the house.'

'Where is it?' she asked.

'Well, for me that's the exciting bit. It's at the old Black Friars Grange on the hill.

4 – The Grange

Things were changing at The Grange. Christine had noticed. Every day if there wasn't fog or rain, she had a good peer through her window at the happenings. She saw a local gardener cutting the grass once, other than that she saw no evidence that there were people at Black Friars. But there were definite changes. Repairs had been made and she had seen a painter and decorators' van leaving the lane once, as she was on her way back from a business meeting in Manchester. Christine had a pair of opera glasses that she had liberated from a theatre in London and had no shame in standing for long periods of time trying to see into the house. She would often sit for an hour watching, whilst eating a plateful of jam sandwiches and drinking a bottle of wine. The walls upstairs had definitely been painted a rich red. Very nice. The woodwork looked to be polished rather than painted wood. Downstairs was harder to see as she was higher than the house. But she thought that the walls were painted dark too. Maybe a racing gPat, she thought.

She was still desperate to get a look inside and to meet the owner. She hoped they didn't have children. She hated them. They would be going up and down the lane on their bicycles, being cheeky. She liked to sunbathe in a tiny bikini in the summer and she wasn't a tiny woman. She wouldn't be able to do that if there were children about.

One morning, she heard the letterbox go and then surprisingly saw Wayne, the postman, going past her back window, towards The Grange. She rushed towards her back door and flung it open in the fog. 'Wayne, darling, could I see you a moment.' She saw him stop mid step and drop his head slightly. She thought she heard him mumble something and he turned around and starting walking back towards her, with a professional smile on his face.

'Miss Baker,' he said.

'I've told you before, darling, you are to call me Christine. We are friends, aren't we?'

Wayne couldn't think of anyone less he would like to call his friend as Christine. She was not his type of person and she was a downright annoyance. And she got too much post. He thought that the least you could do if you lived this far up the hill was make sure you didn't get much post.

'Do you have a letter for The Grange?' She asked.

'Electricity,' he said. Probably best to keep dialogue to a minimum.

'Could I ask you the teeniest favour? Could I ask that you give me that letter and I will say that it got delivered to my house by mistake. I would really like to get to know the owners.'

'I'd better not, Miss Baker.'

'Christine!'

'Christine,' he paused, 'I could get into a lot of trouble if anyone found out.'

'No one will know, Wayne. I was thinking, one time maybe you would like to come in for a little drinky after your round. It gets very lonely up here.'

He looked at her, his eyes big and round.

'I could get into trouble for that as well. Here's the letter.' He shoved it in her hand and made a quick getaway.

She shouted after him, 'don't forget to call in a couple of weeks for your Christmas Box. Chrissy might have something special in her stocking for you! Compliments of the season, if you know what I mean!'

She thought she heard him say 'I'd rather do without,' but it was probably the fog muffling his words. She looked down at the letter in her hands. It was indeed a letter about the electricity supply. Addressed to Mr Norman Morgan. There didn't seem to be a Mrs Norman's name on the letter. Maybe she would be in The Grange after all.

She had to go out to a hospital check up in the afternoon and by the time she had got in and made herself very presentable, it was five thirty and it had been dark for over an hour. She took a last look at herself in her mirror and decided to add an extra layer of her favourite red lipstick and dangly earrings. Christine liked what she saw but as an afterthought, she decided to open another couple of button's on her blouse. Once she had found her big torch, which she used for her cellar, she set off with the letter, down the bank. She was pleased to see that the gate was unchained and she opened it with a loud squeal of its metal hinges. They've not seen to that yet, she thought.

She walked up the drive. There was a large Mercedes parked behind the boundary wall, which she could not see from her house. There were curtains up at the windows now, at least downstairs. They looked expensive with a heavy lining. Not a chink of light came through. There was however a square of stained glass in the front door and its light shone down onto the drive, in a large oblong. She thought this was new. Christine stood for a moment and took a good look round the garden. A mercedes in the drive of a great house? They were asking for trouble. She would have had a security light here. But no such light came on as she walked up the three stone steps to the door. She thought she saw something, move quickly from the roof to the ground, at the right side of the house and quickly hide itself around the corner. That was strange. She looked again from where she stood, without moving and stared at the corner. Well, it had gone now, she thought, but even more reason to have a security light.

There was a large knocker on the door and she knocked three times. She waited and no one answered, so she tried again. Just as she had finished the third knock the door was quickly flung open and a very attractive man stood facing her. She would say he was in his fifties. Obviously wealthy as he was very well groomed and his clothes were immaculate and were made to measure. He didn't speak. He just looked at her. She couldn't tell if he was angry for her disturbance or happy to see her. He was totally expressionless.

'Hello, Darling,' she gushed.

No reply.

'I live in the house just up the lane and I have a letter of yours that has been delivered to my house by mistake by that stupid post man.' *Backstabber*, she thought. But she quickly dismissed it.

'I'm sorry. How rude of me. I was quite taken aback by your arrival. I am Norman Morgan.'

'Christine Baker,' she said and stretched out her hand. She gave her very best wide smile. He looked at her for a moment then took her hand in its greeting and smiled widely too. She noticed he did not smile with his eyes. Just his mouth. His lips and gums and tongue were very red too. Maybe he had just been eating beetroot.

'Please come in, Miss Baker. Is it Miss? I am sorry to presume.'

'It is Miss, for the moment, Norman. Can I call you Norman? You can call me Christine. We are neighbour's after all.'

She fluttered her eyelashes at him. He had seen a film a while back that reminded him of this woman. *Whatever happened to Baby Jane.* She could prove very useful to him. He would keep her alive until it suited him for her not to be so.

She walked into the large hallway with its sweeping staircase and black and white tiles. He gestured left and she went into his sitting room. Racing green it was. With dark wood furniture and expensive sofas.

'Take a seat. Would you like some refreshments?'

'If you are offering, it would be rude not to, wouldn't it?' She giggled.

'Would you like some English tea or wine or something else...Christine?'

'A glass of red, if you have it, Norman.'

'Of course. Red. I only serve red.' He left the room and Christine looked closely at her surroundings. The floor was highly polished wood, with expensive Persian rugs on it. The walls were painted and so was the ceiling but the ornate work on the ceiling was clearly remaining from when the Friars had lived here. Norman returned.

'I see you are admiring my ceiling, Christine.'

'It's very impressive, Norman. I would never have known there was such a beautiful house hiding behind those big walls and grass a few months ago.'

'Ah, a beautiful house is like a beautiful woman, it just needs care and love to blossom.'

He's coming on to me, she thought. *It's in the bag.*

He handed her a cut crystal glass of red wine. 'From my own vineyards in Switzerland,' he proudly said.

'You might think I am ignorant, Norman. But I didn't know they made wine in Switzerland. I know I've never had any.'

'No, Christine. I do not think that. The Swiss

are very clever people. Their wine is so good....they keep it all for themselves.'

'Ooh, Norman. I can see we are going to get on. That's my philosophy as well.' His mouth really was so red. He must be drinking too much of his red wine, she thought.

'I am very glad that you came to visit me Christine, as I was shortly coming to visit you. You see, I was going to invite you to a party.'

'A party. I love parties, Norman. I'm a very popular lady. Say no more. Do you need any help?'

'I could do with a little help in one area, Christine.'

'Fire away, Norman.' She took another sip of the wine. She could tell he was foreign but he spoke English very well. *Probably better than a lot of people that were actually born round here* she thought snootily.

'I have been abroad for a long time. I lived in the land of my ancestors but I decided that, as I got older. This was not for me. My businesses do not require me to be there and I have very capable workers. So I have been looking for a place I can retire to. A place I can make my own. I travelled to many countries and have not felt welcome but here on this Island of Great Britain, I think I have found everything I need. I have visited a few villages, especially in the north, but not stopped for a while. I had an extended stay just over the hill in Yorkshire and made a few friends. However, for certain reasons that I cannot explain, I was drawn to here. To Saddleworth, and then on to Friarmere. To the remoteness and the wildness and the hills. It reminds me somewhat of my own country. So I have found this comfortable house and want to integrate into the community, so to speak. I have learned of a festival of Guy Fawkes that is happening soon, is that right?'

'Ooh yes. Bonfire Night. It's this Saturday,' Norman refilled Christine's glass.

'I have some entertainments coming. I have organised for your local brass band Friarmere Band to attend and play. I am looking forward to having them. I came across them just by chance too.' He paused and took a drink from his own glass of wine. 'And I have lots of fireworks. I have invited some people that I am very interested in meeting. Local celebrities and such. But I just have one problem.'

'What's that?'

'Food. I do not know what you people eat for this festival. Or do you not eat anything special on this day? Food and festivals are very particular, where I was born.'

'You've come to the right person, Norman. Meat and potato pie, red cabbage, black peas. Jacket spuds. Parkin. Maybe we could get some of your wine and mull it.'

'Mull it. What is that? You mean like the eighties hairstyle. The footballers, they had it?'

'What? Oh no. Not Mullet. Not a hairstyle. Mulled wine.'

'I still do not know.'

'Erm, spices and oranges and stuff.'

'Ah like the gluhwein.'

'Yes. That's it. I know where to get all that

from. I'll sort it. I'll just give you the receipt.'

'Thank you Christine, but I just need the list and I will sort it myself. I have troubled you enough. I have workers here in England too. I would like to add my own twist to this food you see. I just have more thing to ask.'

'Yes?'

'What is a black pea?'

5 - Bonfire

It was a dark, rainy and starless night. Bonfire night, full of expectations had been its usual disappointment. Wet piles of wood littered the land, topped by many sad and soggy ragdoll Guy Fawkes'. However, the show must go on.

Black Friars Grange had never seen a party such as this. Black Friars Grange had, in fact, never seen a party at all. Outside, one half of the substantial front garden had a giant gazebo erected so people could stand and watch the fireworks and bonfire in comfort. The house was lit up and candles in jars shimmered all over the garden. A large pile of wood and branches was covered by plastic sheeting and under a large tree, sat a roly-poly Guy Fawkes, happily sheltering from the rain. The garden, was still quite wild, even after work done by the local gardener. But after years with no one to tend it, and it also being November, it was the best it could look.

Peter Woodall, affectionately called 'Woody' by everyone who knew him, was struggling down the dirt path, to the Grange, with various parts of his drum kit, strung about him. He was a large man and the walk up the hill, from where Michael had parked the car, had made him red in the face and short of breath. They were descending now, on the track to The Grange.

'At least I'm warm now. You want to get that

heater fixed in your car Mick.'

'Michael hasn't got the money for that, Woody.' Stephen said.

'Shut up Stephen!' Michael snapped.

'Well I can't accuse you of spending it on fast cars. What about loose women?' Woody jokingly said.

'He'd have to pay them, wouldn't he Woody.' Stephen said and nudged Woody with his elbow.

'Less of it Stephen, unless you want to walk home,' Michael grunted.

'Eh Mick. What's crawled up your arse?' Woody asked.

'I am not having my younger brother talk to me like that. He knows what he will get'

'Bloody hell!' Woody exclaimed, wanting to diffuse the situation now. 'He's twenty-nine years old'

'So he should have learned by now then, shouldn't he?' He boomed. He said it way too loudly and Woody thought he sounded like he knew he was wrong but was trying to convince himself that he was right. Michael quickened his pace and Stephen quickened his too, so as to keep up. There was no way that Woody could walk that fast, even downhill. So he decided to put his drum cases down for a second and catch his breath. After a minute he heard voices and recognised them as some of the band, so turned around to look up the hill. There were no street lights here at all and it was drizzling again, so he put his hood up and waited. He knew the rest of the band would help him with his kit. The Thompson's had never offered to carry a thing.

Soon he saw Liz, Diane, Vicky and Colin. They all picked up a case from Woody, apart from Vicky. There was a much better atmosphere and conversation straight away. Woody thought that this was partly due to the fact that they had already had a few in the pub earlier. Diane especially was quite unsteady on her feet and had a big grin on her face, with flushed cheeks.

'You got stuck with Thompson, didn't you Woody?' Liz asked.

'Yeah. And lucky me, there was no heating in the car. We had to have all the windows open because of them steaming up and I was in the back. Getting the full force of it. Then to put a top hat on it, Thompson Senior just had a go at Steve. It was really awkward.'

'Well you might get a lift back off Keith. I don't think he was bringing anyone.' Liz said.

'Yeah and he won't take anyone back either. Miserable bastard. I'm not asking him. A refusal often offends. Besides that, I never feel comfortable around him, being a copper. I always think I am going to admit to something I've never done.'

They all laughed.

Michael and Stephen carried on in silence. They were soon at the Grange and Michael thought *I should be living somewhere like this.*

'Can you smell that, Stephen?' He asked.

'What? Have you had egg?' Stephen quickly covered his face with his sleeve.

'No. Stupid boy! There is a reek around here. But it's money. Lovely money.'

He walked confidently up the steps and rang

the bell.

A young woman answered the door. She was very attractive in a sexual kind of way. She had long, shiny, chocolate coloured hair. Dark almond shaped eyes and full cherry red lips. She wore a simple red sweater, which clung to her figure and a tight red skirt with black boots. Michael thought he recognised her, but that she was slightly different from the person he thought she was.

'Good evening and welcome to Black Friars Grange,' she said in a light voice.

'Evening. We are from Friarmere Band. I am your point of contact.' He offered out a business card. Ernie didn't know about them. Michael had gone to a machine on a service station on the M62 motorway and had had them done. She took it in her hands and read it.

'Michael Thompson – Band Manager. Come in Mr Thompson.' She opened the door further and they stepped in. She shut the heavy wooden door behind them.

'This is my brother, Stephen. He plays the Baritone.'

'That's wonderful. If you would like to follow me.' She turned on her heel and walked away from the door. She gestured to a dark green room and said, 'You may go into there after you have played to join the party. You are playing in the blue room,' She walked past the green room, past another door that was closed and then opened the next door and gestured inside. This was a dark brown room and along one wall was a long table, heavy with food.

'These refreshments are just for the band and no one else. If you would like to change here and when you have all arrived and are ready, I shall return and take you all to the blue room. The two men entered the room and she shut the door behind them. Behind the door stood Keith, Darren, Maurice and Vincent, all with plates piled high with food from the large table and a glittering glass of red wine each.

'Oh. I thought I was the first.' Michael said.

'You're always wrong though, aren't you Thompson,' Keith said.

'Yeah and don't tell Ernie, we had a drink before we played. We will know it is you, if we get in trouble.' Darren added.

Michael ignored him and went to the table, it was beautifully set out with an expensive cloth.

There were various kinds of hot pie including cheese and onion, and chicken and beef. A steaming terrine of soup, jacket potatoes, pickled red cabbage, treacle toffee, and black peas. Plus an enormous chocolate fudge cake with a jug of cream. On a separate table at the end were about twenty bottles of wine and crystal glasses. All red. And what seemed like a ridiculous amount of crisps in a china serving bowl.

'You can put a couple of bottles of that wine in your baritone case and carry the instrument home,' he whispered to Stephen.

'I would rather take the crisps actually. You know I like crisps. Anyway, what if I get caught?' Stephen asked.

'Don't get caught.' He replied.

'Eh Stephen, that bird was a bit of alright

wasn't she?' Maurice said with a cheeky wink.

Stephen nodded, finishing his mouthful of crisps, before laughing.

'Yeah Maurice, I would,' and winked back.

'Er, I am getting myself sorted out before you, Stephen,' Michael said crossly, 'she looks like a woman that would appreciate an experienced man, like myself.'

All the men laughed and just then the girl in question entered the room. They all looked embarrassed and it was clear that they had been talking about her. The other band members followed her in and she quietly left the room. The group of men erupted with laughter.

'Let me guess. One of you thinks you might end up with her,' Liz said.

'Michael thinks he's in with a chance,' Maurice said in between gasps of uncontrollable guffaws.

The new group looked at each other and joined in the laughter.

'Cat in hells chance.' Griped Keith. 'She looks like she actually has taste.'

Michael sat at the other end of the room. He drank his wine and ate his pie and thought how wrong they were. And *how* he would show them.

After about fifteen minutes, which was time for everyone to have at least one glass of wine and a plate of food. The woman returned and asked them if they were almost ready, as most of the guests had arrived. They followed her to a large room on the other side of the house, which did indeed have blue walls. They all walked in with their instruments and started to take a seat. Michael was the last to enter and the lady put her hand on his shoulder and said, 'Mr Morgan is very eager to meet you Mr Thompson. Could you come with me?'

'Oh yes, yes. Lead the way, Miss….er…er….' he said. Hoping that she would give him her name.

'Kate,' she said, 'just Kate.'

'Beautiful.' He replied. They walked back the way they had just come and Kate went to the door, which was between the Green and Brown rooms. She opened the door and gestured inside. The interior was quite dark and through the door he could only see the edge of a desk.

'After you,' Kate said. Michael walked in the room and Kate pulled the door shut quietly behind him. He also heard a quick metallic noise, which he thought was the door being locked from the outside with a key. This room seemed to be an office of sorts. But not the kind he had ever been in. This was a luxury office. Expensive solid wood furniture with leather upholstery in a deep burgundy colour and it was lit just by the light of a green bankers lamp on the desk. As his eyes adjusted to the half-light he saw that there was a middle-aged man smiling at him from the other side of the desk.

'Welcome Mr Thompson. We meet again.'

'Pleased to meet you, Mr Morgan,' Michael said. He offered out another business card and Norman took it. 'I am sorry, Mr Morgan. I don't remember meeting you. You have me at a disadvantage.'

'Ah yes. But of course. You won't remember. Never mind,' Norman replied still smiling. 'Please have more wine,' he said this as he was already pouring a glass for Michael. 'I do insist that you enjoy my hospitality.'

'Thank you very much' Michael replied as he took the glass and greedily took a big slurp of the wine. 'I hope you are happy with the band's performance tonight. We should go into the other room really. You want to enjoy what you have paid for don't you?'

'The band is for my guests tonight. I will enjoy them wholeheartedly at a later date'

'Is that what you want to see me about. Another booking?' Michael asked excitedly.

'No I wanted to meet you. I want to make myself at home here. I would like to find out about you and what makes people *tick* around here. So to speak.'

'I'm your man then,' Michael said quickly and took another drink of his wine.

'I thought you might be. I *sensed* it.' Norman said. As he did he moved his finger slowly round and round in a circle on the desk and Michael watched. 'The people here seem to be very old fashioned and I like that. They seem to be very interested in each other and in marrying each other and then having children who then grow up and settle in this oasis amongst the wilderness. I wonder about them and their habits and how to *integrate* quickly and efficiently. I need people who will help me do that and I had my eyes peeled for such men and ladies. I would like them to be of a certain type. Ambitious, insightful, articulate. Pillars of the community. But I also know when there is an extra special quality in a man. Maybe raw unused talents that I once possessed myself, many years ago and I think you are that man. I know you are him. I tell you what I think, Mr Thompson.' Norman moved forward quickly, from sitting behind the lamp, to being fully illuminated. The bankers lamp made shadow's on his face. His eyes looked black and hollow, inside his mouth was endlessly deep and dark red. 'I think you are a man, who should have power, and wealth and respect. A man who would like those things and more. For people to look at you and envy you and maybe just a little… fear you, yes fear you, Michael. For them to look and say I wish I was him. I had his life and I had everything he had and his woman. Maybe someone like the lovely Kate. Or even Kate herself.' He trailed off and then looked at Michael full on in the eyes and stared at him. 'Am I right in what I *sense*?' Norman asked.

Michael swallowed hard, his throat rasped dry with no words in it.

'Yes,' he said quietly and took another drink.

'And that is where we come to the *meat* of it, so to speak.' The vampire rose out of his seat and walked around the desk. He walked to a cabinet at the end and took out a bottle of wine, in an ornate bottle and two glasses. He returned to the desk and sat back down. Slowly opening the wine, which had a jewelled stopper in the neck and not a cork, he poured a full glass and a half glass of wine. The full glass he placed before Michael.

'My very best wine, for our toast. We must seal the deal.' Michael immediately took the glass and drank half its contents. 'What if I told you I could give you all that. That your life could change from this moment. Because of me. What if I said, you could have Kate tonight. Anyway you liked. I could make that happen for you.' He considered the man across the table. 'What if that could be all yours now? What would you say?'

'What do I have to do?' Thomson asked hungrily. It seemed the second drink of wine had made him find his voice.

'A lot of self-development, a few chores. Everything must have its price. I think though that you might think the price is not too bad. In time you will grow to love it, I can assure you. And I think that there are many that should also go through this *self-development* too. Growing and changing can be painful but *no pain no gain* as they say.' He filled Michael's glass again. Michael took it and drank it all the way down.

'I want it, tell me what to do.'

'You are already on the way, Michael. I will call Kate. She will entertain you, and then after, enjoy my party. I will be in contact about the price.'

Michael noticed that Norman hadn't touched his wine. He also began to feel a little nauseous and dizzy. No wonder as he had drank a lot of wine really quickly. He sat in the chair and must have lost consciousness for a moment because all of a sudden Kate was standing next to him and putting her hand in his.

'Would you like to come upstairs with me, Michael? Do you want me?' She whispered as she bent to his ear. He could smell her cherry lipstick and another smell, earthy, like soil.

'Yes' he said slowly. But it seemed to him that he could hear his own voice from afar. The vampire stood and laughed and nodded towards him.

'Good man. Good.' Norman said. A very joyful expression on his face.

He could hear his blood rushing in his ears and it sounded like the sea. He felt himself get up, go out the room and walk up the stairs. It felt like the time, he had had his wisdom tooth taken out and his cousin came to get him. He remembered going to the car. But just floating and going through the motions. Not because he wanted to, or realised what he should do. But just because his sister told him what to do. He found himself in a bedroom and he thought *I feel quite cold actually.* Kate told him to sit on the bed and he did. She sat down on a chair nearby. She took off her boots, and then her skirt and sweater. Underneath she was smooth and white and naked. She was truly beautiful, and he had never had a woman like her in his life. She slowly walked over to him, but in his state of mind, he felt like she glided, and he reached out and took her hand and kissed her soft cold skin. She started to undress him.

Downstairs the band carried on.

After they had played, their Host walked in and stood in front of the band clapping his hands quietly.

'Thank you Friarmere band, that was

wonderful. Let me introduce myself. My name is Norman Morgan and I am the owner of Black Friars Grange. I have thoroughly enjoyed renovating this house and have received a warm welcome from many of the local people here. Some of you, I have already met and some of you I hope to be able to call you my friends after tonight. Please enjoy my hospitalities. We are going to light the bonfire soon and set off the fireworks. I believe tonight we have the largest 'Catherine Wheel' in the North. There will be a disco later, and do not be afraid to stop until dawn if you so please. My home is yours tonight.'

There was a short round of applause and Norman walked out of the room. Some people went into the Green room and some people started to put on their coats and hats to watch the bonfire and fireworks. The band went back into the brown room and put their instruments into their cases. Some of them started to eat more of the pie and peas that were there, which had been kept hot on warmers. Diane went straight for the wine. After a short while they collectively decided they would go and mingle, apart from Keith or said he would rather stay in the room on his own with the food. He was determined to try one of each pie and decide which was most delicious.

When Diane and Liz and Vicky went into the Green Room, Diane noticed that Christine who lived up the lane was talking to Norman. She was fluttering her false eyelashes at him and had a very ill advised amount of fake tan on. She drank a wine with one hand and with her other hand she twirled her peroxide blonde hair with her fingers whilst gazing at Norman

'Look at that, Liz. That fat Christine is talking to him,' Diane said under her breath.

'So what,' replied Liz.

'Well I wouldn't have minded a go on that,' she nodded her head once in Norman's direction. 'And she's got in first. 'I think you ought to have a 'go' on the black coffee and slow down a bit,' said Liz.

'Knickers!' Diane stated rather loudly and walked over to the wine table. Liz sighed.

'I wouldn't mind Vicky, but it's everywhere we go. She has to get drunk.'

'I know what she means though.' Vicky said looking at Norman with a smirk on her face. 'I wouldn't mind a go on that either. He's very fit for an older bloke. He looks like he would be right filthy between the sheets,' she laughed quietly.

'Vicky, he is twice your age. Old enough to be your father. At least him and Diane are about the same age. You're sex mad.'

'Many a good tune played on an old fiddle,' Vicky said and took another sip of her wine, whilst looking at Norman over the top of her glass.

Just then they noticed Stephen was right behind them, listening to their conversation. 'What's that Vicky, are you changing instruments? Going on a fiddle. They don't have them in brass bands. You would have to leave.' The two women looked at each other but didn't answer. 'Anyway, have you seen my brother?'

'He's probably outside on the Bonfire.' Vicky said with a smirk.

'I'll go outside and look then,' he said.

Liz sighed then said, 'We'll come with you Steve,' she looked around the crowd. 'It's a bit dead in here.'

They didn't find Michael for the next hour. One by one the band left. Stephen was getting a bit worried when he went back into the band room and found Maurice, just getting all his stuff together. He was struggling as he was trying to carry his coat, his instrument, some music and two paper serviettes tied together full of food. He planned to have this for his lunch the next day. It didn't make it easier as he was in his late sixties and had a significant limp from an injury in a motorbike crash fifteen years ago.

'Have you seen my Michael, Maurice?' Stephen asked.

'I haven't lad. Not since before the concert. Have you checked outside?'

'Yes. No sign.'

'Ooh, I don't know then.' Maurice started to walk to the door. He seemed to stop and have a second thought. 'I bet I know where he is. I bet he's with that lass we saw earlier.' He laughed. 'I haven't seen her since then either.' He carried on laughing and shaking his head as he walked out the door.

Stephen decided to have more pie and quietly sat down to eat it in one of the seats. He looked at the objects left on the seats and realised there was only his brother's and his things left. Then he had a second thought, got up and picked up the bowl of crisps, set it on the seat next to him and began to munch away, quite contentedly.

Norman stood in a dark upper floor room, overlooking the front entrance. He watched the last few guests walking up the track, happily unaware of what was beginning in their village. Kate joined him and they both stood together for a moment, before she spoke.

'You have offered the man, Michael, all his wishes, and eternal life? I do not wish to question you, Master but I have seen many men here tonight, who are more worthy than him.'

'Yes, more worthy….but not as pliable.' He replied. 'They will all get their chance for transformation, one way or another. But Michael is just a pawn in my game. He will never become as great as you or me. Once he has served his uses, and there will be many, I will discard him. You see Kate, most worthy subjects, require the full act of turning to do my bidding, as you did. And that sometimes puts them in a less than useful position. But you see, Michael, he craves respect and power so much, just my blood being inside him and a bit of gentle persuasion will control him. Thus, making him a useful pawn by day or by night. Did you not enjoy making his dreams come true?'

'Out of all the things I have done, in my life before death and my ascendance since death. Of all the things I have done, in disgrace and shame, that is the worst.' She said quietly with a hint of anger. Norman laughed loudly.

'My dear Kate, it was a great thing you did for

me, and the cause tonight. Believe me, if he was so inclined I would have done that job, not you. But he considers himself a virile red-blooded male so it is a lady he would like. I wish I had better news and could say I won't ask you to do it again, but I must keep him sweet and you must play your part in that. I will say to you though, as recompense, I will give you a plump child to drink for every time you must humiliate yourself with him. How is that for a deal? Would you like that Kate?'

'Yes please.' She smiled and he noticed her teeth and mouth were already tasting the child. She was easily controlled too.

6 - Prawns

Tony, Susan and Bob drove up to the bandroom in their Landrover the following Wednesday for band practice. As they got twenty feet from the entrance the security light came on outside the bandroom. Tony turned his steering wheel suddenly, swung them in the space and screeched to a halt. Gravel was flying up and he stopped. He looked at the others cars

'Are we early, Sue?' Tony said.

'No. The usual. Why?'

'There are usually more people here by now'

'Maybe there is a zombie invasion and everyone has been eaten,' Bob said wickedly.

'More like a pub invasion,' replied Tony.

They got out of the Land Rover. Tony opened the back of the Land Rover and in amongst tools, a few old coke cans and some oily rags, there were a few bags, full of different collections of items. A bag for the charity shop, a bag of cat litter, Sue's bag for band and others.

'Get my bag for band, will you?' Sue asked. They each took out what they needed for the rehearsal. Tony picked up his trombone and Sue's bag and Bob got his stick bag. Sue had bought some chocolate digestives and some fig biscuits for the biscuit barrel. Tony locked the car and went into the bandroom. The security light went off.

Ernie was in his usual position behind the desk, counting money and filling in accounting books.

'Hi Ern. Where is everyone?' Susan asked.

'Well, I'm not positive, but I think the ten piece got food poisoning the other day.'

'Are they all off?'

'Not heard from Liz yet, but there's still time, or Diane and Sophie. Not heard from the Thompsons either.'

'I bet it was prawns,' Tony said. 'Sue eats them and is always lucky, but whenever I have them, I am having conversations with the toilet pan all night. Anything that you have to pick the poo out of, I think you should avoid!'

'Nice. Tony's got the bag for the barrel' Sue said. Ernie took the bag from Tony and put his hand in it. Taking out the contents. Metallic and long. He looked shocked then dropped it on the table.

'What the bloody hell is that?' Sue rushed over and looked at the object on the table. She couldn't place it. Then it hit her right between the eyes.

'It's a spare part for my washing machine. Tony, you picked up the wrong bag.' She said. Ernie sat down mock clutching at his heart.

'Blow me....I thought it was a marital aid!' Sue burst out laughing.

'I don't need any help in that way.' Tony said. He walked towards the door to get the other bag.

The door banged open and Liz and Andy walked in. Liz looked white and weak. Her hair was stuck together in clumps and she was wearing her jumper inside out. Andy is carrying both instrument cases.

'Liz! You look terrible!' Ernie said.

'Thanks a bunch Ern. Glad I made the effort now.'

'It's much appreciated but if you have a bug, I would rather you be at home and not infect the others.'

'It's not a bug. Andy hasn't got it. I just don't fancy any food and I feel shaky and want to sleep all the time.' She drops herself into a chair near the counter and weakly starts to get her instrument out.

'Maybe you are in the family way,' says Ernie.

'No!' Andy and Liz reply together.

'It's not that at all. It's since the weekend. The day after the party. I have been having such weird dreams too.'

'Did you eat prawns?' Tony asks knowledgeably.

'No.'

'Pork?' asks Susan.

Liz thinks hard and then says, 'I had a vegetarian hotdog.'

'There's no pork in them. Only earholes and eyelashes. The same as real hotdogs,' laughed Ernie.

'Thanks. That's taken the queasiness off completely,' Liz said as she rolled her eyes.

'Why did you let her come in, Andy?'

'She bloody insisted didn't she. Said if she didn't come with me, she would drive herself here, in her car, after I had left. So I had to bring her. This is Liz you are talking about, you know.' Andy shakes his head.

'I see that would be difficult,' Tony said,

winking at Andy.

'You probably just need a Tonic. One with iron in it,' Sue says. 'Or an old fashioned posset.'

'Oooh. A posset. I fancy one of them,' said Ernie.

'What's one of them?' Asked Andy. 'If it will help Liz, we will get it.'

'Well, you take half a pint of milk in a pan, warm it, not boiling though.' Said Sue.

'Or you'll cook the egg,' shouted Lynn as she came in from out of the music library.

'What egg?' Asked Liz.

'Ok, while you are warming the milk, you take an egg, beat it, stir in about a tablespoon of black treacle.' Sue said.

'Not golden syrup either, never!' Ernie interrupted angrily, looking at Lynn. 'If you don't have the ingredients, don't cobble it together, like someone I know. The black treacle is important.'

'Then you add the warm milk to the egg and treacle combination, and stir it gently together, melting the treacle. Finally you sprinkle a bit of nutmeg on the top.' Sue smiled.

'Not cinnamon. That is forbidden too.' Ernie looked at Lynn, shaking his head.

'I did all this, one time. And you have never let me forget it, have you. It must have been fifteen years ago now.' Lynn said

'I can't forget it Lynn. Anyway, Liz, take it to bed, drink it down, go to sleep. It fixes anything.'

'That sounds nice. I'll call and get something on the way home tonight. Thanks Sue and Ernie.

There's not many here tonight.'

'No. They are dropping like flies. Not heard from Sophie or Diane. Or the Thompsons. Various tales about all the others, but they were all members of the ten piece so this food poisoning theory of mine, might be right….even if that food wasn't prawns.'

They could hear a car engine outside and Tony looked out of the window as he was just beside it, getting his trombone out of its case. The security light came on and he recognized the BMW 4x4.

'It's Roger,' He said, and drew his nose even further towards the window, straining his eyes to see through the darkness. 'He's got Sophie with him.'

'Talk of the devil,' Ernie said grinning.

Roger entered. An elderly wealthy man, who was always well dressed and liked the finer things in life. Sophie was just behind him. They shut the door and Sophie announced breezily 'Me Mam's not coming. She's ill.'

'What's up with her?' Ernie asked, 'I can guess that it's probably food poisoning.'

'No Ernie, You're wrong as usual. It's migraine.'

'Oh. Fair enough,' *cheeky madam*, he thought.

Sophie stood by the coat rack and started to take off her coat. 'She's been in her room with the curtains closed since t'weekend, not seen her going the loo, so I think its migraine. She's had them before.'

Liz got up wearily out of her seat and walked past Sophie. 'Yeah, usually after every weekend.

To be fair Sophie, she was really drunk at the concert and we all know she likes a good time,' Liz said.

'Piss off Liz. I see you are looking gorgeous as usual,' she snapped.

'Didn't you ask, what was wrong with her or ask if she wanted anything?' asked Sue.

'I've been out with my mates, most of the weekend and I've looked in, but she looks asleep.'

'She could be dead as far as you know,' Andy said.

'Just leave it.' Sophie snapped back.

'Lets get on with the practice, everyone' Ernie said diplomatically.

Everyone took their seats. Liz and Sophie, shooting daggers across the room at each other with their eyes. They had never been the best of friends. Ernie walked to the front to make his announcements. 'Right everyone, we have got a few absent after the other nights food poisoning or shenanigans – I wasn't there, I don't know. I have heard that the band played beautifully, and that's all I am bothered about. Not heard off the Thompsons yet, which is unusual. I will keep you informed. We are practicing a few new Carols tonight amongst other things for the Christmas concert with Friarmere Primary in December. Barry has got a few things out of the music library for us to go through and those are in your music pads, courtesy of Fred. Ok. Over to Barry.'

'Right band, get out Carol of the Bells,' sighed Barry.

Woody sat in his living room. The room was just lit by the light of the television. Even that got too bright at some points. The sound was off and Eastenders was on. He wasn't watching Ian Beale in the Café though. He felt like he was falling into a bottomless pit. Desperate to eat, his stomach groaned, but he knew he couldn't eat or else he would be sick. He hated being ill. Plus, he was in a vile temper and didn't know why. His wife, Janet wanted to stay at home and look after him. Or make him soup, or tea or put a blanket on him. But every word she said, even her presence in the room made him want to kill her. Not just kill her, no....rip, eviscerate, destroy her. He had never felt like this in his life and never wanted to again. He loved Janet. Sometimes he felt lucid. He knew what he was feeling was only temporary and alien. Then 5 minutes later, he would want to embrace these feelings, still in anger and immense hunger again. He definitely wasn't going to go into work again tomorrow. Or even to the shops. He didn't want to go out. Didn't want to see anyone. Didn't want Janet to come home. He was too afraid. Too afraid of her getting to close to him and what he might be capable of.

Diane lay in her bed the pillow was wet with cold sweat. She had felt dreadful the next morning after the party. She had a bad hangover. It seemed it happened less and less these days. But this was bad. She couldn't face food, or water. It was lasting much longer than usual. But after many hours of tortured dreams and tortured wakefulness, she knew what would make her feel better. The hair of the dog that bit her. It crossed her mind for a split second, that she was becoming an alcoholic, but then she discarded that notion with a snort. She had taken a bottle of wine from the party when there was no one else in the room. Stephen had clumsily taken two and Diane thought she would blame him, if questions were asked. She weakly reached into her bag and took out the bottle of wine. The corks had been removed, to let the wine breathe and a stopper had been inserted. As she removed the stopper, the slightest scent of salvation came from the bottle. She shivered all over and took a sip. The effect was almost orgasmic. Each drop was wonderful, but she knew she could not take a lot at a time. Tonight this tasted so rich, even thick. So she had another wonderful sip and put the cork back in the bottle. She felt so much better, but then had a sudden realization. Had Norman drugged them? Diane had experience in drugs and knew that she had been craving something that wasn't just alcohol and was withdrawing from it. That substance was in the bottle. She thought she cared, then realized she didn't. Then sleep finally came to take her.

Keith felt like shit. He refused to stay at home. Absolutely refused. He had always said he would go to work with two broken legs if he had to. He had been brought up by a strict father and old fashioned mother and they had instilled in him that you attended school and work every day. Spare the rod, spoil the child. The adult Keith thought that weakness or illness were to be despised and he was pompous, loudmouthed and unpopular. Tall and unattractive, with the kind of skin that told of many acne plagued years, he was a heavy smoker and recently had become quite hunched in the shoulders. At fifty-three he was a Police Constable, regretting he hadn't achieved a greater rank. One of many source's of his bitterness. He also wished he was a better musician and had never been a father, so a child had never softened his approach to the young either. His wife Yvonne, who he thought might turn into some kind of sex kitten had ended up just like him. Shrew-faced, bitter, childless, selfish. At least they had someone to talk to at night as they had no other friends, apart from the people at Friarmere Band. There was no one he spoke to. The other officers avoided him and he was a very negative energy. Life was tough enough in the Police Force, without some misery bringing everyone down.

So, apart from all Keith's other natural and normal ways, there was a certain added blackness about him tonight. No…more than that. A need to inflict pain, misery on others that he had not experienced before. The rain and cold matched his mood. As he started through the streets he was determined to suffer no fools gladly tonight.

Maurice didn't feel too well. Like indigestion but a bit different. An acidic taste in his mouth definitely. But a hunger that was fierce. A man of his age knew though, if you have acid indigestion, you don't put more food in your belly for it to raise the acid levels further. He thought back to when he had had a last meal. Maybe it was when he had that left over food from the party. Yes, yes that was it. Obviously too much pastry. Or maybe it was on the turn. He couldn't quite remember when that meal was though. Maurice remembered the following morning feeling very unwell and forcing himself to eat that food for strength. After all, he lived on his own, so if he got into a proper state, who would help him? He had to walk everywhere, even in the house, with his stick. Immediately after that food, he had a good sleep and woke up feeling quite refreshed. He felt like he might have a headache on its way though, probably too much sleep, and he hadn't opened his curtains. Coming to think about it now, he hadn't opened them since the weekend. Tonight he had rang Ernie and said he couldn't blow his cornet with a load of acid at the back of his throat and Ernie agreed. He thought for a while about fixing himself up. Now, did he have a couple of rogue antacid tablets in his medicine box? It was quite full of all his other medications and he hadn't needed them for ages. Getting up, he walked slowly to the kitchen and opened the cupboard, containing his tablets. Rummaging around for a minute in there he wondered if he had thrown them out and had forgotten about it. Just when he had lost all hope, he saw the bent packet underneath an old tin of Fiery Jack rubbing ointment. Luckily, there were two tablets left. Popping them out of their blister pack onto the kitchen counter, the smell of mint was overpowering. He fumbled about with them, on the counter and wondered if this was such a good idea at all. The smell of mint made him more nauseous. Flaring his nostrils he took deep breaths to try and not succumb. He waited a couple of minutes, deep breathing but it wasn't going away. In a decision of all or nothing, taking the tablets in the palm of his hand he threw them into his mouth and started to chew. Almost immediately he started to heave, his gag reflex showing its immense strength by forcing him to disgorge his mouth's contents, straight back up onto the counter. *Oh bloody hell, that's the end of that*, he thought. Wiping his mess up with some snowman kitchen paper he put the medicine box away. Wondering what on earth to do next. Deciding it might just be best to take his mind of it, he walked back into his front room, switching the Radio 3 on as he passed it. There might be some brass band music on. Sitting down, his hand touched his stick, his old friend for many years, which has been there for the whole time he was in the kitchen. That stick had been his old friend for years now. Unable to get up out of the chair without it, never mind walk into the other room. Well fancy that!! Swings and roundabouts he thought. I might not be able to eat and have a chest and throat that feels like fire, but I've just bloody walked at least fifty steps without my stick. Like everyone, he always took his health for granted when he was younger. Running, walking, dancing, weren't things to be grateful for, were they? That was until his motorbike crash. Everything changed then. His leg was damaged forever. The knee, useless. The leg was thinner, the muscles unused and wasted. There was very little sensation and a general sense of numbness about it. Maurice was just thankful at the time that he hadn't lost it.

Stephen sat in his bedroom on the end of his bed. Opposite him, was his games console which he was playing on now. This console was a 'collective' Christmas present about five years ago and it was getting pretty old now. Being old had its advantages as he could buy games cheaply. This made the fact he could not complete any game not hurt as much. At least not financially. This wasn't because he didn't want to, but because he had thick clumsy fingers and his hand to eye co-ordination was slow. This meant he got frustrated when he came to a difficult bit and got angry at the game and at himself and would not play for a while. He got angry about a lot of things. That he was made fun of at most places he went to, because of his slowness. That he could not play the baritone as well as the other baritone player. The fact that he lived with his brother, at twenty-nine years old. Most of all, it was because he wanted a girlfriend. He was lonely. Everyone he knew from school, had someone. Some were married, or even had children. When was it his turn.

He hadn't felt like going to band tonight. Which was very unusual. He never missed band. They were his only friends and he really enjoyed talking to Liz and a few of the others. But tonight he couldn't' face it, but not really knowing the reason why. He was distracted, floating from one thing to another. He had ventured out of his room to find his brother earlier and to say he would have to give his excuses to band tonight, but Michael wasn't in. The car was missing. Stephen supposed he would be back before band, to pick him up and at that point, he would tell him he wasn't going. Needing a distraction from the way he felt, he started to play. It did distract him and playing for so long he lost track of time and did not realise that the time for band had long gone. Carrying on playing, he wasn't getting sick of it tonight. Stephen had never got such high scores before on this game, he was killing zombies left right and centre, his fingers reacted to every impulse his brain sent, a stone cold killer tonight. He started to laugh, and laugh. Large guffaws, which got louder and louder. If there was anyone left in the house, they would have said it was maniacal.

Keith felt that if people weren't committing crime on the streets, they were trying to hide it from him. He hadn't found anyone up to no good tonight and it wasn't enough for him. It couldn't be true that all people were law abiding and some preparing to go to bed. He wanted, no needed to get someone good and proper.

Michael stood outside the bandroom in amongst the trees. He didn't need to camouflage himself really and there was no one outside or even due to come later. But even if there were, they would never see him as he was so far back in amongst the undergrowth. Norman stood beside him. They stood in silence for a while. Then Michael spoke.

'What are we doing, here, Master?'

'It is rude to question me, Michael, but I will forgive you as you are in training, and you have been chosen for other qualities. I am your teacher and will make you into a fine predator. I am here to study my prey. I do not presume to know everything about them or their habits. And Michael, I can hear them. I hear their plans and it will make it easier for me to snare them, yes?' He lifted his hand, palm upwards and seemed to grab quickly at the air as he pronounced the word 'snare'.

'Oh, yes. Of course. I knew that. I feel I am already far greater than I was. A much better man. I feel King of the World already. You have made me, what I always should have been and I thank you from the bottom of my heart. Also for giving me the lovely Kate, who I definitely feel is my soulmate.'

'Michael, Michael,' Norman laughs, 'you are nowhere near what you will become. You are just a shadow of what you must be. But we will get there, will we not?'

'Yes. Oh yes. But I was wondering. When will I be like Kate and the others?'

'When you are ready. Such a gift has to be earned and I think you should be honoured to know that I have picked you amongst all others to be my special servant. You may see others get turned before you, but they will not be in the same class as yourself. I need you to be just the way you are for the moment. You still have Kate to keep you content for a while.'

'Ha, Ha. Yes. Whilst it's just us guys together, wow, what that Kate can do.....she does this little thing with her..'

The Master turned to him quickly and sharply said, 'I do not wish to know'

'I thought we were friends,' Michael said in a whining voice, sounding rejected.

'We are Teacher and Pupil. Or Master and Servant. Whichever you understand better.'

They stood in silence for while. Michael's mind wandered on the thoughts of the lovely Kate and whether he would see her again soon.

'When I first met her, I thought I had met her before, you know, Kate.'

'Yes, she is from somewhere not far from here. You may have met her before she turned.'

'Oh right,' Michael was quiet for a moment and then murmured, 'You don't seem to be in as good a mood as you were the other night.'

'I am quite perplexed about a matter, Michael. The other night, I started the process of ascending a small group of people, towards what they will one day thank me for making them. Just a small group, you see, who will be part of my army. If I had made many subjects, well...... it would be a lot of work for me to look after. So if I make a small amount, they can recruit others and look after their own. Plus. We need to leave some for our refreshments, yes? So, the food that was especially made for the band, had a special ingredient. And the wine that was supplied.'

'I ate some of that food too!'

'Yes, also you alone drank from my special vintage, which was in my office. Not only do you, and the others have a special place in the world now, you also have, what you might say, a scent or marker on you, that I can find anywhere. And nothing can wash it off or wash it out of you.'

'Fair enough,' Michael said and shrugged his shoulders. 'So why are you perplexed then?'

'Because I expected all of my protégé's to be at home, as until I help them along, they might feel unwell due to the marvelous changes beginning in their body. In their soul. But one is not at home. One is here and I did not want that. A female. And I want to know why and I am how you say *cross* about it.' He seemed to be straining to hear and had his head cocked to one side. He sniffed the air a lot and sometimes opened his red lips, with his mouth wide, he would take in a gulp of air even though, it was clear, he did not breathe. He would then click his tongue on the roof of his mouth like he was tasting something. He then came out of this sensory phase and turned to Michael.

'I want to eat them. To look inside them. To immerse myself in their warm blood. It arouses me. I can do that every day soon. And I will Michael,' He shivered at the thought. It seemed almost orgasmic.

'Us red-blooded males eh? Woman don't get it do they,' Michael said. He had no idea of how intense this perversion was. Norman seemed to shake himself out of it.

'However we have work to be done, places to go, visits to make. You and I, Michael. The night is young. My confusion about this human can wait another day. They will not deter me from my path.'

Tonight, there were two people being very naughty on the canal path. Nick Smith was up to quite a lot with his best friends wife. It wasn't the first time either. They were only about six feet on to the path and Claire was worried they would be seen. She stopped kissing Nick and pulled his hand out from under her dress.

'Let's go a bit further, baby, we might get seen.' She said.

'We won't get seen, we might get heard though, you get too carried away, ohh Nick…ohh Nick,' he mocked in a breathy girls voice.

'Cheeky!' she laughed and grabbed him by the hand and pulled him further down the path. They were so drunk.

She leaned against the wall, and put her arms around him, chewing his ear.

'Hard and for a long time tonight, Baby.' She asked.

'Your wish is my command.' He bent her over the wall and they were both soon groaning. They were hot and nearly fully clothed and didn't feel the cool November air. Even though it was pitch black they both had their eyes closed in ecstasy.

Keith removed his baton and tapped the wall with it. They both looked at him, definitely inebriated and the woman giggled.

'Shit!' she said.

'What are you looking at Pig,' grunted the man as he continued with what he was doing. 'Are you jealous? You don't look like you get much. Just give me a few minutes and I'll be done. You won't put me off. Nothing does. I could probably even manage to give it to your wife after this one, if you can't manage it. '

Keith's eyes flared and he snarled through his teeth.

'You have just made a very serious mistake,' He raised his baton. Keith narrowed his eyes and he looked at the woman who was trying to pull up her underwear. 'Run. Now.' He hissed at the woman. And she did.

Maurice sat listening to the radio, the sounds of Strauss echoed through his house. He was considering trying out his legs again. There was an insatiable hunger in his stomach, he would kill for liver and onions, but knew he didn't have the ingredients, and wasn't prepared to test his legs enough to the shop and back. His mouth was watering, just thinking about it. On second thoughts, even though he fancied if…..well, the onions would only add to his indigestion. By the time he had made it and eaten it, it would be time for bed. Then he would be trying to sleep on a full stomach. No, no. It was a silly idea. His doorbell rang. Looking at the clock on the mantelpiece, it was now 8.45pm. Very unusual to get callers at this time. Maybe it was Mrs Williams next door, having a funny turn and needing his help. He got up slowly out of his chair. Carefully, but without his stick, using the walls for balance, he made his way to the front door. When he opened it, he was faced with two people. One man he knew well, and one man he had only met once. Both were smiling. 'Come in,' he said.

7 - Turning

As she looked out of her French windows, across the Hills and down to the village below, Christine reflected on the information she had received from the Hospital this morning. She wondered which would get her first, the Alzheimer's or the bailiffs. The race was on. Everything she had fought, lied, cheated and begged for would soon be gone. She had few options left on the bailiff front and little hope for a recovery from the Alzheimer's. A drop of condensation ran down her window and she traced it with her finger. *Why was she so lonely?* No one was here to help her, get her out of her financial mess or give her sympathy or help after her news today. Nevertheless, she would always fight to survive. She turned her direction to The Grange and decided that it wasn't going to be the bailiffs that got her first as least. She wiped her tears away, sniffed and reached for her red lipstick.

Diane was feeling tired. All she was doing was sleeping but never felt refreshed. She really had to kick the habit of drinking so much. She lay in bed with her eyes closed, but awake. She squinted through her eyelids towards the window and realized it was daytime as there was a faint light coming through her curtains. A gap was open at the top, where they were not drawn properly and the light lay across the bottom of her bed in a large triangle. She guessed that she was hung over, but couldn't remember drinking last night. She heard a faint knock on the door and said, 'Yeah?' Her voice sounded small and far away. The door opened, but Diane didn't open her eyes. There was only one person it could be.

'Are you alright?' Sophie asked.

'No, I still feel shit and tired and weak,' she whispered.

'Should I ring the doctors?'

'No. I just need some rest. I've felt worse than this many a time.' There was silence for a moment then Sophie said,

'Your voice sounds really hoarse and quiet, do you want a cuppa?'

'Just a drink of water please, Soph. Is it Thursday?'

'Yeah. Everyone who did the ten piece at the weekend has come down with something. Loads were off last night.'

'That's shit. But at least I know where it came from and it's food poisoning or a bug. I was worried it was more serious than that. Can you straighten my curtains at the top, its bugging me.' Diane murmured.

'Yeah. Will you be alright tonight? I was going to go out.' Sophie crossed the room and sharply pulled the top of the curtains together with both hands.

'I'll pull myself together later and get myself downstairs Soph. I'll be fine.'

'I'll get your water and some tablets,' Sophie said softly as she closed the door behind her, leaving Diane with her thoughts.

Peter Woodall sat in his living room and had not opened the curtains. His black mood spread outwards from him, immersing each room in gloom and anger. He had not spoken to his wife since they had awoken this morning.

'Woody, you look really pale.'

'I feel like shit, that's why, Janet. You don't have to be bloody Sherlock Holmes to work that out,' Woody snapped back at her.

'I'm just saying. Maybe you should get some fresh air. Have a walk or something.'

'Have a walk outside in the cold grey morning, when I feel like this? I'm ill. You're not very bright are you? I don't feel like it and I'm not doing it.'

'It's forecast snow next week. If you wanted a walk, you would be best doing it now.'

'I don't want a walk. It's you who wants me to have a walk,' his voice got louder, 'you go for a bloody walk. Stop annoying me.'

'Why are you being like this with me?' She asked.

'This is me, holding my temper. You wouldn't' like to hear what I really want to say.'

Janet sighed, 'This isn't like you. You will have to get yourself sorted for tomorrow night. You missed band last night, someone will be sitting in your seat if you don't watch it.'

'Ernie can replace me if he wants to. I'm sick of everyone there and they can stick it up their arses.'

'Why are you saying this? You love everyone at band. Did you have a row with them all at the weekend that you didn't tell me about? Did something go on when I was out last night?'

'No. Just go for your walk, woman,' Woody snapped.

'At least open the bloody curtains. It stinks in here as well,' she said as she walked away. Woody muttered something under his breath about having an off stomach, but she felt she had had the last word on the matter. It was time to ring Liz or someone and tell them about this, before it got out of hand.

Keith was sitting in an old chair. One that he had saved when his wife, Yvonne, was on a spring clean and declutter a few years back. Sticking his heels in and he said he wasn't getting rid of it. It was comfy and he liked it and it fitted his body. She said she was changing the living room décor and if he wanted it, it was going in the basement or to the charity shop. So it was in the basement. It had deteriorated somewhat since and now had several strips of black tape holding the stuffing in, but that didn't bother him. After he had taken a lamp down there, he could sit sometimes and do a crossword or read a book. Other men had got their garden sheds and he had his basement. The lamp wasn't on now though. It was dark. Inky black. But he could see. He was thinking about the previous night. The pleasure he took from beating the man and leaving him bleeding on the ground. About later meeting two kindred spirits on the canal path. One more welcome than the other. He had never been friends with

Michael Thompson, he just tolerated him and only spoke when he had to. That seemed to matter less this morning. He definitely saw eye to eye with Norman though. Maybe more than that. They had come to an understanding.

Keith had returned to his broken human on the path. Nick now lay on his basement floor on a piece of carpet. The carpet was red before but redder now. Keith needed to see where humans gushed blood most. He had found out. Nick was still alive, but unconscious and not doing well. His mouth was taped with the same tape that held Keith's armchair together. Confident that he would be a good source of food for a while, Keith felt secure. He rubbed his thumb over the side of his neck discovering he could barely feel the bite now. Feeling powerful, stronger than he ever had, he was angry that his wife was at her sister's for a few days. He could have practiced on her in the comfort of his own basement. Tonight he would have to go out to feed, if he didn't want to finish off Nick. He knew that going out tonight wouldn't be a problem and he leant back in the chair, looked at the ceiling and waited.

Maurice had been busy in the night. First he went to his paper recycling bin and got out a load of newspapers. Then he taped a double layer on all of his windows and shut his curtains again. People would think he was decorating. Then he walked two miles to an all night supermarket. He had made a list. The liver he needed and a loaf of bread. That was it. Trying the self-service till for the first time, which he had avoided before meant but he would have no questions from the till staff. Maurice cleaned them out of liver and took three large carrier bags full, and carried them home, using both his hands, as he had no stick. Without pain, or indigestion or tiredness. He got back about five am and put all of the liver in the fridge apart from two packs. Then he put the kettle on. He set himself a place at the kitchen table. Then put out a knife, fork, plate and salt and pepper. He checked the table, something was missing, what was it? Ah yes, of course, the Brown Sauce. The kettle boiled and he made a pot of tea. Putting the teapot, with it's knitted tea cosy next to his place setting. He tipped the raw liver on his plate and placed it down, looking down at the trays that the liver had been packaged in. Picking up his loaf of bread, he dropped chunks into the empty trays, soaking up all the blood that was at the bottom each tray. He then tipped these red and white clouds of bread onto his plate. On top of the pile of food, he used the salt and pepper and finally plenty of brown sauce. Maurice sat and ate his breakfast heartily. After that, he washed up and cleared up the kitchen. Very contented, he reclined in his usual chair and switched on Breakfast TV.

That evening, Norman was mulling over his recent work. His turning of the old man was easy and he thought he would make a good vampire. Maybe an unexpected vampire to some. Very non threatening. However, the other one, the

Policeman, was a violent human just this side of sane. He would take a lot more controlling and could prove a little problematic. But unfortunately, he had been a member of the band, thus consuming Norman's blood, so he had to be turned after that. Not to mention that he needed to get The Police on his side at some point anyway, for his plan to work. He would keep a close eye on that one. He didn't want to show his hand too early. That could be disastrous.

He heard footsteps on the gravel of his path. This was unexpected, as he had told the waste of skin Michael to call in two hours time at eight o'clock. He walked to his front door and before the person could knock, he opened it. Christine stood in front of him smiling.

'Could I have a word please, sweetie,' she asked and stepped inside without being invited. He moved aside.

'Of course, my dear. Come in.'

She clacked her way across the wooden hall floor. She had high heeled sandals on, and no tights. He noticed she must have gone through some mud on the way down and it was all over her toes. All this in November, too. Hmmm… he sensed a hint of desperation. It was looking good for him. She went into the green room and sat on the sofa. He followed and took a chair that was nearly opposite the sofa. She had a cotton handkerchief in her hands, which was certainly not fresh. She twisted it this way and that in her hands.

'Would you like a wine, Christine?'

'No thank you Norman,' she twisted the handkerchief again, 'I was wondering if you wanted to go into partnership with me? I can see we are alike. You have obviously done well for yourself and we are both business people. I have a few ideas, lots of contacts and a superb business interest that just require a little bit of capital to get off the ground.'

'Yes? What business interest?'

'We will save that for another day, sweetie. You know you can trust me, don't you?'

'Oh Christine. I have heard many things about you. People talk. People at the party for instance. People who work here. People in the bank. One thing I have heard from all of them is that I should never trust you.'

She opened her mouth to speak. Changed her mind and closed it again, then opened and closed again, like a fish trying to breathe.

'You need to start again, if you want my help.'

'It's hard to know where to start.'

'We are perfectly alone. You can be open and honest with me.'

'Alright. In recent times, my affairs haven't quite been in order and it has led me to get in a bit of trouble money-wise. Chrissy can't afford Champagne any more.'

'Or Prosecco from what I hear,' he interjected.

'Well, yes, and then other things have happened and I...I...need help.'

'Would this other thing be, that you have been given shall we say, a long death sentence?'

She looked back at him and he saw her eyes begin to fill with tears.

'How did you know? No one knows. That postman throws his letters into anyone's postbox, willy nilly! '

'No, it was not from a letter, I can assure you. I sense it. Surely you have wondered about me. I know you watch my house and my comings and goings. I aren't your usual neighbour. I am in fact, an unusual neighbour. Which could be good or bad, according to how you look at it.'

'Well, I did notice something's but I didn't like to pry.'

'Not prying is good. But I feel now that I see all your cards on the table and you shall now see some of mine.'

A slight shiver ran up Christine's spine. She felt a little scared, in fact her animal instinct was saying *make an excuse, say you have made a mistake, run home, lock the door and hide under the duvet.*

'Norman, I think I should go now. I am getting rather tired and it's been a long day,' she shakily said.

'Nonsense, my dear. You came here for help. I will help you.' She looked at him with wide eyes and he returned her gaze. He rose from his seat and walked slowly over to her. Their eyes remained fixed on each other. As he sat down beside her, their heads turned towards each other. He put his arm around her. 'How much do you want to live. Would you give your life, to live?'

She swallowed hard, 'I don't understand you….I.. I don't understand you'

'Oh I think you do. I think we understand each other.'

'No, no…this isn't what I want,' *What was he going to do? Was he going to rape or even murder her? What was he talking about when he said she would have to give her life.* She started to move away then became paralysed with fear. His arm around her becomes tighter and then he moved the other one to hold her too. He was so much stronger than her.

'You know too much now Christine. You cannot refuse. You will be helped, but MY way. Which isn't what you wanted is it? What did you expect? Who do you think you are? You are nothing.' She looked up at him. The whites of his eyes had filled with blood. She screamed and then felt as if her breath had stuck in her chest and she couldn't breathe or make any more noise. He roughly pulled her head to one side and bit hard into her neck.

'Michael, I told you my guts are off, why have we got to come here?'

'Stephen, I have got a little extra job now with Mr Morgan and he might have a bit of work for you, so has asked that I bring you.'

'I don't want another job, I've got enough with the one I've got, and band.'

Michael turned towards him and stopped him in his tracks, 'What if this job made you irresistible to women?'

'I wouldn't mind that, but he can't promise

that. That will never happen, and you are daft if you believe that line.'

'It can happen and it has happened ….to me already.'

'Who have you got off with then?'

'A gentleman never tells, Stephen. Remember that, but she can't get enough of me.'

'What's the job?'

'I don't know, but as my job is to do as he says and he said, bring you to him, then I won't be doing my job, if I don't bring you to your job, will I?'

'You're talking double dutch now.'

'That may well be so. But it will all become clear when we get there, because Mr Morgan is very good at expressing himself and you will be very certain of your job then, lad.'

'Fair enough, then.'

They carried on down the path, then through the gates and up the gravel drive in silence. It was very cold and Stephen thought he would be glad to get into the warm.

They rang the bell and heard clattery footsteps coming closer, which they could tell weren't Norman's. The door opened and a large lady opened it. She looked flushed and was giggling. Maybe she even looked a little tiddly.

'Come in, sweeties. Norman is expecting you.' They followed her up the hall and she was indeed unsteady on her feet.

Michael said out of the corner of his mouth to Stephen, 'Don't you call him Norman. It's Mr. Morgan to you.' Stephen replied with a nod.

'He's in his office,' Christine said.

'I know the way,' said Michael and pushed past her. She giggled, which annoyed him and then she walked away. Michael knocked on the door and heard nothing, but entered anyway. Norman was at his desk, both hands on the blotter.

He said in a very relaxed way, 'Just show the boy in, then wait in the other room.'

'Oh, I thought we could have a chat about stuff.'

'Not tonight. After this, I have to go out again. Strike while the iron is hot. Show the boy in.' He then got up from his desk and started to walk towards the door.

He turned round to Stephen, put his hand on his shoulder and said, 'It's for the best, honestly.' Stephen stared at him curiously.

'Eh!'

'Go in then, fool.' Michael pushed him through and Stephen strolled in, and shut the door in Michael's face.

Michael heard a scuffle, just the other side of the door. Then what sounded like a person hitting the other side of the door and sliding down it, to the floor. It didn't bother him one bit.

8 - Garlic

Ernie was on the phone again. He had probably been on and off for about three hours. His wife Lynn was supplying him with constant coffee and homemade biscuits, so there was a silver lining to every cloud. He was making sure that there would be enough tonight to make a viable rehearsal. Some people he couldn't get hold of. He didn't know if they were over their illness or at work. But he wanted at least one in the smaller sections and more in the larger ones, or it wasn't worth pulling Barry out of the pub to do the rehearsal. Cornets were sorted. He had done those first. It looked like Diane was still ill, but Sophie was coming and as she was Principal Cornet and that was all he was bothered about. Liz was going to turn up, *'although not functioning at full capacity, so don't expect too much,'* Andy had said. Maurice was coming. Ernie had expected him not too. As the oldest member that had attended the function on Saturday and, as he was off on Monday, Ernie thought he would be a definite absentee. But no, according to Maurice he felt as right as rain. All the other people, who had played on Saturday were not coming, apart from Liz and Maurice. Keith said he felt better but had had his shift changed at work, so wasn't coming. Ernie couldn't keep up with him, but often the atmosphere in the bandroom was better with him not there, so that was fine. He had the other trombones coming, so he wasn't bothered. He had one euphonium, one baritone, two horns, one of each tuba and four percussionists out of five. That was plenty. He hoped though that this bug, or whatever they had, cleared up soon as it was due to snow next week and he would hear every excuse in the book to get out of band. Rehearsal time was short for this carolling job with the school. He was just thinking about putting extra vitamins in the pot of tea for band, when the phone rang.

Geoff was an ex-serviceman, always pristine in appearance and very stern. He didn't suffer fools gladly and had no sense of humour whatsoever. Other people found him very hard to get along with, which was fine as he didn't get on with most of the band either and got extremely annoyed when people didn't *'pull their weight'*. Geoff was also, in time determined to take over the band and then he would crack down on this lackadaisical behavior. He had a list of forbidden actions. Firstly, not turning up to every band job and rehearsal. Secondly, not practising their parts at home. Thirdly, tea breaks, they were out. Tea was for the sick and infirm.

His son Shaun played on percussion and tonight, they were on their way to band practice with brass band music playing on the CD in the car. Shaun was a very decent young man. Although, since young Bob had started, he had noticed Shaun and Bob being a little disruptive at the back of the bandroom, especially during 'march season' when they had little to do. Tonight, Ernie had told him he was flying solo as

Darren was still off due the mystery illness contracted on Saturday. Geoff thought this mystery illness was probably alcohol related and thus, shameful, to miss two rehearsals. That was unheard of, in his book. He thought that there was more to this than meets the eye about this matter. This required more investigation. Then a sacking.

Gary set off in his old Land Rover. He was big friends with Tony who had persuaded him to get one for himself and he had never looked back. It was especially handy for his plumbing business and it always started. Even if it didn't, Tony knew what to do about it and would come over, then it would be soon chugging along again. Tonight, Gary was giving Danny a lift to band. Ernie had said it was like a Friarmere Plague and he was glad (and so was Ernie) that he hadn't played on Saturday as he was the only flugelhorn and would be sorely missed.

Danny would be the only baritone tonight as Stephen was still ill. Probably the band wouldn't be able to tell as Stephen wasn't the best musician and, half the time, kept his instrument in his lap. So, it was only usually Danny that you heard anyway. Gary pulled up outside Danny's house and, as Danny was looking out between the curtains for him, he came straight out. He opened Gary's back door and put his instrument on the seat, then got in the front, rubbing his hands against the cold.

'Alright Gary?' he said.

'Aye, I am. Are you? Not come down with the lurgy have you, from band?'

'No. I've not seen anyone since Wednesday. Can you smell garlic on me, I've had Bolognese?'

'Yeah I can. I'm glad you're not sitting next to me at band. You can't have garlic lad on the nights you're going band. Smells like that stick for ages down your instrument. You want to do what I do and have a chippy tea. Pudding, peas and chips.'

'You can't have that every time, Gary.'

'I do,' Gary replied, 'You can't beat it.'

'I'd be making other smells if had peas every night,' Danny laughed.

'That is why this cat, lives alone. No ladies to moan at me. Free and easy I am at night. A waft of the duvet, and it's away. It's only natural,' Danny laughed. 'Actually, I would wind your window down, just to be safe.' Gary said, slightly embarrassed. Danny didn't laugh at this and wound his window down, as the waft of digested peas began to get to him.

'Are you having a pint after Danny? I was going to.'

'Oh yeah. We'll have a pint. There is always something to moan about after band.'

'There is indeed. How's the motor?'

'I think she is going to the big scrapyard in the sky. I am going to have to sort another one out.'

'Get one of these. You will never look back. Join the Tony and Gary club.'

'I'll definitely think about it. I don't want another one of those pieces of crap anyway,'

Danny said. Gary indicated right and started to slow down to turn down the road to the bandroom. As they bumped down the country track, Danny nearly hit the ceiling with the combination of the bumps and the suspension on the Land Rover, as he was a good six feet four inches tall. 'On second thoughts, I might not survive one of these Land Rovers.'

'Just brace yourself on the dashboard,' Gary said.

They pulled up outside the bandroom, got out their instruments and went inside.

'Right,' Ernie said, 'Looks like everyone who is coming, is 'ere. A couple have made the effort to come even though they have had this illness from Saturday. So can we show our appreciation for Liz and Maurice.' There was a quiet few seconds of clapping from the rest of the band. Ernie waited until it had ended then spoke again.

'Very important that everyone tries to make all rehearsals as so many are off and we need a balanced band to practice this music for the school gig. So watch who's germ's you're breathing and don't do any skiing.' This was a little joke of Ernie's, but it didn't raise any kind of appreciation.

'It's Armistice this Sunday, so I need everyone fighting fit. Anyway, very kindly, the bloke who booked us last week has sent a few bottles of wine for us to have. Maurice bumped into him, just by chance. Can I stress that only non-drivers can have a glass at break. Whatever's left will be going for raffle prizes at Christmas.' He walked back to his chair at the back and Barry took control of the rehearsal.

They started with a Hymn, ran through Land of Hope and Glory and had just started Jerusalem. When Barry stopped the band, holding his hand over his nose and mouth.

'Someone's bell stinks of garlic!' He shouted.

Gary looked over his glasses at Danny and their eyes met, he gave a brief nod. *Told you so*, it said.

'Sorry Barry,' Danny said quietly, 'I've had bolognese.'

'Hell's teeth lad, my toes are curling. Point your bell elsewhere.'

Everyone laughed and Danny blushed a little but laughed along with them. He tilted his chair more to the right.

'Bloody Nora!' Pat squawked, 'This is the one time I wish Stephen was here, in between us, blocking that stench!'

Everyone laughed again.

Liz looked at Maurice, he could see that she was taking deep breaths as off to stave of vomiting and her eyes were full of tears. Her fingers were holding on to her instrument so tight that the knuckles were white. He looked up and their eyes met.

Maurice stood up, then picked up his stick. 'Sorry Barry, I think it's a bit too much too soon for me. I'll have to get off home.'

'Do you want someone to take you. Make sure you get in ok'

'No, no. You'd better not. Probably safest.'

'Er...ok. Fair enough. Get to bed. I'll ring you tomorrow.'

'Yes, alright. Night everyone.'

'Night', they all called back and Maurice quickly shut the door.

They waited a few seconds then Sophie said, 'I hope it's nothing catching because he has been sitting next to me for half an hour. It's bad enough I've got my mother ill. I don't need old man disease as well.'

'Watch it,' Ernie said. 'He could be right outside the door and that's rude anyway, Sophie. Besides that he has got what your mother has anyway and you haven't caught it off her, have you?'

Sophie hummphed and started fiddling with her music.

'He didn't look good, did he, poor fella?' said Andy.

'No, and I was thinking how good he looked when he came in earlier. He was walking a lot faster than usual and didn't look as tired. He must have just gone off,' Ernie shrugged.

'I think he got a whiff of that garlic. If he's been sick, that will put him right off, especially if its his stomach that is dicky,' Pat grunted.

'Thanks, that's made me feel loads better about my bolognese,' Danny replied.

'Don't have it again on band night,' Barry said shaking his head, 'they are dropping like flies as it is'

Maurice got outside the bandroom and took in the fresh cool night air through his nose several times. He didn't breathe it in. He didn't breathe anymore so he couldn't. The smell of that garlic was terrible. It was all he could do to not just run out of the room, without his stick, screaming. Starting to relax, the fresh air was slowly wiping away the smell of the garlic. So, this was one of the new things he had discovered about himself. There were positives, yes. He felt healthy, he had no pain or stiffness in his leg. In fact it was as good as the other. His eyesight had improved. He had worn his glasses for band, but looked over the top of them to read the music, so as not to be found out. The negatives, well, he couldn't bear garlic, which he used to love. He couldn't go out into the daylight, which was going to stop him visiting one of his old friends in Whitby, the week after next. And he was going to spend a fortune on meat if he didn't want to bite someone. He didn't want to name what he was. Maybe he was in denial, but so what. Rome wasn't built in a day. Did he mind? Hmmmm...that was difficult. No, it wasn't difficult. He did mind. That is why he was lying in word and deed to just keep his old life. He wasn't exactly embracing it was he. Plus, he had just worked out that his cornet mouthpiece had been pressing on his new teeth. That wasn't good either.

Sandra Jones, or Mrs Jones, as she was known to her pupils walked out of the bright fluorescent lights of the school foyer into the dark cold night. She loved this time of year. Her favourite term was the Autumn Term. New pupils, Harvest, Halloween, Bonfire Night and now on to Christmas preparations. She had stayed late with Mrs White, who was Head of Music and Mr Shufflebotham, Headteacher, to sort our all Christmas activities. There was the Christmas Party to organise, talent show, buying the Christmas tree, the fancy dress competition, the school Christmas Fayre and three concerts. One for the school only, inside the school hall. One in the Church including a Christingle service and a joint one in the village with the local brass band. This was always the best one and her own children enjoyed it because both parents were involved as her husband Simon, played with the brass band.

As she walked, her mind drifted. She wondered what time Simon would get home tonight. He said he was going for a few drinks with the others. She knew they often had a few drinks. However, she had gone one time, about three months ago to surprise him, and he hadn't been there. She stayed for a 'quick one' with the others but she felt they were tense and hiding something. Some of them were over enthusiastic which made it worse. Her spider sense was tingling. When she got home, Simon still wasn't in. She waited up, which was unusual. He didn't get back for another hour. She had asked him if had enjoyed band and he said yes. Then about going for drinks after and he said he had been talking about mouthpieces with some of the lads and the benefits of a fourth valve. Then he quickly went upstairs and had a shower. She followed him up and examined his clothes, smelling the ladies perfume on them, that definitely wasn't hers. She looked at his phone and found messages from someone called Tracy. What was in the messages left her no doubt. But what could she do. Confront him, and he could go and be with this Tracy. She decided to sleep on it. Although she didn't sleep much that night. In the morning, after thinking about the children, she decided to leave it and see what happens. The following practice she followed him and saw where he went. Tracy answered the door and from what she could see from the texts and how Tracy had greeted him, he was pulling the wool over both their eyes. She thought she would hate her, but she didn't. Only pity and sadness about the whole situation. She had driven back towards home and felt strangely alright about it all, so had called for a drive through meal, from McDonalds. Turned her music on and ate her burger and drank her milkshake, singing aloud all the way home. She knew where she was at least with him, now. Sandra knew, deep down that tonight, he would be late.

She was halfway down the school drive when she saw some movement up ahead, near the hedge. A crouched figure could just about be seen in the darkness of the November night. It pulled her right out of her thoughts of Simon. Her stomach tensed. *Oh no, what if it is a pervert or a group of druggies or something.* She looked back at the school entrance and the light was

was still on but no sign of Mrs White or Mr Shufflebotham. It was so quiet here, they would definitely hear her scream.

'Hello?' she said quietly. No answer. 'Hello?' she said a little louder and moved two steps backward. Then she something glitter or glint on their body, in the reflections of the school lights. *They have a knife!* She held her breath. She took another step back. They moved and suddenly stood up, tall. *Run!* Then at the last moment she noticed that the silver was buttons were on a uniform and it was a policeman. She let out all her breath in relief.

'Hello, you had me worried there,' she walked further towards the policeman, then realised who it was, especially with the height. He bent down again, away from her to examine something in the bushes. 'No band tonight, Keith?' she asked.

'No. Come help me with this, I think it's a hurt animal,' She walked up beside him and looked down at the place he was looking at.

'Where? It's too dark. I can't see anything.'

He looked up at her, smiled, then reached up, grabbed two handfuls of her coat, and with his immense strength pulled her down until she was beneath him. Where was the scream that was in her throat a minute ago? Gone. Just a strange a..a...a......a....a.... noise came out. It wasn't enough to save her.

When Mr Shufflebotham and Mrs White wound their way down the long drive in their cars, ten minutes later, the hedge was empty. All was peaceful again.

The Thompsons were walking along the lane, in the rain. It ran across the highest peak in Friarmere. To the left, there were just moors, black now and silent. To the right, the village of Friarmere. From the lowest part of the village if you looked up with all the hills and streets, way past them upwards to the farms above it, this lane looked like the hairline to a giant face. A long punctuation, civil from uncivilized.

Michael had parked half a mile away. There were no street lights and very few houses along here. Thus, very few cars. There was no pavement on this lane, and it was lined with dry-stone walls and high trees at either side. This meant that in November, it had thick clumps of rotting leaves at the side.The scent was strong of damp wood, mossy rocks, leaves and soil.

They arrived at their destination, which was a lovely farm with its entrance on this highest point but it went down and lay on the side of the hill. As they stood at the entrance to the track, the natural break in the trees, meant they could see the whole of Friarmere, stretching out beneath them. All the little lights, making straight and curvy patterns, like a toy village. How many parents were telling their children fairy tales where good triumphs over evil, then to tuck them into bed with a drink of hot chocolate, to dream of dragons and trolls and adventures that would never happen in real life. No bogeymen here, of course. What a perfect and lovely village they lived in. What an idyllic setting, a place where children were safe to play in the streets, where so many happy memories were made. Nothing could ever happen here. That was for other places.

One of the bogeymen, Michael read the sign out loud to his brother. 'Lazy Farm,' this was the one he had thought of. He had noticed this place on one his walks and thought it was ideal for his purpose.

'Come on Stephen,' he said and they began to walk down the cobbled path towards the farm. Within five minutes they had passed over the cattle grid and were well and truly on farm property. Michael knew there was a public footpath here that led back down through the village. It was definitely less work, better parking and flatter ground. However, it came out right in the middle of a large settlement of detached houses though, so he knew he would have to enter and exit from this way, to risk being discovered. He was just wondering if he had gone too far when he noticed the styal on the path, which gave entrance to the corner of the field on the other side of the wall. He looked over the wall squinting, trying to see through the darkness into the field, but he could see little. He thought he could hear movement though. Before getting his mobile phone out, to use as a light, he quickly glanced towards the farm to check all was safe. He switched on the light and in the distance could see the milky white oval shapes of a few sheep.

'Go on then, they're in there.'

'What are?' asked Stephen.

'Sheep, and that's what you'll be having from now on.'

'Norman said that for the moment we should keep a low profile and just eat raw meat. I thought he meant from the shop.'

'Yes, he did, but we aren't made of money, and you don't get fresher than that in that field. I am assured you can cope with any eventuality, from The Master, but as I aren't turned yet, I won't be partaking. Norman has told me I am meant for great work with him, so he is keeping me alive for the moment.'

'I don't think I am going to like doing this.'

Michael thought for a moment then said, 'how do you know if you haven't tried it?'

Stephen nodded. 'You're right there. Have you got a penknife or something like that, Michael?"

'Why are you going to whittle them something first?

'No, to stab them.'

'Er...no. You will have to bite through the wool, Stephen.'

'Oh, I don't really want to do that.'

'It is on his orders to eat raw meat and it is on my orders that this is the meat you are eating. Get used to it, because until he tells me otherwise, this is your dining table.'

Stephen took a couple of steps forward towards the styal and seemed to be squaring the notion in his head. Then he put one of his hands on the top of the styal and vaulted quickly over using the one hand. He must have easily jumped six feet into the air. He started to walk forward.

'By the way, Stephen,' Stephen stopped and turned towards him, his face white and his eyes dark and hollow in the night. He was changing for the kill and Michael was scared. He was always in danger, whilst he was still alive. He cleared his throat and coughed. 'Bring the carcass back up with you, it will only get covered in maggots and stuff here. I am partial to a bit of mutton. I'll see you at the gate, when you are finished. Don't come up until you are satisfied.'

He quickly walked away and out of the corner of his eye saw Stephen turn back and walk towards the flock. Ten seconds later he heard a dreadful scream of pain and knew Stephen had begun his evening meal. The next time would be easier. He walked quickly up the track, his chest really taking the strain as he gasped to cope with the steep incline to the top. At least it had stopped raining now. He could hear the rest of the sheep running from the carnage, bleating in panic. *Run and hide little sheep. You won't escape your fate. He will get you next time*. He chuckled to himself. As long as he could control Stephen, until he was turned too, this was going to turn out great. But he didn't like the look on Stephen's face when he was standing in that field. That scared him. He was different, changed, pale, freakish. This wasn't his brother anymore. For a slight instant, he thought he had made a mistake. What had he done? Was it worth it? There was no going back now. No taking anything back to the shop for a refund and setting things to rights. His brother was a monster. Plain and simple. In fact, he didn't have a brother anymore. His brother was dead and he was now an only child. He reached the top of the hill and stood with his hand on the gatepost of the farm, looking down towards the track. He couldn't hear anything and wondered what was going on. Looking up to the sky he felt that nothing would be the same again, which was great as his life had been shit. His mother had left them when they were younger for his father's best friend and when he was seventeen his father died. Little Stephen was only six. So he had looked after him, hadn't he? That's what the rest of the family all expected. His aunties and uncles and cousins and the odd grandparent. They wouldn't have accepted that he should go into care, and he agreed. But it wasn't easy. They brought around quite a few cooked meals for a few years, money and looked after Stephen whilst Michael had worked. Somehow he had coped, got him to an adult age, where he could look after himself. Surprisingly now looking back, it seemed a short time. But it had left him changed. It was hard to make and sustain friendships, never mind romantic relationships when you had to look after your younger brother every night. And look at him now forty, no friends, no wife or children of his own. He just had Stephen. And at twenty nine, Stephen just had him too. Well, their luck had just changed, hadn't it? This was where they started, getting the women and the power and everything they always wanted.

He thought he saw a movement in the field to the right of him and after a few seconds recognised that it was Stephen coming towards him. It was hard to see him because he looked so dark, as he got closer, and a cloud moved itself away above him, he noticed in the moonlight that it was not just dark, but a dark red and Stephen was covered in blood. Michael's breath caught in his chest as he absorbed the macabre sight. His face, the front of his hair, his shirt, shoulders, arms and hands. The top of his jeans were still blue, but his knees were black with a combination of blood and mud. In amongst the strong smells that emanated from him, there was also another whiff – maybe sheep poo. He swallowed, his throat, very dry.

'What the bloody hell,' said Michael.

'I've made a mess.'

'I can see that. How am I getting you home, like that?

'I don't know. Have you got some baby wipes in the car?'

'I think it might take a bit more than that, you can't see yourself can you. Where's my fresh mutton as well?'

'Back down there. I've come up for the bin bag you said you would put him in.'

'You could have brought it up here, you bloody fool! Saved your legs.'

'No. I must have gone a bit mad and it's in pieces. Er...you know chunks and bits of lumps and stuff. It's still good meat though, definitely the legs are still whole.'

Michael stood with his mouth open and thought long and hard. He unrolled the roll of bin bags that were in his pocket.

'One or two?' he asked.

'I'd better take two,' he replied.

Michael rolled off two bags and tore them quickly at the perforations. Then handed them to Stephen who turned around and clumped slowly back down the field. Michael rolled a few more bin bags out and started to open them flat, he would put them on his car seat. The baby wipes would just have to do, until they got home.

9 – The Pub

Maurice was considering an evening walk. It was hard not to run down the street clicking his heels together. He didn't have to use his stick, he didn't get tired, he didn't have to avoid the cold which troubled his joints so much or slippery conditions where he would end up breaking his neck. But oh, how he felt guilty. He knew what he was now, of course he did. But he was determined not to let it control him. He would control it. If Liz could do it, so could he. He knew she was infected, but didn't know if she knew how, or why, or if he was. But he knew she was carrying on with her life and so would he. Of course it would be more difficult when she was finally turned.

It was Saturday evening and Maurice knew that this meant a gathering of the clan, so to speak, in the local pub.

It was a lovely pub. Unchanged by time, real fires, real ale of course and tasty pub grub. They always sat in the same alcove too. They would take turns in going down early and saving the seats. But, even if they didn't, most people knew that it was their place for the Saturday evening and left well alone. If a visitor came, well, they talked so loud and laughed so heartily amongst themselves that they soon felt uncomfortable and found another seat.

Maurice wanted to go, but he couldn't trust himself around them yet. *What if he had an uncontrollable urge and bit one of them?* He had to know his new self better first. The other matter was, he didn't know what he would be able to drink. *What if he vomited blood all over them after having a pint of mild?* He also felt like a spy, in fact he decided, he was a spy, after turning on them by giving them all that wine. Maurice knew what was in that wine, of course. But he was compelled to do what The Master told him to. This was not too bad, he supposed. He could have been ordered to bite or kill one of them. At least this didn't make him a criminal and he decided he had spent his entire life on the right side of the law, why change things now.

He also missed his best friend Freddie. He really hoped he hadn't drank any of that wine. But knowing Freddie, he hadn't. Now if it had been ale, well, he would bet all his savings that Freddie would be infected now.

He decided he would go for that walk and thought about what he should wear. He didn't feel the cold anymore, so didn't need the warm coat, scarf or cap. If fact he could go out in his underpants and he wouldn't have one goosebump. Appearance mattered very much at the moment though, so he gathered together all of his various bits and bobs. He picked up a couple of spare carrier bags and stuffed them into his pocket, deciding to visit the supermarket for some more liver, which would save him a journey. He opened the door and it was a fine clear night. Lovely. Out he stepped, closed the door and walked smartly down the path. As he opened his front gate, it suddenly struck him.

Blast it! My stick! That wouldn't do at all, so he turned back towards the house, went in and picked it up. As he closed his front door again, the next-door neighbour was just coming in with a takeaway pizza box and a six pack of beer.

'Are you fixing her up?' he asked Maurice.

'What? What do you mean?'

'Your house?'

'No. Why do you say that?'

'The newspaper at the windows. It must be really dark in there. What's that in aid of?"

'Oh, yes. I am decorating, you were right the first time. I was miles away Eddie.'

'Ah right thought so. Do you want a slice of pizza, you are welcome to one. I will be eating the leftovers for breakfast anyway.' Maurice could smell each and every topping on the pizza.

'Extra garlic, no thanks. I'll pass.'

'Going out on a hot date are you and don't want to knock her out before you have had a goodnight kiss?'

'Something like that. See you later Eddie.'

'Bye' Eddie said and went happily through his door to enjoy his tea.

Another time, I would have really enjoyed that pizza, Maurice thought. He shook his head and set off towards the village.

Bob was on the phone to his friend Adam. They had been discussing the merits of which gun to use on a zombie game and they both had different but valid opinions on the merits of each.

'What are you doing tonight?' Bob asked.

'Just Xbox. My Mum is meeting her new

friend, so I have the house to myself. I have got a massive bag of popcorn and a big bottle of Coke, so I'm set. Are you off to the pub, you alcoholic.' Adam laughed.

'Yeah, just going for a few hours, as usual. I will be on the Coke too though. I will be back by nine, if you want a game?'

'I will still be online at twelve, mate. She will be out for ages, so I will see you later.'

'Prepare to be well and truly thrashed,' Bob taunted.

'You and whose army?' Adam replied.

The boys both laughed and Bob put down the receiver. He made out to Adam that it was a bit of a chore going down to the pub and sitting with all the 'oldies' and drinking Coke but he loved it. He took out his best jeans out of the drawer and pulled on a t-shirt. He hoped it wouldn't be just them tonight down the pub, that would be boring. The way things were though, everyone was getting ill these days.

Freddie was off to the pub. Saturday, actually, the whole weekend would be very boring without it. The highlight of the week for him. He quite readily would volunteer to go down first and save the seats. Plus on Saturdays, his wife liked to watch reality TV shows about dancing, and he couldn't abide them.

He enjoyed being band librarian. He had never played an instrument, or wished to. He was best utilised on the periphery, and lets face it, some people had to be the workers whilst others were the queen bees. His wife had no interest in it, so band was like his garden shed. Plus, she was always doing things with her three sisters, so everyone was happy.

When he was about two minutes from the pub, he saw a familiar figure coming in towards from the opposite direction. Short, stocky, with a cap and stick, he knew that person anywhere. His old friend, Maurice.

Maurice saw him and waggled his stick at him in greeting and the both closed the distance between each other.

'How do? You are going in the wrong direction Mo.'

'I'm crying off tonight, Freddie. I'm not right yet, just off to the shop to get some essentials, you know.'

'You need some lubrication down your neck, that's what you need.'

'Oooh, I couldn't face it. Really.'

'You must be ill then! I hope you have had some medicine.'

'I'll get something from the shop. I will be as right as rain soon, Freddie. Don't worry.'

'I will be, until you are sorted, Mo. Ring me if you want anything.'

Freddie set off and was soon at the pub. He opened the door to the foyer, walked in and let the swing door shut behind him. The dark was outside and in here it was like a gentle caress of tasty food smells, beer and salt and vinegar crisps. It was always warm, sometimes overly as the fires were quite large and it also had the benefit of central heating. He took off his overcoat and laid it on the chair at one table, hat on another chair and cardigan on another. Freddie went to over the bar and spoke to the barmaid who he had known for thirty years, hell, even his children had gone to school with her. She knew his tipple, so it was already halfway poured when he got there. They spoke about the weather for a moment, then she gave him his pint. He picked up a menu from a pile off the bar and sat down. He always ate the same meal here, but liked to think that he wasn't stuck in his ways so still had a look. He sat down at another table so in fact he had occupied several tables. He wasn't worried, as there was only a young couple in the bar who were situated in another alcove so he was in no danger of feeling he should move or make room. He looked at the menu, whilst having a drink of his beer and thought *mmm…what shall I have, curry? No. Scampi and chips? No. I know, what about steak and ale pie, with puff pastry and chips? Yes, that's it.* He slowly got up after having another sip of his drink and walked over to the bar.

The barmaid said, 'Steak and ale pie Freddie?'

'Yes,' he said, 'steak and ale pie, for a change,' he winked at her.

'Ok, I will bring it over when it is ready.'

'Thank you very much,' he replied and returned to his seat, knowing his pie would only be fifteen minutes at the most, and by that time some of the others would be in. Some ate meals there and some didn't, but no one cared really what the others consumed as they were just there for the conversation and company. He had just settled himself when he saw two friendly faces smiling through the little windows into the pub. They noisily came into the small vestibule, there was a waft of cold crisp air and they began hanging up their coats. Irene, was a very slim, small Scottish lady, who was dreamy, spiritual and referred to herself as *'Wee Renee'*. So that is what everyone else called her too. She always wore strange clothes that didn't match and had an other-worldly aura about her. Her friend Pat was the opposite. Large, loud and a woman of great appetites. She drank stout and tales were told of all the husbands she had had before moving to Friarmere, but no one dared to ask her the truth. Opposites attract however and Pat and Wee Renee were the very best of friends. They played in different sections of the band, Wee Renee on cornet and Pat on horn but they always stood together when it came to opinions on music and everything else, whether that was politics, tattoos or which washing powder was the best.

They went to the bar and ordered their drink and meal. Wee Renee went for a small sweet sherry and a cheese salad sandwich. Pat went for half a pint of stout, large fish and chips, bread and butter with chocolate fudge cake and fresh cream for pudding.

'I'll get the cutlery,' she said. Wee Renee picked up both drinks and came straight over to sit down with Freddie. She had a shopping bag with her which contained all manner of secrets and everyone knew she liked a seat at the back so she could get her flask of herbal tea out and drink it later. Pat followed a minute later, three sets of cutlery in one hand, salt and vinegar in the other hand, tomato ketchup under one armpit and brown sauce under the other. She dropped herself down on one of the soft chairs and unloaded her burdens.

'I brought you one Freddie, you know you always forget until it arrives,' she nudged him.

'Thoughtful as ever, Pat,' he said.

'And brown. I know you like brown on your pie.'

'I might not be having pie. I am a man of mystery. No one knows my next move.'

'I'd bet my best knickers you are having pie. I've never seen you eat anything else.'

'Alright. I am having pie,' he laughed, 'you can keep your knickers on.'

'They are wee pink ones. I've seen them on the washing line,' Wee Renee joked.

'Nothing of mine is wee, Rene,' Pat replied.

Freddie took a drink of his beer at that point, and kept quiet, which was best. He thought that was enough talk about Pat's knickers. Freddie liked them both very much and they were very good company on their own, but especially together. They really bounced off each other and many times it was like watching a cabaret show.

Outside, Maurice looked through the window. He watched Freddie, Pat and Wee Renee laughing and ached to be inside and part of it all. It made him feel immensely sad for his old life and wished for his old knees back and all his frailties. He hadn't realised how much he enjoyed his life until it was gone. Walking to the shop he had had an idea, he had bought four packets of liver, which he thought at this time of night, didn't look too suspicious and he had also bought one bottle of Guinness. Maybe, if he tried it at home, and it gave him no severe after effects then perhaps, cravings withstanding, and if he hadn't attacked the postman, next week he could come to the pub and join in with everyone else. Maybe just live in hope that no one ordered garlic mushrooms. Just then the landlord came round and shut all the curtains, not noticing Maurice as he was laughing at something Pat had said and his eyes were on her. Maurice drew back. He felt shut off from the band, in more ways than one now. He sadly went off into the night, to his dark house, with the newspaper on the windows and the solitary prospect of his liver and Guinness supper.

One by one they came into the pub. The biggest group being Bob, with his parents, Tony and Sue. Soon the alcove was full, and tables were loaded with glasses, plates and crisp packets. Bob had wanted the foot long *'dog'* which he had foolishly put too much ketchup on, and had splattered everywhere. Wee Renee was trying to get it out of Gary's fair isle sweater with some baby wipes.

'I'm so sorry Gary,' Sue embarrassingly said, 'he won't be told, you know.'

'It's not a problem, I have got everything on

this. That's why I always wear patterned ones. They last longer until the wash. I have egg and everything on this, you know.'

'I think it is wise for me to take it home and give it a wee wash in fairy suds,' said Wee Renee, giving up on the baby wipes and putting them back in her bag.

'No, Wee Renee, it's good enough that is,' he replied without even checking the stain.

Bob was on his phone texting his friend, ignoring all the fuss that he had caused. He had tried this tactic many times to avoid trouble and it mostly worked.

'I saw Maurice earlier, on the way here. He is getting himself some medicine, so should be on the mend soon, Ernie.'

'Good news. I said to Lynn, that he looked very peaky last week. You're here though, Liz. Always the trooper.'

'Yeah, I couldn't face being in on my own and Andy was coming anyway. I thought it would be good for a distraction.'

'Janet rang Liz yesterday. She is really worried about Woody. He hasn't been to work, still ill from last week.'

'She is really fretting, bless her, because she had to go on a weekend residential course with work this weekend and you know how funny they are if you don't go. She wanted to look after Woody even though she says he is in a mood with her. He promised her he would come out tonight and meet us. I am wondering if he is too ill or too miserable to come,' Liz said.

'I'll give him a ring,' Ernie assured her.

'It's like a wee plague,' Wee Renee whispered.

'Yeah, a zombie plague,' said Bob, with an interested look on his face. 'Or vampires.'

They all laughed.

'You with your horror club. You and Adam, want to watch some spy films or adventure films, or something. You pair are horror mad.'

'Rest assured lad, if they rock up to our front door, I still have my gun!' Tony said loudly.

'Shh.....' said Sue, poking him in leg, 'you won't have it long, if you keep shouting about it.'

'What's this, Tony?' Pat said excited, 'I never knew you were pistol packing!'

'It was his grandad's, Pat. It probably doesn't even work. It was from the war.'

'It does work, I've taken it up on the moors and shot some tin cans up there.'

'Oh, have you now? When was I going to hear about this?' Sue asked.

Tony didn't reply and looked up to the ceiling for inspiration.

'Guns are useless on things like that, Dad. You need to join horror club with me and Adam.'

'He's right, you know. Guns don't work. I, myself have witnessed all sorts of weird and strange things roam these moors. On this plane and from beyond the veil, believe me,' Wee Renee said in a quivering voice. Looking around them all with large eyes in distress.

Pat surveyed the others, waiting for someone to dispute this. Then when they didn't, she sniffed and finished her drink.

'Has anyone here considered it could be

aliens.....or pod people,' whispered Gary.

Bob stuck two thumbs at Gary.

'Brilliant.'

'Anyone for another?' Tony asked.

Woody lay on top of his bed considering what Janet has asked him to do. He didn't feel like going to the pub and making conversation with people. He was generally an amiable bloke, always had been. Not this last week. He had told her just what she wanted to hear so she would go and not worry about him. She had rang today. He didn't want to answer the phone, speak to her or anyone else, but he knew if he didn't she would be straight in the car back down to him, to see what was wrong. As he preferred to be on his own, he had chosen this option and put on his best *I am okay* voice, to quickly get free of the situation. He never had any intention of going to the pub. She had left him all his meals for the two days she was away - food on separate plates, covered with foil, in the fridge. Each plate had a sticky note with the instructions on how to heat it, stuck to the top. He hadn't ate since she had gone and was used to eating quite a lot. So what he did now was rub his stomach and just think about how ill he was and how he just wanted it to go away. The thought had crossed his mind that he might be getting depressed as he had never felt like this before. Trying to cheer himself up, he got off the bed, slowly went down the stairs one at a time, holding tight to the banister, and sat down in his chair, exhausted. He put on the football that he had recorded earlier. He thought he might drop off this morning so had set the recorder. In fact he had been asleep all day. He had no energy, and knew usually he constantly ate large meals, snacks and fatty foods, so he could transport his body to work and band and to do the garden. No wonder he felt so weak as no food was inside him. He decided to make an effort, now he had got as far as getting downstairs and wandered into the kitchen. He even struggled to open the fridge and when he did, he leaned with his other hand on the work surface to support him. He peeked under all the circles of foil and decided to eat a couple of sausage out of the one that contained sausage and mash. As usual Janet gave generous portions and there were six fat cooked sausages in there. So he ate three, standing there by the fridge. They tasted good and already he felt a little better. He stood for what he thought was a minute but was actually ten minutes daydreaming, looking into the fridge, but not seeing it. He reached under the foil again and ate the other three, took the plate out and put it on the table, removing the foil. He stared at the plate, the mashed potatoes, peas, onion gravy. No, he couldn't manage that. But then something that his mother used to say, crossed his mind. What was it? *What the eye doesn't see, the heart doesn't grieve over.* He laid the foil flat on the table, and scraped the rest of the meal on top of it, folding the foil over the top, to make a parcel, which went straight into the bin. She would only tell him off if she found the mash in the waste food container. He was just thinking what else he could try to eat out the foil containers when there was a knock at the door.

The Master stood looking through a chink in the curtains at the people in the pub, with one red eye. He could hear everything they were saying and could smell their delicious blood above the food and alcohol. Michael was with him and was trying to look over his shoulder.

'I have plans for them all, you know but in particular I would like that boy and his family. I have never collected a whole family. You would think I have, but something has always happened and I would only get one, sometimes two. Isn't it strange, after all this time, that I haven't done it? I have a special interest in them, but I get the feeling, this is my time and I will get many in this village. Just something on my tick list, Michael.'

'It's good to have goals.' remarked Michael. 'Didn't any of them have your wine?'

'No. Alas, only two had wine the other night. A lot less than I anticipated.'

'It doesn't shock me. A lot are tea drinkers in this band. And if truth were told, I only have wine if someone else is buying. I can be found brewing up more often than not. What are you going to do then? Just wait for them when they go home? Get them all at once?'

'No. it is not what I am about to do it at all. Quick is to be discovered and that is not what I am wanting to do, am I? I am playing the long game. No quick gains. I have made that mistake before. This time I can have it all and that is what

I want, so can wait my own sweet time.'

'Can I ask what you are planning to do with Christine. How does she fit into your plans? I don't like her very much. She thinks she is better than me, and she isn't!'

The master detected a hint of jealousy from Michael. He knew that many people became obsessed with him and wanted to be in his best favour. To be his special one above anyone else. Wasn't that human nature, and Michael was still human. He had to reassure him.

'That is not certain now but she is a good pawn is she not? She has connections. She is useful to our cause.'

'That isn't what you are doing with me is? Using me as a pawn?'

'Of course not,' The Master replied, 'but we all have our roles in this war, even me. I have plans for many of you. For instance, tonight's visit we made. He will make an excellent servant of mine and spreader of the word, so to speak. I think he will be able to be undiscovered for a while. He has control.'

'Ah, Woody yes. Nice bloke is Woody.'

'You see, prior sanity is the biggest part in how they will become. If they have the predisposition to become violent, this will become great once I have made them my own. Some will hide it, some will become terrifying.'

Michael gulped. He could see an aspect of this in Stephen, who before, let's face it, was pretty normal.

'What you don't know is that I have done this many times before. Quite recently in fact so I know what I am doing, no need to be concerned. I think you need to go and check on Stephen. He is still in need of guidance and support.'

'Can't you do it? I don't know what I am doing. Why do I have to have the uncontrollable sibling?'

'You aren't the only one. Maybe I have one too, but that is for another night. Needless to say I have better things to do and more visits to make tonight. I have to visit my friends over the hill. Kate is there at this very moment, visiting her family and chewing the fat, so to speak. Earlier she informed me that other matters require my personal attention there. I will need to do that and back before morning. Tomorrow, I will try to tie up the some loose ends and get to the last few people that I marked on your Bonfire Night. Let each of us attend to our own business.'

10 - Miracle

The following rehearsal night was drizzly and misty. Sue had considered wearing her sheepskin boots for five minutes, when she looked out and saw that it was cold, grey, dark and moon-less. But, thinking about previous mistakes, and boots she had ruined, she had changed her mind. *There will be an inch of mud to step in on the band car park*, she thought. So she traded warmth for waterproof and wore her brown leather boots. She had more on her mind than boots and she hadn't told Tony. This rash of illnesses that were affecting the band was really worrying her. What if Bob caught it? He wasn't fully grown and it might hit him harder. What if it Spanish Flu or Bird Flu, or worse. Some idiot might have released a kind of germ warfare on them. No. It had to get better soon. She decided she had an overactive imagination.

The bandroom was three-quarters full that night. Ernie was pleased with the attendance and the relief of thinking that he wouldn't have to cancel any future concerts. What was unsettling was the fact that Barry looked ill. He slowly walked from the back of the room by the toilets to the front, holding onto each chair in the row as he passed to the front. They all looked up at him in silence.

'I feel bloody wretched,' said Barry exhaling. 'Awful. Anyway as I am here I might as well get on with it.'

'We don't mind a night off,' said Gary.

'I am not that bad, that I can't manage to stand here and wag my baton in front of you.' He opened the front page of his music score. 'I might have to have a chair though. Ernie can I have the high bar stool from the back, so I can see 'em all.'

'I'll get it,' said Shaun with concern. He picked up the stool over his head, carried it past the other musicians and put it beside Barry.

'Thanks lad,' Barry muttered and lowered himself down on to the stool.

'I'll brew up early,' Sue said as she started to fill the electric kettle.

'Thanks Sue. It might put a bit of lead back in my pencil,' he sighed.

After ten minutes everyone had a cup of tea or coffee made for them and they were laid out with a plate of biscuits and fruit cake that Lynn Cooper had made. They all put their instruments down, and wandered over to the table, or outside for a cigarette. Pleased for the early break, whatever the circumstances, they were in the best spirits that had been since the previous week's concert at The Grange. Lynn was trying to force Barry to have a beef tea that she had made for him. All of a sudden Andy looked at Maurice and then back at where Maurice was sitting.

'Oh my god, Maurice! You haven't got your stick!'

Maurice looked down as if to see it. Then

realization spread all over his face. *They've outed you*, he thought.

'Ah yes…the stick….mmm…the stick. Yes, yes I was meaning to tell you. I've been having intense physiotherapy. My Doctor put me forward to the consultant and I feel ten years younger. I didn't know if it would help, so didn't tell you. Surprise!'

'I am so pleased for you,' exclaimed Freddie, walking over to shake his hand. 'You even managed to keep it from me. Well done!'

Everyone went over to him congratulating him, patting him on the back and asking him all about the physiotherapy. He felt an awful fraud and a liar. But what could he do.

Liz sat in her chair exhausted. She had asked Andy to get her some cake and coffee, but he had become distracted by Maurice's new found vitality and she was still waiting. She felt apart from the group, apart from even herself really. She felt like she was looking down on herself sitting on the chair with her instrument in her lap. Looking down on the situation and seeing it all. *By heck, I hope I am wrong or going mad. I must be*. She thought about what Maurice had just said. Ten years younger? She felt Ten years older, at least. Certainly last time she had seen herself reflected in the tv, when it was off, she looked it and had avoided looking into the mirror these last few days, it only depressed her. Liz was tired, weak and sick of fighting it. She knew what Maurice was. Is this what it did? Made you feel so ill, and weak and desperate that you caved in and became one of *them*? You need to stop feeling so wretched and you know there is only one way out. Well, she wasn't going willingly. She wasn't going to be on her own ever, either. Liz made sure she was always in the room with someone. Determined that she wouldn't miss band practice, that was when they would get you. She was questioning her sanity again, when Andy plopped himself down in the next chair to her with her cake and coffee. Liz jumped up in her chair.

'Sorry!'

'I was miles away, Andy.'

'Great news about Maurice, isn't it,' he chirped happily.

'Yeah, great,' She uttered unenthusiastically.

The Master and Michael were standing outside the band room watching the band in the mist. Again the Master was sensing the air with his mouth open. He turned to Michael and spoke angrily.

'She is still inside I don't understand what has happened. She is fighting it better than anyone I have ever known. Like she is not craving the meat. But I know she is feeling the infection within her. Why doesn't she stay alone so I may help her?'

'Oh, do you mean Liz? Yes, she won't crave meat, will she. It will be her first time if she does. She's a vegetarian. She only eats vegetables and rice and tofu and them mung beans.' Michael shook his head at the silliness of this.

'How perplexing. I had heard there was such

a thing but I didn't think it was true. I want to know how I am going to turn her. And what will she eat. She will need blood or else she will wither like a rose in the winter. But I have shown my hand to someone for once, in error, and this time it may work against me. I already have a problem elsewhere and a new violent vampire to try and control. I don't need two albatrosses around my neck. To think of it like that, it might be for the best all round, if she was Stephen's first real kill.'

'He might not like that. He liked Liz and Andy a lot.'

'He might not for now. But his old life and feelings with be replaced with his new strength and power. Slowly it will ebb away, as he *becomes*.' He stood with his thoughts looking the place over again.

'There is one other inside that is also affected but we will get around to him at some point.' A rustling in the trees behind them made them turn, and Stephen joined them. Even in the darkness they could see he was in a horrific state. Covered in blood and other matter, but smiling.

'I've put the bin bag in the car,' he said, pleased with himself. Michael turned around to look at him and Stephen winked at him.

'What the bloody hell is that dangling from your forehead,' Michael exclaimed as he naturally picked it off Stephen's head. 'Is it a bit of grass?' He looked down at his hand, tilting it to pick up a bit of light from the bandroom. All of a sudden he dropped it on the ground. 'No it's a bloody vein! Gross! How did you go on tonight? I hope it is better than it looks. Which is a monstrosity!'

'I think I did a lot better. You'll find that it is mostly in one piece.'

'What do you mean by that?'

'Well I was only just starting and being really careful and the head came off. Just like that!'

'What do you mean? You say *it just come off* like it wasn't it on properly.'

'No, it just come off. So you've got the rest of it.'

'What have you done with the head?'

'Thrown it in the canal. I had eaten the eyes anyway.'

'You will have to go with him next time,' said Norman quietly.

'Do I have to?'

'Yes, you do.'

'Please stop playing,' said Liz and put her hand up in the air. They all immediately stopped. 'Barry I feel really sick.'

'Best get to the lav then,' said Barry.

She stood up, put her instrument on her chair and walked a few steps, then her legs started going wobbly and she felt herself losing consciousness.

'She's going to faint!' Lynn said from the back and sure enough she did. Pat looked over at Wee Renee and mouthed the word *pregnant*. Wee Renee replied *no, cursed* and made the sign of the cross with her hand across her chest. Tony coughed and said the word 'Bullshit!' At the same time Gary and Danny had also witnessed this mouthed dialogue and they both burst out laughing. Pat looked at the three of them, lifted her fist in the air shaking it at them. All this was going on as Ernie, Lynn and all the other members of the band were trying to rouse Liz from her faint.

'She grows weaker, good,' the master drawled menacingly.

'You should have asked me about her. I would've told you she was a vegetarian. Let's plan who we are going to pick next. I know all about them, I can help you.'

'I do not need you to help me I will do it all by myself. I will pick who is best in my game and won't be swayed by someone who you have a grievance with, for example.'

'Can you mind-read, Master. I was just thinking, if you aren't bothered who, well, Tony and Gary annoy me. Ooh, and Pat and Wee bloody Renee.'

'I cannot stand here talking with you all night I have more than one visit to my new children to make.'

The Master arrived at the house with all intentions to knock on the door and be invited in. However, the band member was outside in the back garden sitting on his garden bench waiting for the visit. In fact, he didn't want to miss it, hoping it would happen tonight. The man felt everything that was happening to him and embraced it. He relished the metamorphosis, which the master was going to give him. The other night one person had had a small glass out of the bottle of wine and he had drunk the rest of the bottle. The amount of The Master's blood inside was great and multiplying, his journey was fast and he quickly needed The Master to turn him. He rose from the bench and stepped forward towards The Master with his arms open.

'Hurry. Please. I need you,' he said in a quavering voice. They locked together and he was happy.

Diane loved the way that her new state made her feel. As a woman in her late forties, she had felt time pulling away at her face and body muscles, making them slack and sag. She did as much as she could to prevent them getting worse. But hair dye and makeup couldn't cover bingo wings or what she called her *spaniels ears*. You can't fight time. But now, how wonderful, she had noticed a difference in muscle tone and smoothness of skin since her transformation. Her boobs were definitely firmer and higher. So were her buttocks. The lines had gone from her neck and she would never need Botox. Now, she had a body to die for. Quite literally, and she was going to use it. She did need to feed however. It needed to be something bloody, that is one thing she was certain of. Something nourishing and refreshing. After much soul searching Diane had realised, she didn't want to harm her daughter or, for the moment, some stranger. She decided unfortunately that it had to be next-door's dog that ended up her first meal as a vampire. There was no question of her not being able to overpower him, as she just knew she could. Diane hoped this would be enough to nourish her and she wouldn't have to do it very often. Lets face it, if she took a pet a night, it wouldn't be long before she got discovered. It was hard getting used to this new way of living, if that is what you could call it and she didn't know the rules. There should be a rulebook, instead of being left to discover it all. Maybe she would suggest it to The Master and offer to write it. That would be fun. She realised that when she was in one of these visceral states she needed to ask The Master about what she should do. Or maybe she would ask one of the others, form a small support group. Knowing their numbers would grow day by day, a rulebook would benefit many.

Diane couldn't control herself much longer so decided to get on with the job. She removed all her clothes. That would save on washing, besides that, the chances of getting caught naked were minimal. There was no fear of being seen as her next-door neighbours were always out at this time.

Walking into the kitchen, she took out her largest knife, just to make it easier. *Rule number one* she thought. *Are you able to use your teeth or do you need a weapon?* That was one for the book. Maybe not number one though. Diane had already had to work out about ten things before this.

She went through the adjoining gates and Dino was chained by his lead outside his kennel. A fluffy brown terrier, with glittering black eyes. At first he started wagging his tail, he knew Diane, and his first thought was *doggy treats*. Then as she walked into the light, he knew it wasn't his old friend any longer. He hunched down, cowering, and with a low whine retreated into his kennel. She quickly covered the distance, walking silently on the cold wet grass in her bare feet. There was a very small part of her left that felt regret and guilt, but if it came to the choice of this dog or her daughter, and it did, there was no question to which she would have to choose.

11 - Dogs

'The first stage is done, it is been very successful,' said The Master. 'It has worked on some. The rest will be turned. Then we will take out the remainder of the band. Those that resist, we kill.'

'Yes, Master,' said Kate.

'So I just thought I would just show you a preview of further attractions.'

They were outside the Primary School, looking through the window at the lines of children, practising for the Christmas Concert. A huge school choir, singing a Latin Christmas Carol.

'Look at all those lovely children. I am so looking forward to it,' whispered Kate.

The Master watched the light shining in her dead eyes and chuckled. He took her in his arms and waltzed her around the school playground as the children sang.

Maurice was out on one of his nightly walks. A regular mission to the shop, so that he could buy his liver. It was cold but he was enjoying being outside for once and was taking his time. As he was walking along he saw a picture, and A4 photocopy of a missing dog pinned to a tree. A few steps further and he saw another picture of the same dog on a lamp-post. He stared at the picture, taking it in. He was there quite a while thinking about this the picture and what he should do about it. Or if he should do anything about it all. The street was so quiet, apart from an owl hooting every so often. It gave him plenty of space to think. The picture had a phone number and an address and he knew exactly where this address was. After walking along slowly, looking down at the pavement and his feet walking on it, he decided he would make a visit after he had been to the shops. He needed to give someone a little bit of advice. The owl hooted in agreement.

Bob was on the telephone again to Adam he was discussing the recent absences from band.

"That is really creepy,' said Adam, 'and, yeah I think it is suspicious too. Why do you think it is vampires? Have you seen any punctures?'

'Well, no,' replied Bob.

'They could be kidnapped.'

'They aren't being kidnapped because no one has asked for any ransom and their families aren't rich either.'

'Are you sure you aren't being paranoid. Anyway, don't you have to be a virgin?'

'I don't know. I don't think so. Not if this is right because some of these people are definitely not virgins. But I really think that some are vampires and some are on the brink of becoming vampires. I have just got a really weird feeling about it Adam.'

'Do you think we watch too much Horror?'

'No, not enough and I want you to find out as much as you can about vampires and how you kill them.'

Janet had let the phone ring about twenty times before Liz had picked it up.

'Hi, Liz. It's Janet. How are you?

'I am not well at all.'

'Still got it then? Sorry to hear that. How's Andy?

'He's fine,' Liz replied tiredly.

'It doesn't sound like it's catching. At least that's something. I want to talk to you about Peter.'

'Yes, how is Woody?'

'He's not well. He hides away most of the day. I don't know how he feels really. He won't talk to me or tell me about it. In fact, he is nasty to me and aggressive. He won't let me help him. I don't know what to do.'

'That is not Woody. What about getting him to the doctors?'

'Any mention of it and he goes berserk. But I thought I should just tell you, you know. A trouble shared is a trouble halved.'

'Let us know if we can do anything and try and keep cheerful Janet.'

'I am trying, believe me. Bye'

'Bye, Janet,' Liz said sadly.

Keith sat in his basement. At the side of him, on the cold cement floor he had a large hessian shopping bag. In it, were three cats that he had caught one by one. They were pretty hard to catch, even for him. When he had caught them, he had broken their necks. Then he had placed each one in the bag. *For the moment, this would have to be enough* he thought. He did not want his friends or colleagues investigating a whole lot of murders. Norman had spoke to him quite strongly and left him in no question about how far he could go. Keith had lost control twice now, and The Master had to bring those two into the fold, before their time. There was enough going on, with the missing people at band and those that were ill. If anyone checked the infected, and how their symptoms presented themselves, it wouldn't take much for some people to put two and two together. He had to make sure there was nothing else suspicious going on, The Master was right. His survival depended on it too. Everyone would know soon enough.

Woody was not ready to take the next step. He was lying in bed again, analysing how he felt. He felt so powerful, just like when he was a teenager, perhaps even better and he was enjoying that. *The best thing to do was to try and seek out some of the others and find out what he do,* he thought. Staying locked in his bedroom forever was not an option. How many times could he say to Janet, when she came to bed at night, that he would sleep on the sofa and watch his video collection, as he couldn't sleep. If he stayed in the bedroom all night, he *would* harm her. He was making the choice, when she was asleep, to go out and feed on animals, but this would have to end soon.

Colin wanted to bite his wife too. He did not know how he was going to stop this. It was a compulsion stronger than he had ever had. He had always been a small and gentle man, and so was his wife. Why had this happened to him? He decided when he did it, and it would be *when*, he would make it as painless as possible for her.

Keith picked up Yvonne from the train station. It was rainy, and after she got in, the car windows started steaming up, which made him angry. She has been visiting her sister, and as soon as she got in, she was yacking on about this and that. What her sister had got and how lovely her brother-in-law was, and their new car. He was already annoyed as her train was late, so he took the route through the moors, furious because he had had to wait for his wife to come back. Keith had made a plan in his head of how all this would go down. It wasn't going to be tonight, but he realised that this was his ideal opportunity and he was going to go for it. Pulling the car up at a graveled area at the side of the moors, he switched off the engine. It was bleak and insanely dark. He had left streetlights behind about three miles ago and was relieved that the night would veil any *tell tale signs* that he had changed. The rain still came down out of the heavy oppressing clouds. He knew just how to push Yvonne's buttons.

'What have you stopped for?' She asked.

'*What have you stopped for?*' he mimicked in a woman's high voice. 'If you shut up for one minute you will find out!' He shouted.

'Don't you dare shout at me like that,' she said.

'You rude bloody man! My sister never gets spoken to like that!'

'Shut up. I have stopped the car to tell you, you are not allowed to go to your sisters again!'

'How dare you! Who do you think you are? Just because you can tell people off at work, it doesn't mean you can tell me what to do. I'll go to my sisters even more now. I was happy there, you pig!'

Keith smacked her across the face.

'Now you've done it!' She screamed at him whilst she fiddled frantically with the seat belt, and picked up her handbag, before getting out of the car. She briskly started walking down the road away from the car. *That was just perfect,* thought Keith. Attacking her on the moors would ensure minimum clean up and maximum fun. No one would hear her scream. Keith got out of his car and turned his face up to the rain and smiled. It didn't matter how much of a head start he gave her, because he would still catch her. This would have the added bonus of her being weak and less likely to scratch him up. If she thought she could hide, he had a surprise too, his eyesight was even better in the dark. This was just so perfect.

'I'm coming, dear,' he shouted.

'I'm coming to get you,' he laughed madly and raced towards her. A chill ran down Yvonne's back and she started to run.

Ernie had called every band member in the afternoon, but had only managed to reach about ten of them. He had made thirty phone calls.

Surely two thirds of his band was not ill or indisposed? Generally he had a ninety percent success rate. Lynn came in to his office then with a cup of tea and two chocolate digestives. She could tell by his face that all wasn't well.

'Not had much luck, Ern?' She asked.

'No. Only managed to reach ten,' he said gravely.

'What do you think they are up to?'

'I don't know, but they can't all be having a bit of afternoon delight,' he smiled.

'Oh Ernie,' she laughed.

He laughed loudly and she walked out of the room and shut the door. He soon stopped laughing and looked out the window. *What the hell is going on?*

'I have just been having a quick look about vampires on the internet,' Adam said to Bob.

'Okay,' said Bob.

'Has there been any interaction with blood or any sharing of it?'

Bob thought hard and chewed his chewing gum very loud. Adam knew this helped Bob to think and let him chew down the phone as loud as he wanted to.

'Not as I know of,' said Bob, 'but there might have been.'

'Alright. Have you seen any of them react negatively to garlic?'

'Well, I told you about the old guy Maurice. He is back at band but he certainly didn't like smelling garlic when Danny had bolognese the other day. He couldn't get out of the room quick enough. But neither did anyone else so that could mean anything.'

'Any shying away from crosses?'

'Again, can't verify that. My mum wears one, but it is usually under her polo neck.'

'Well, she's not one then,' said Adam.

'I think I knew that. Or my dad.'

'Have you noticed pointy teeth on the suspects or marks on their neck?'

'No. But I wasn't looking that close. I will from now on.'

'Hmmm, very interesting,' said Adam whilst rubbing his chin.

Having little else to do that night, Ernie systematically drove past each band member's house that had not answered his call that day. He parked up. At a lot of them he saw that their car was in, and the lights were on with the curtains closed. He called them but they did not answer. Some looked like they were out, fair enough. Some had the lights off, with the car in and the curtains closed. He rang them too. Still no answer. He wrote all this down and would ponder on it later.

Maurice knocked on the door and half expected that he would get no reply. He was just about to walk off when Sophie answered the door. Maurice was quite surprised, and very pleased that she was obviously still uninfected and human, especially when he knew what she was living with.

'Can I see your Mum?' He said. 'It is very

important, or I wouldn't come, but you see, I had what she has got, and as you can see I am as right as nine-pence now. I have bought her some medicine.' He shook one of the carrier bags at Sophie.

'You had better come in,' she said. He followed her into the hall.

'She is upstairs in her room. I will ask if she can see you.'

'Yes please. If you don't mind,' he replied. Sophie disappeared upstairs and he could hear a brief dialogue through the floorboards. He then heard footsteps on the first couple of stairs.

'You can come up,' Sophie shouted down. He looked up the stairs and she was standing on next to the top step. 'I am going out, so I have to get ready,' and off she walked, back into one of the rooms. Maurice got to the top of the stairs. There were three doors. One was open and he could see that it was the bathroom. Sophie was looking through her wardrobe for something in another room. So it must be the shut door. He knocked lightly, and entered.

The lights were off, and from the brightness of the landing light he could just make out the form of someone lying on the bed. He entered and shut the door behind him and as his vampire eyes got used to the darkness, he could see everything very plainly.

'It is alright Diane,' he said quietly so Sophie wouldn't hear, 'I know what you are. I am the same as you, whatever that may be.'

'Are you really?'

'Yes, I am. I have come to see you, to help

you. To give you a bit of friendly advice.'

'What about?' She asked. 'What do you mean?'

'I happened to notice that your next door's dog has disappeared. Now I don't think it's much of a stretch of the imagination to imagine what has happened.'

'What do you mean?'

'You know what I mean. Just be truthful with me.'

'Well yes, okay, I do know what happened to it.'

'That is enough of that, Diane. I have been coping now for a while and I am here to give you advice.' He dropped one of his carrier bags on to the bed.

'What's that?' She asked.

'Liver. I feel great on it. I eat it raw. You will be absolutely fine if you live on that and you won't have to resort, in desperation, to eating everyone's pets. Try to keep as much of yourself as you can. If you succumb to these feelings you will never come back and Sophie will be in great danger.'

'Okay,' Diane nodded, 'anything else?'

'I find it is even nicer with a bit of salt and pepper.'

12 - Lust

Ernie did not expect any surprise returnees at band and, for the most part, the usual crowd was in attendance. But he was delighted with a visit from Michael Thompson who just turned up out of the blue.

'Hello Michael!' Ernie said, 'I am really surprised to see you. I've had a right time getting enough players for rehearsals since Bonfire Night. Although a couple are making it in, Liz and Maurice. It gives me hope that I will see everyone else soon.'

'Oh, I haven't been well at all. I have been having right conversations with the lavatory bowl,' said Michael, 'and our Stephen has got it worse than me, so I don't know when he'll be back. Anyway, I happened to see Norman out the other day and he said that he had given you some wine. Have you drank it all?'

'Why, do you want some? I have a bottle or two left,' said Ernie. 'I was going to put it in the raffle. People didn't really drink it because they were driving.'

'That explains it,' said Michael pushing his glasses up his nose with one finger. 'No, no, I am alright, I don't need it.'

'Fair enough.'

'So I thought I would come out and try and push myself you know.'

'You want to watch yourself. Liz tried to do that and obviously did a bit too much last week.

She went and fainted.'

'Ah, she did, did she? She wants to get some meat in her.'

'Don't let her hear you say that. You know how she can get about vegetables and the like.'

Liz was listening. One thing that happened was that her hearing had got better even though she felt constantly nauseous. As the days went on, more and more she realised what was happening to her and all the others around her. No, she wasn't mad. The facts kept building up. She knew what was happening and she knew what some people were. For the moment she couldn't voice that, because then she would have to admit what she was. Or nearly was. And she was not ready to hear those words or for anyone else to hear or judge her. She just wanted to carry on and be normal.

Barry was back tonight although he still did not look well. He talked quietly, when he did speak and struggled to sit on his high stool. Vincent had returned about five minutes after band had started and looked very pale but, again, he was trying. He just came in, sat down picked his tuba up, and kept himself to himself, quietly getting on with it. He was keeping up with the music so there were slight improvements, but he kept frowning and it was clear he was finding it hard to concentrate.

Ernie looked around the band. Certainly, there were a couple more people here but they were very pale and looked like they could keel over at any point, just like Liz. He really hoped this thing wasn't catching or was not as serious as it seemed. So that he didn't interrupt band by making a phone call, he decided to go outside and check on arrangements for the concert at the Civic Hall. Picking up his mobile phone, he walked outside. It was very cold. Colder than earlier. The bad weather was definitely on it's way. He quickly rang Stuart, who was also a colleague of Keith's. A fellow policeman. Stuart confirmed everything was still on for that day. Tea and coffee would be provided and Ernie checked the fee for the hall, as well as opening and closing times for him and the band. He was going to mention Keith but thought that Keith would go mad if he sensed that Ernie was checking up on him. *Sod him,* he thought. He shivered and went back into the warm.

The Master watched him do this from the trees and listened intently. People here certainly do have patterns of behavior. They made it so easy for him. This time it was actually going to work. How wonderful. He laughed loudly, no-one could hear him over the band.

Stephen Thompson did not have his brother looking after him tonight, after giving him the slip. He also did not have The Master watching over his shoulder. He knew that some people were infected with The Master's blood as he could smell them too and felt it burning in his veins. He knew of a member of the band, Vicky, who he would love to visit. He had always fancied her. She would never look twice in his direction though and had a boyfriend, Jake, who also played in the band. It really made Stephen angry to see them together. He was so jealous and had fantasized about Vicky and himself for a few years now. Maybe tonight was his night.

Her house looked empty with the curtains closed and the lights off. He knew she was inside, the smell drew him like a magnet. His mouth watered. Stephen tried the front door, which was a latch type and it was locked. The back door, however, was unlocked and he swung the door open. There were advantages to living in the country and open doors was one of them.

'Vicky?' He called but there was no answer. He was about to call again when he heard movement on the stairs. The kitchen door opened from the hall and she was there. 'Stephen,' she said with a sigh, not surprised to see him at all.

He gazed at her, a lust and longing that had needed to be satisfied for so long.

'You are like me,' he said quite plainly.

'You have called for me haven't you?' She smiled.

'Yes, take my hand' he said. She walked to the back door and took his hand. His eyes had never left hers since he had opened the door and she looked at him, unblinking.

'Let's go upstairs.' He said, and stepped in.

Stephen realized that two things were

apparent here. Firstly, he had absolute power over her and he loved it. Secondly, she also knew he had power over her, could do nothing about it and loved it too. She was compelled to do what he commanded. *Cool,* he thought. She walked up the stairs as if in a trance and he followed her. They went into her room and she stood by the bed, turned around and looked at him. As if she was waiting for his next instruction, unable to do anything unless he said it. *Simon says? No this game was Stephen says.*

'You might as well take your clothes off. It would be easier in the long run.' She took off her dressing gown and slipped off her pyjamas. She stood naked in the moonlight, her beautiful body gleaming in the light from the streetlamp, which came through the window and illuminated half the bed. Vicky was very curvy, her voluptuous body was even more fantastic than he had imagined. He stared at her breasts and then between her legs. For a long time he did this. She waited. He did not move from his position. Stephen had never seen a real woman naked and had not been intimate with one in his life. Knowing that he was going to enjoy it this so much, he walked over to her, pushing her down on the bed with one hand and lay down beside her. Unable to delay this any longer he immediately bit her neck. His first taste of human blood and his first woman. They locked together in eternal death and lust.

The rest of the band had gone and Michael

stood outside fiddling with his car keys whilst they all drove off. He could see The Master in his usual place and was desperate to be with him. The Master wanted a word with him too. As soon as the last taillights had disappeared, Michael ran over to The Master. He saw that there were others around him and he started back towards his car.

'Come now,' The Master said to Michael. He didn't want to go over there. That was a proper pack of hyenas. Some he knew and others he didn't. He stood where he was.

'It's alright, er… I'll see you later,' he said, swallowing, and backing away to the safety of his car.

'No need to be worried about this, Michael. You are fine. It is just because you are still made of human flesh. But you have my protection.' Michael was not fully reassured about this but would have to accept it. He walked over to the pack, with a wary look on his face. They all smiled back at him, menacingly.

13 - Sheep

Stephen was in trouble. He had not had the permission of the master to go and visit Vicky. Yes, luckily he had done a good job and had turned her fully into one of their flock. But it was a close thing. He had drained her very low before enjoying her sexually then finally turning her after several hours. The Master said that Michael had to constantly be with Stephen to try and control his behaviour.

That evening one of the Thompsons neighbours who shared a food waste bin with them, went to empty some potato peelings into the bin. As she opened the bin, the smell that wafted out at her was terrible. She looked in the bin and jumped back immediately. She took a deep breath and then warily looked back into the bin. Yes, there were real heads in there. Two sheep's heads. Eyeless, uncooked and bloody. Underneath that she was also surprised to see lots of raw bones. *This wasn't good enough,* she thought. *Disgusting.* She always put food waste in the caddy bags then put them in the green bin. Now that she had seen this monstrosity, not even in caddy bags, she was determined to have a go at the Thompsons. Without thinking twice she went straight to their door and knocked on it. Michael answered.

'Can I come in?' She said abruptly.

'Yes,' he replied and opened the door so she

could get through. She had been in before, many times because she had often been very useful on the neighbourhood watch, where he was the organiser. This time he could tell something was wrong though. Stephen was in the kitchen and the door was shut. This was a good thing, as far as Michael was concerned, as Stephen looked dreadful today. Chalk white and demonic. He was also in a foul mood.

'Take a seat in the living room.' She stomped into the living room and sat down. He could see she was frothing herself up for a confrontation. *Let's get it over with,* he thought. 'What can I do for you, Mrs Welch?'

'Micheal, have you been ordering whole sheep from the butchers, by any chance?'

He thought this was a strange question and then just before he answered, he realised where it might be going.

'Yes I have,' he said boldly. Pleased with her quite innocent, conclusion about the sheep. It could have been a lot worse.

'Can you please not put the raw bones in the communal bin without putting them in the green food bags? Flies will land on there and the next thing you know we will have maggots to try and get rid of. The bin is already smelling very bad.' She sniffed as if this was a final punctuation mark. Mrs Welch waited for Michael to reply. Michael opened his mouth to speak, but then Stephen walked in, silently sauntered past her, all the time glaring at her and sat in the armchair. Michael thought, *oh no, this is going to kick off.* As Michael hadn't replied to her yet, she went into her next rant. 'There was something else in there too. You've been putting loads of cotton wool, from what it looks like, in there too. That does not go in the green bin either. It is not food waste.'

'It isn't cotton wool, it's sheep's wool,' said Stephen openly.

'What do you mean?'

'You heard. The…wool….off….a …sheep.' He said slowly and loudly, defining every word as if she could not understand him or was deaf.

'What?! When you get a lamb from the butchers, it arrives skinned. I have had one before. You can ask for the head and make sheep's head broth. I've never made it but I understand that. However, it never comes with the wool. I know that isn't what have you been putting in there.'

'I tell you it's the wool, I skinned it myself.'

She then saw Michael and Stephen take a quick glance at each other, and straight away she knew something was wrong. Something had been unearthed here and she was going to get to the bottom of it.

'What are we talking about here?' She asked.

There were more looks between the two of them. Micheal ever so slightly shook his head at Stephen. *Please leave it,* he thought.

'You two have been sheep rustling, haven't you?'

'No, we haven't!' Said Michael defensively.

'Yes, we have.' Stephen said at exactly the same time. Michael quickly looked at Stephen and knew he was going to go for it.

'What are you going to do about it?' Stephen said.

'First, I am going to ring the farmer. Then I am going to ring the police.'

'Oh you are, are you?' Michael said, 'You have made a very big mistake saying that to him,' he said sadly.

Stephen stood up and in one second was upon her, ripping the front of her coat open. The big orange buttons flew off across Michael's living room. Michael stood watching, frozen to the spot, unable to make a sound or move. He started to press onto her chest with his strong fingers and as if by magic, Michael thought, her chest began to open. Stephen put his mouth to the gushing wound and began to drink. She was making a gurgling noise and her hands were twitching, squeezing the air. Stephen held her like a rag doll. Her eyes both slowly turned and looked at Michael.

Her hands clutched out to him and her eyes rolled back to Stephen. Even as he looked at this scene he saw the life draining out of her and she slumped backwards, lifeless. Stephen stepped back, dropping her onto the sofa. She bounced a little and the top half of her flopped forward so she lay folded over on her own lap. She looked like she was closely examining her own feet. Blood still came out of her chest and ran down in between her knees onto their carpet. Stephen looked over to Michael.

'So that is how you always get it all over your face?'

'Yes,' said Stephen, 'That is what I usually do.'

'Well we are in a right pickle now. What were you thinking of, putting them sheep bones in the bin?'

'You just told me to get rid of them. That's where we put the stuff isn't it? What we aren't going to eat.'

'Not your carcasses,' he said, 'It obviously was going to incriminate you sooner or later and now look what has happened! What if a gang of bin men had seen it?' Stephen shrugged.

'She won't be telling anyone, now will she?'

'No, but you need to get all them bones out before the bin men come or put them in plenty of caddy bags. Go upstairs and wash your head, whilst I think about what we should do about all this.' Stephen wandered out of the room. Michael looked at the state of his living room and was at a loss of what to do. There was nothing for it, he would have to tell The Master now. This was an actual murder that had happened. He rang the number at The Grange and Kate answered.

'Hello, lovely lady,' he said, 'It's Michael. When are we meeting again?'

'Soon,' said Kate, 'But you know how things are. We are all very busy here and I suppose you are too but we will get together, I promise.'

'I cannot wait. Anyway, can I speak to Norman, please? Important business and all that, you know.'

'Yes, just one moment,' said Kate and he heard her footsteps walk away with the phone. Within a few seconds Norman was on the line.

'What has he done?' Asked Norman crossly.

'How do you know I am ringing about that?' Michael replied astonished.

'Lets just say, I am getting the measure of you and your brother. I just know something has happened. What has he done now?'

'He has killed the next door neighbour,' he blurted out, 'She came and complained about our bin because the silly bugger had been putting sheep bones in there.'

'Right, how bad is it?'

'To be quite frank, she is all over our living room.'

'I will come at once. Keep the boy there, where you can see him.'

Within ten minutes The Master strode through the front door. Stephen was sitting in the chair looking at Mrs Welch with a look of amusement. As if he couldn't remember what she was doing there or how she was in this state. Michael was pacing up and down the house worried about the trouble they were going to get into, and how The Master may punish them.

The Master was very angry when he saw the mess in their living room. He stared at them for a long time, his eyes protruded and a vein twitched in his head. Neither of them dared to speak. He realised they were not good enough to be his disciples. After a while he spoke but it was through gritted teeth.

'Have you not heard of the old saying - don't shit where you eat?' They both shook their heads. 'I will dispose of this body as I am used to these matters. I will also dispose of what you have been putting in the bin. What I am saying to you Stephen, because of this, is from now on, you are not allowed out without me or at least your father and he is in trouble anyway for letting you do this.'

'What was I supposed to do? When he got going he went at her like a freight train. I couldn't have stopped him.'

'I was already angry with the boy because of him turning the girl, the other night. I wished to turn her, in my own time. We were lucky we did manage to turn her, the state he had left her in. Especially after seeing this.'

'No,' Stephen laughed, 'I didn't want to eat her that time I wanted to ...'

'I know what you wanted to do and you did,' The Master said, interrupting him, 'We have that situation with the girl and now on top of that, we have all this. I will clean up this mess. I have done this before but from now on, you are to come and live up at the Grange where I can keep my eye on you all.'

'That is fabulous. It will be like a holiday,' said Michael.

'No, not really. I have several rooms that have not been done up yet, and that is all I have. They do have beds in them however and a lock on the door, which you will find more useful, Michael. You will find there are other people up there that are kept for this very same reason. *To keep my eye on them.*'

'I for one am happy about this scenario,' said Michael with a smile, 'I can't control him on my own, so I need you and some of the others to help me. And I'll be able to see Kate every day too.'

'It is done then,' said The Master

Vicky had called her boyfriend Jake and asked him to come over for the evening. She said she had been to the shop and got some lovely, naughty underwear. She wanted to wear it for Jake that night. Jake was on his way over. He had stopped at the shop for some chocolates, and had seen Maurice in there, buying meat and had had a little chat with him. Maurice did seem on the mend and this put Jake in a good mood. Things were looking up all round. He happily picked up the largest box of chocolates, thinking they were a good thank you for a totally unexpected evening. Whistling all the way to her house, he was even happier when she answered the door in a red silky robe, under which he could see she had very little on underneath. He lifted up her hand and kissed it.

'You're cold,' he said.

'You will have to warm me up then, won't you stud?' She said cheekily. 'Go straight upstairs.' He walked up the stairs, still holding the chocolates under his arm. The bedroom door was open and there were candles lit inside.

'Would you like a glass of wine to relax you?' A large glass was on her beside table and she poured the wine until it was nearly full. She offered out the glass.

'Aren't you having any?'

'I have already had some. Quite a lot in fact.'

He drank his glass down in one, instantly he

felt how potent it was. It certainly made him feel warm and even more amorous towards Vicky. She stepped forward and she opened the drawstring of her silky robe. It fell open and the red satin shone against her skin. It seemed like, in here with the candles and the wine, Jake thought, that her eyes nearly glowed. It was a moment he would take to his grave, Unfortunately that moment wasn't going to be a long time away.

'Come to me,' she whispered. He walked the few steps towards her and she began to undress him. Then he started to kiss her. She opened her mouth and her tongue went in to taste his lips. He did the same to her and noticed that she had quite prominent teeth that tasted like pennies. She lowered him down onto the bed as they still kissed. Her hands moved his head down to her chest, where he still carried on kissing

'Go further,' she said gently and moved his head down until he was just above her small red panties. 'Kiss my thighs,' she said and he started to do that with her hand on the back of his head, which was a tad insistent. Not as he minded. His eyes were closed so he did not see other hand come down towards him and touch her thigh. He felt something hot in his mouth. All of a sudden realising that she had heavily scratched herself on the thigh and the blood was running into his mouth. Strangely he was quite enjoying this, but in the back of his mind, he knew it was wrong. He lifted his head up, his mouth smeared with her blood. She quickly rose up onto her knees pushed him backwards on to the bed, he felt like he was falling forever. A combination of the walk in the cold, the wine and her blood, *what was happening?* He looked at her, he was sinking downwards. She looked so far away, but all the time she was coming closer. The last thing he heard before he closed his eyes was

'Forever, you and me.'

Sue was looking through the window at the houses opposite for her oldest cat. She surveyed the gardens for his little white and ginger body and was starting to get worried. Some cats had been going missing. When she couldn't see him after five minutes she closed her curtains and so missed the car drawing up at the house opposite to her. The owner of the house was a lovely old lady that Sue knew well, named Alice. They often had a chat when they were both out in their front gardens weeding. Sue heard a noise and went into the kitchen. In through the cat flap came Basil. She smiled, all was well in the world. Picking him up, she kissed his ginger head and shut the cat flap for the night.

The man knocked on Alice's door and she happily opened it and let him in. As she walked into her living room, chatting away, the man behind her struck her on the head with her carriage clock that he had just picked up off the sideboard. All of it took eight seconds only. She fell to her knees. He stooped over her, did something to his mouth and then bit down on the back of the neck and started to feed. The old woman did not stand a chance. After five minutes he was satisfied but she had already gone, three minutes before that. He stood up, put his false teeth back in over his new ones and sadly looked at what he had done with unblinking eyes. He stepped over her and walked over to the fireplace, picking up a picture of himself and the older lady who lived there. It was a picture of him and his mother, who he had just killed. He was the first vampire in Friarmere to realise that he could cry.

14 - Wolves

The following Saturday teatime, Sue rang Ernie about the band situation.

'How many people are ill, do you think?'

'That's hard to say. How *ill* are you talking? You have got what I would call the walking wounded, Liz, Maurice etcetera. Then you have got the taken to their beds, like Woody and Diane. All in all, between ten and fifteen. I've made a spreadsheet,' he said quite proudly.

'Go on then, tell me all about it,' said Sue. Ernie told her the list one by one. 'What do you think about it all?' She asked after he had told her his findings.

'Well I don't know,' he said gravely. 'It is something I've never come across before in over thirty years of running this band. It is getting very serious, Sue,' Ernie said.

'There is one question. Is this just an illness or could it be some other person or persons picking us off one by one? Stalking us even... I have asked around, nearly all the cases of this are in our band.'

'Do you mean another band, trying to nobble us?'

'Ernie, this is bigger than band. No. I don't think it is another band. But it is a conspiracy.'

Ernie was quiet for few seconds whilst he thought.

'I would discuss it with Keith, but I can't get hold of him. It amazes me that none of them want to go to the doctors. Yes Sue, I think you're right, there is something fishy going on.'

'Although I don't want to face it, I am thinking that the type of stuff Bob watches could actually be coming true.'

'Do you mean out of those horror stories?' asked Ernie.

'Yes, something like that. I think that could be a little far-fetched but there is definitely something amiss. We have to think outside the box to solve this.'

'We will keep our ears to the ground. I'll do a bit of snooping around,' said Ernie.

Ernie picked up his telephone directory to decide whom to call first. He called Keith again and there was no reply. He called Sophie and Diane's house. Sophie was just about to go on a night out and said her mother certainly looked better, but was staying in her room most of the time and had told Sophie that it was a ladies problem. So, she was keeping well out of it. Ernie, thought that was good advice for him too, but wondered if it really was ladies problems after all. That couldn't be what was wrong with Keith or the other men who were ill. Or he hoped not.

He called the Woodall's and Janet answered the phone.

'How is everything. How are you?' asked Ernie.

'I am absolutely fine, but I am so worried about Peter, he just locks himself away all the time. If I am in one place, he will make sure he is in another. It is so out of character, Ernie. I don't know what to do.'

'Maybe I will come round to yours, for a little visit,' said Ernie after a thought. 'Yes, I'll bring Lynn and maybe a couple of the others. Bring him a get well soon card. Maybe that will cheer him up and change this situation. Act like a catalyst for recovery.'

'Yes please Ernie. I don't know where to turn. I have been telling Liz about it but she isn't well either, so I don't want to burden her too much.' Ernie could tell that Janet was getting upset and soon she was full blown blubbering down the phone.

'I tell you what. I will call on my way to the pub tonight, maybe we can persuade him to come out and pull him out of his mood.'

'That would be great,' said Janet and put the phone down with a relieved sigh. Everything would be fine now she had help and an outside intervention. She felt a hand on her shoulder.

'You silly woman,' Peter said with a growl. She turned quickly towards him his face furious and wild and waxy white. His lips pressed together like an uneven gash. He grabbed her by the shoulders. 'We do not need interference at this stage. Now I have to do what I must, but then it was only a matter of time after all.' She could not believe that earlier, she had thought he looked so weak. In astonishment, she looked into his face for the last time. With amazing strength he pulled Janet towards her sticky end and bit down hungrily on her neck.

About an hour later, Ernie and Lynn Cooper

drew up outside the Woodall's house. They both got out and walked up the path towards the front door. The curtains were closed and there was no light on. However, Ernie had said he would call and he always kept his word. It was quite clear he was needed here. He knocked on the door, rang the bell and waited a minute. Ernie looked at Lynn.

'They're not in.' She said.

'They are supposed to be and we're expected,' he said to her and knocked and rang all over again. When no one replied this time they walked back down the path with a heavy heart. *What was going on in Friarmere?*

Tommy Proctor, one of the local farmers was in the pub talking to the barmaid. His head was in his hands and he was on his fourth pint of beer. He stood at the bar against the bar-stool. There was no one else in the pub as it was bitterly cold tonight. They could hear the wind roaring down the chimney.

'They are all gone,' Tommy said weakly, 'I don't know what has happened. The police say they will look into it. But what am I supposed to do with myself. I have no sheep left in my field. They have either been taken or torn apart. I keep finding bits of them everywhere. It has cost me thousands of pounds. I just don't know how to stop it happening in one of my other pastures.' He shook his head and drank another half pint of his beer straight down. 'My best bet is that it is wolves.'

'Wolves? Here on the moors? You are

kidding. What did the police say?' The barmaid had become fascinated once Tommy had mentioned wolves. This was becoming a very interesting tale.

'They are about, I've heard them the last month. Never before. But now I do. It makes me shiver in my bed. The police think the same as I do. Some wolves or a pack of dogs.'

'You know, it may be some of those banned breeds that people have let loose,' she said as she wiped the bar.

'I'm not ruling anything out. If it is wolves or banned breeds, it would spread like wildfire on the moors. I need to let everyone know, being the first victim of it all. It's only responsible. I don't think it is foxes. There would have to be an awful lot of them if it was, and I have not seen any signs of them on my land whatsoever.'

'How many foxes would it take?'

'I don't know. But at a guess, with the carnage I found, I would say a pack of twenty or so. But they are solitary creatures. Foxes doesn't tally up at all.'

Freddie came into the pub, took off his hat and coat and placed it on the chair in his usual manner, then stood in front of the fire for a moment rubbing his hands, to get warm. He walked over to the bar and picked up a menu. 'It is a bitter night.' Freddie said to the barmaid. 'You can smell the snow on its way.' He ordered his pint. 'Alright Tommy?' When the farmer looked up at him with baleful eyes he realised he had asked the wrong question. The farmer told his tale again to Freddie, who was shocked. He had obviously heard of livestock going missing but not a whole field full so quickly.

The first people to come in that night ten minutes later were Tony, Sue and Bob. There was already the first light grains of snow falling and Bob was excited about the prospect of school being called off for the following Monday. They sat down and Freddie beckoned them closer, so he could speak secretly.

'I have got something to tell you when everyone is here.' They were intrigued, so ordered their drinks and food and waited for the news.

Ernie and Lynn came, then Liz and Andy, Gary and Danny and a couple of the others. The last being Wee Renee and Pat, who had seen this snow before they had left their houses and seemed to be dressed for the Arctic.

Freddie poked the fire and looked around the pub. There was no one else in there still, only Tommy, who was still at the bar. He said to them all 'We need a chat.' Everyone nodded in agreement. Freddie said 'Gather in a bit. I don't want to shout it out.' They all moved in a bit and he told the tale of Tommy's sheep. Afterwards they all looked over at Tommy, his back hunched over his glass. He was now on his sixth pint of beer and considering going on to the hard stuff. They started to talk about the current situation at band.

'I have rung Keith, Diane and Woody this afternoon,' said Ernie, 'I didn't get to speak to any of them but spoke to Sophie who seems to think that Diane is on the mend. When I spoke to Janet she was very concerned about Peter, so me and Lynn called round on our way here. She knew we were coming and wanted us to try to get him to come out of himself and get him to the pub tonight. But, when we got there the lights were off and they didn't answer the door. It is so strange.'

'So let's go through the evidence we have.' They nodded. 'Several people ill, most of those went to the party and we are assuming that they got some kind of food poisoning. Then there are a couple of new people who feel ill, but they did not go to the party. It does not seem to be airborne, as Sophie would have it, so I am wondering if this is a disease at all. Even people who are ill are acting very strangely. Not just physical symptoms, but a change in behaviour. To add to that, now we have this flock of sheep missing.' Ernie picked up a beer mat and tapped it on the table. 'I don't see how there is a connection. But there could be.'

'Tommy hearing wolves? That's hair-raising. You know how isolated his farm is. Can you imagine lying in bed and hearing that?' Sue said.

'I feel that there is a general sense of dread and I don't like saying that. That is not me,' Ernie admitted and he was right. He was the most level-headed man, they knew.

'There is definitely something weird going on,' said Wee Renee.

'Oh yes. As sure as eggs are eggs,' said Pat, 'Me and Rene have been talking about it. There is something afoot but we can't quite put our finger on it.'

'That isn't the only thing. Have you noticed that there are animals going missing? Pets, not livestock. I have seen posters for missing cats and a dog around. What is happening to them? That can't be wolves, they are in the village. People would have caught sight of them.' Said Gary.

'I am telling you now,' said Bob, taking a deep breath. 'I have been talking to my friend Adam about this and the more you think about it, and then realise it can't be this and it can't be that, ruling everything out, the only thing we can think of is vampires.' There. It was said.

'But what we are forgetting,' said Freddie, 'Is that there is one person sitting here that was in fact ill, and is still coming to band. She isn't a vampire. Or not that Andy has informed me,' he chuckled. 'What is your take on it Liz?' He asked.

Liz had been quiet during this whole conversation. Looking back, she had been quiet for the last few weeks. Deep inside her heart she knew what was going on. Were they ready to hear it? What the hell.

'I do know more than you think and you won't want to hear this, but I think Bob is right.' She paused. 'Or *may* be partly right. We are being slowly taken over and controlled. I have so many urges now that go beyond human comprehension. I feel low, animalistic... subhuman. I want to do things I know I shouldn't and have constantly stopped myself.' They were all dreadfully shocked at this. 'I'm actually, just the last couple of days, starting to feel stronger and getting myself back. Maybe this kind of infection is slowly coming out of my body. I haven't acted on any impulses but I did want to eat raw meat, which as you know for me is a terrible thing. But I have managed not to do it. I have spoken to Andy in the last couple of days, and he knows the way that I feel. What I think has happened is that someone or a group of people put something in the food and drink at The Grange. I don't know why, but since then we have been dropping like flies. I feel there are two stages to the descent. One is urges, needs and illness and a desperate cry for it to stop. It's torture. The solution or medicine is the second stage when you act on the urges and you can become something else. The torture will stop. I do know some people who feel like this amongst our band, but it is up to them, not me, to tell you. I don't think that's fair, to out them. After all, it isn't their fault. I also think it would hurt some people, if they knew their friends were infected. And maybe they will fight it like me. I don't know.. maybe it is some kind of germ warfare, I am so confused. But from everything I have felt, know, or sense from the last few weeks, I think that the vampire line sounds the best.' Andy put his arm around her and Sue rubbed her hand the other side.

'I can't believe we are talking about this!' Danny said. 'This is a load of old codswallop'

'You have got to agree Danny that there is a dividing line between what we know to be fact and what we have yet to discover. Perhaps we are about to step over that line.' Wee Renee said.

'I suggest that we all watch each other very carefully. To protect each other and also watch for changes,' Ernie said. He then looked Liz straight in the eye and shook his head. 'I am sorry Liz, but I think you should tell us everything you know. I don't care, if you think you are *outing* them. These are peoples lives we are playing with. So exactly who are all these band members that you have come across who we need to worry about.'

She looked around the group and knew she had no choice to tell them now. She knew she would feel better if she did anyway. Her gaze fell on Freddie.

'You won't want to hear this but of course one of them is Maurice. He was there that night and he did not fight it. He is the only one I am sure about, as I have been in his presence. I am unsure about Keith and Diane, as I haven't been close to them in a while. And of course Stephen and Michael'

'In the end we need to find out as much as we can about vampires, even if it is just to rule it out,' said Tony.

'I mean, as much as it grieves me, it seems the easiest thing to believe. The one thing that answers all these questions is the classic vampire,' Gary said.

'Add to all that this fact. We all have heard that vampires don't like garlic. The night that

Danny had bolognese and you could smell garlic all round the bandroom, I was nearly sick. It was so hard to stave off. But did you notice that Maurice had to go home? I think that garlic is definitely something that works and it ties in with the vampire mythology,' Liz said.

'What is their next step?' Ernie said. 'How does it happen if you *don't* resist it? Do you know?'

'No. I know that it takes an outside intervention for this but obviously that hasn't happened to me. To tell you the truth I have stuck to Andy like glue and felt that I have been watched a lot of the time.' They all turned towards the window. The curtains were shut apart from about two inches in the middle, so they could just see the snow coming down outside.

'Did you see something then?' Freddie asked quickly.

'No, it is just the shadows,' said Danny. But it wasn't and they all felt it.

'This is making shivers run up and down my spine!' Lynn said.

'I think they must have run over from mine,' said Pat.

'The problem is, if they are coming to get us then the only thing we can do is kill them,' said Bob matter-of-factly.

'That is something we would have to be sure of, son, before we started taking that kind of approach,' said Tony.

'Yes, I agree Dad. What we know is that garlic repels them but does not kill them. So how do we kill them?' Bob asked.

The Master had crawled down from the roof of the pub. His head faced downwards, looking through a chink in curtains. They couldn't see him. His legs were splayed above him either side the upstairs window of the pub. He had slithered down from the roof. It was harder to night-crawl in the snow, but not impossible. Thankfully for him, he could still manage to slyly watch them. These people were cleverer than he thought. They were piecing it together and his plan would have to move along a little quicker than he thought. He had someone to visit tonight and that would be another one in his clutch. Norman wouldn't learn much more here. Now to the escalation of the game.

In a moment he crawled backwards up to the roof, his head low, smoothly retreating last from the street. He had disappeared into the snow. But outside the pub, the malevolent atmosphere remained.

15 - Police

There was a chalk dusting of snow on the ground for band practice on Monday. It was dry snow, with a mixture of ice crystals. The ground was ice cold, the air frigid too. Ernie sat in his sitting room, listening to the odd car go past, crunching on the crispy snow and cracking the ice on the odd puddle. There was nothing to prevent anyone from coming to band tonight, it wasn't slippy and it wasn't deep. He was expecting a good turnout.

Ernie sighed and took a drink of his tea. He looked out of the window from his seat and was miles away in thought. He picked up the phone and called the police station, hoping not to get Keith but to get Stuart, the only other local policeman. There were only two police officers in Friarmere. Ernie did not trust Keith. He wasn't his favourite person at the best of times, but he just knew that Keith was involved in all this. He spoke to Stuart who was quite shocked and dumbfounded by Ernie's story. Keith wasn't mentioned. He hadn't ever been called about missing sheep or a rash of illnesses in the village. He would have thought that the local doctor would be the first to know about this, not him. Stuart also wondered what Ernie expected him to do about it.

'Do you think that there are any suspicious circumstances regarding these absences?' He asked.

'Well, I don't know,' he swallowed, 'I thought that would be a matter for you, not me.'

'I'll give it my full attention,' Stuart said, winding up the conversation. He put the phone down, smiled and shook his head. There certainly were some funny folk in Friarmere. He carried on writing his report.

Ernie wouldn't tell him about the band suspicions. Why or what was making this happen? He thought he would leave that to Stuart to find out. He also neglected to say that he thought Keith was involved because he thought that Stuart might not believe him. He would probably think he was going mad and if he did find any clues it might put all the other evidence in jeopardy. Let him sort it out with an open mind. Stuart should have a more investigative brain than him so he would let him put it together piece by piece. Turn it over to the professionals. Get it off his plate.

Sue had made a list over the weekend of all the players in the band. Then marked off people that went to the play at The Grange that night in green highlighter pen. After that, she had taken her red pen and marked off those that were not coming at all, or those that had come and now weren't and it was very worrying. It was all of them except Liz. She tapped her pen on her lip, forgetting that she hadn't put the top back on. *What had happened that night? Could they be right?*

That night Liz was in attendance as usual and felt slightly better than she had even on Saturday. In fact, a little bit of colour was in her cheeks and they didn't look as hollow as they had. As if to make things worse, there was a bad cold going around at the moment and a couple of them had come down with this. Danny had decided not to come to Band that night. He had taken a look at the freezing cold day and put his head back under his quilt, telling Ernie that he was concerned about spreading it around. However, Barry did have it and had picked up a pretty bad case of it. Luckily, as he didn't have to blow down an instrument he had turned up anyway, and was back on his stool with his conductors baton poised and ready. The last band job they had done had been for Armistice Sunday, which was particularly cold this year. Never to be put off, they had still played and placed the Wreath of Remembrance. It was wicked cold that day though, and had got them deep in their bones. Everyone was sniffling in the band.

Freddie was wiping his nose and was also looking to the prospect of going home to an empty house. That day his wife's sister, who lived over the hill, had called his wife to say how very poorly she was. She couldn't even get out of bed and look after herself in a basic way. Also there was a little dog to consider. He needed feeding and walking. His wife Brenda, was very worried as this was her older sister who now had just turned seventy. She had two other sisters and the four of them were extremely close. Her eldest sister who had called her, named Doris was very close to his wife, who was the second eldest. Brenda was quite clearly worried and so Freddie had suggested that she go and maybe look after her for a few days. What had also crossed Freddie's mind was that this meant that Brenda would be out of harms way if something was going to happen in Friarmere. Freddie would manage quite easily on tins of tomato soup and bread rolls. He enjoyed having soup with so much pepper that it looked like a black hat on the surface. It made his nose run, but that was the just the way Freddie rolled, head hanging over the soup, sneezing away. But Brenda would tell him off, saying anything that made you do that was quite clearly bad for you. Now he could have free reign with the pepper pot.

He had driven her up to her sister's. Doris was in bed and one of her sisters was already there. Brenda had a key anyway so she got out of the car with her suitcase and some of the substantial medicine stack of theirs in a bag and went on up to the front door. Freddie was happy as she was safe and that meant he could go to Band or the pub and not worry about her being on her own. She was well out of harms way, definitely.

There was a sombre mood in Band that night. Everyone was worried but no one discussed it. Tonight they just played music to take their minds off it, which for a small time it did. They were practising their songs for the carol concert with the school choir. Mrs White, had called to say that all tickets were sold. She said she could have sold double the amount that the hall could hold. They had all been thinking about it over the weekend and called each other a few times to clarify some points. No matter what explanations they tried, really they could come up with nothing that fit the bill as accurately as vampires. Especially with the evidence of the garlic and Liz's testimony.

Stuart was at the station front desk drinking a coffee and eating a custard tart. He was thinking about everything Ernie had told him. He had been on his rounds earlier and seen a couple of people walking around, very pale and acting suspiciously. They seemed not to want to talk or meet his gaze. Once they noticed him, they would dart up a street out of the way. He had a wander to the local shop to ask if the shopkeepers were having any problems. They said business was booming and were very happy. Indeed the place was more packed than usual for this time of day. But all the time he stood there, no one came to the counter. After he left, he doubled back on himself and looked through the window. They had all left the back of the shop where they had been lurking and went to the till in silence to pay for their baskets of shopping. He tried to see what was in their baskets from the window. Only half the till area was visible. From what he could see, apart from raw meat, there was little else in each basket.

How weird. It was natural that people would want to eat protein if they were ill, but why couldn't they pay for it in front of him. Usually, people hid things they were ashamed off. *There was no possible reason to be hiding raw meat from him, was there?* He put this together with what Ernie had said, on the way back to the station. Maybe he had been a little dismissive earlier. He respected Ernie and thought that he would not call him unless he was extremely worried and serious about this. Stuart thought that he would have to you discuss it with Keith and then maybe contact someone from HQ that was higher up the chain to see what could be done. The more he thought about it, the more he thought it certainly looked like a matter bigger than the two of them. He didn't look forward to discussing it with Keith who was generally a miserable sod. Another thought crossed his mind. Why Ernie had chosen to call him instead of Keith who was in the actual band that Ernie was talking about? Keith had been turning up for work so obviously he wasn't infected. Ernie hadn't mentioned if he had been turning up for band or not. Stuart did half of the police hours allocated and Keith did the other and they were very seldom on together. Tonight Stuart had decided to stay behind and wait for Keith to check in. He took out another custard tart and began to eat it. Yes, he would wait for Keith. There was no need for twenty-four hour cover in this small village. They only sometimes had the odd drunk to contend with or a stranger speeding through the village. Most of the time their ships crossed in the night.

He looked at the other custard tart left in the box and considered saving it for Keith. *Sod him*, he thought. Ate it quickly, throwing the box in the bin just as Keith came through the front door.

'Keith,' said Stuart.

'Stuart,' said Keith in acknowledgement. Keith looked like he was in a foul mood and Stuart did not relish this conversation at all.

'I thought you were finishing half an hour ago!' Said Keith rudely.

'Yes, I was. But I need a chat. A bit of advice.'

'Right...' said Keith suspiciously.

'Yes, I have had one of your friends on earlier from Friarmere Band, Ernie Cooper, telling me that he thinks there is something going on in the village.'

'Right.'

'He mentioned something about people being ill and also about a lot of missing sheep which I was not aware of. I had a look through the last few days paperwork, but didn't see a report about it.'

'Ah, yes that was me that Tommy spoke to. He said he has a few sheep missing. I don't think it's anything to worry about.'

'Don't you think that you should be letting me know that. I could be looking into what is going on as well. From what I hear it was not a few but a whole flock.'

'No, no. I've just told you, I don't think it's anything to worry about.'

'Alright, so what about they all these people that are ill and not doing what they should be?

They are not able to carry on with their lives as normal. I have seen some in the shop myself tonight. We should be doing something about that. We may be able to prevent some kind of epidemic.'

'I don't agree,' said Keith.

'So you don't agree that there is a problem with a load of sheep missing? Or that people are coming down with some mysterious illness?'

'No,' said Keith abruptly.

'Well I do think there is a problem. I have a responsibility to Friarmere,' said Stuart firmly. 'So, I am going to call Head Office and ask for reinforcements and more investigations. There could be something going on in a few villages or maybe nationally and we haven't been informed.'

'Just hold on for a moment,' said Keith, using his pass code to come into the office, and slowly walking around the desk towards Stuart. His eyes never left him but Stuart was picking up the telephone receiver, determined to do what he thought was right.

'Why is that? We aren't doing our job, protecting people and their property, if we don't act on this information Keith. This is not like you. I am disappointed.'

'I am so glad that you discussed this with me first. Because, I can't let you tell anyone else or bring any outsiders into this village.' Stuart quickly looked up from the telephone keypad at Keith, who was on Stuart faster than he could have believed possible. He snatched the receiver out of Stuart's hand and hit him across the side of the head with it, striking his temple.

As Stuart's head lay on the desk he aggressively tore at the side of Stuarts throat ripping away his Police uniform, with his fingernails. The Master had said when Stuart became involved, when he started to discover them, then it would be up to Keith to sort it. But that he would have to make the Police Officer one of his own. Keith did not agree with this and so badly wanted to kill this man, as he had never had much respect for Stuart. He thought that there was only room for one vampire policeman in the village. But the Master had decreed it, so Stuart was to become a vampire too. Maybe Keith would like him more as a vampire. They would protect Friarmere's secrets and keep them well hidden whilst they multiplied.

16 - Coffee

It was quarter past six in the morning and Mark was cheerfully doing his usual job of delivering milk to the village of Friarmere. It was extremely cold on his milk float, but luckily for Mark there was no one else about so he was having a nip of rum out of a hip flask. If the police had pulled him over and breathalysed him, he was in fact still over the limit from last night. He had delivered to most of the village and was just on his last stop which was right at the top of Friarmere, at a lady's house called Christine. He did not ever go further than her house to The Grange because it was just a dirt track and his milk float would never have made it. If they asked him to start delivering milk there, he would turn them down flat. Luckily Christine's house was on the corner of the main road and this track, or she wouldn't have got it either. He parked at the top of the track on the main road, picked up his milk crate and walked down to her path. It was still dark and extremely cold. He put her milk and two yoghurts on her front step. As he stood up he had the feeling that someone was behind him. He knew there was. Even in his inebriated state, his hair stood on end. Every fibre of him screamed danger. He froze, holding his breath. He did not want to turn around. He couldn't if he had wanted to. Mark was right of course. But it wasn't someone, *it was something*, and there were three of them. He looked forward and gulped. The door of the house opened and

Christine stood framed by a dull light behind her. He focused on her scarlet lips, so red with lipstick, that they fascinated him. He stared, forgetting the feeling of terror he had had a few seconds before and cocked his head. His breath came out like a mist in the cold morning. Hers didn't, as she spoke directly to him, their eyes locked together.

'I don't need milk anymore, Mark. So I don't need you either.'

He only felt the strike on his head for a second then he crumpled to the frozen floor. A milk bottle smashing on Christine's path, like a scream, that no living person heard. They dragged him down the lane towards The Grange where his fate would be decided.

Teresa stamped her feet against the cold. It was gently snowing again and she thought about how she would love to be back in bed. She was waiting for Laura, who owned this mobile coffee station. They would alternate days, one opening up at six am and the other would turn up at seven-thirty am. Today was Teresa's early day and Laura would still be snuggled up in bed, she bet. She was parked outside the little railway station in Friarmere and they did great business here every day. Usually it was people on their way to work, one way into Manchester and the other way to Leeds, picking up a latte and a chocolate muffin. They would also get the odd dog walker or teenager off to school or college. This was a great job in the summer. She was done by eleven, and Laura paid her well, so she was free the rest of the day to do what she liked. She warmed her hands on the coffee machine. At least she had that. Plus, several layers of thermal underwear. It wasn't that bad. She was waiting for her regulars. Over time, she knew who wanted what, who was in a rush and who wanted to stop and have a chat. Teresa did really like this job. The next train was due in in five minutes and then would carry on towards the city. Not many people got off here, not many people at all. They were on their way from the other little villages, to the city. No reason to get off here and not enough time to get a coffee from her. So when the train drew in and the people got on she was surprised to see one person get off. It was very dark. It would be another hour before it would be a light and there was still no sign of dawn at all. She saw the man coming towards her, from the station platform and thought he was up for a welcome cup of coffee, to keep him warm on his way home, or wherever he was off to.

'Morning. What would you like?' Teresa asked. Turning towards her coffee machine.

'Something sweet,' he chuckled.

'Ah, right you are,' she said as looked in her basket full of goodies. 'We have flapjacks, muffins and some rocky roads, or I could do you a coffee with syrup. Are you after a sugar rush?'

'Yessss...' He hissed as she felt her scarf being grabbed and twisted round her neck. He wrenched her backwards by it, his strength sudden, and overwhelming. She quickly tried to grab hold of the coffee machine to pull herself away and back from his grasp. She saw the coffee machine moving further away from her. He drew the scarf closer to his mouth. When he got it there, no longer useful, he threw it on to the ground and bit into her neck. She yelped in pain as he bit down further and twisted her head. He knew the way to stop that noise.

Laura came early at seven and from a distance saw that there was a queue at the coffee van. *Great! Business was booming*, she thought. She walked up to the front to help Teresa and Teresa wasn't there. Just a long queue of people, looking with hope at the steaming coffee maker.

'Where's she gone?' She said to the others.

'She wasn't here,' one of them said. 'But we thought she would be back soon, so we started the queue.'

'I've got to catch a train soon,' another said, 'but I might as well stand here instead of up there, if there's a chance of coffee.'

'Okay,' she said, 'maybe she's got a problem or been caught short,' she said reassuringly and started to make the coffee for the people that were waiting. When Teresa didn't turn up after a while, Laura was worried that she must have had an accident and decided that she would contact the police. They said they would fully investigate it and she would hear from them in due course. At eleven am she shut the van up and drove it home, nervously.

Norman had asked Michael to take a delivery

at The Grange. He hadn't said what, but he said to just leave the delivery outside. A truck drove down the lane, its sides scraping along the brambles either side. Michael saw it on its way down. It looked like there were two motorbikes in the back of the truck. The truck pulled up outside the front door of The Grange. Michael came out and walked to the back of the truck, where two men were undoing the back of the truck and fitting a ramp from the back down to the ground. One of the men noticed him and turned around.

'Mr Morgan?' He asked.

'No, I am his representative, he asked me to take delivery. He is indisposed. What are these? Two motorbikes.'

'No mate. Two snowmobiles. Like a motorbike for the snow. Great fun. Pretty rare in these parts too.'

'Snowmobiles! I have never seen one.' He peered over the side of the truck into the bed. The snowmobiles were black, shiny and absolutely gorgeous.

'I think I'm going to have fun this winter!' Michael said smiling at the two men.

They slid each snowmobile down the ramp and set it on the drive. Then shut the truck bed up and put the ramp in the back.

'Just sign here please?' Michael signed the paperwork with a flourish. They passed him a copy and a brown envelope that contained the paperwork and two sets of keys.

Michael waved them goodbye and watched until they were at the top of the drive. Then he got on one of the snowmobiles and put his hands on the handlebars. He imagined himself swishing effortlessly through the snow on it. Just like James Bond. Him on one and The Master on another. Michael reckoned Kate would find him very sexy on one of these.

It snowed lightly for most of the day. Lightly but incessantly, it was starting to get quite a covering and the gritting lorries were only just managing to keep the roads open. It seemed to go dark earlier, with the grey snow clouds above them, blocking out most of the light. After tea, the phone calls between members of the band began. Some of these were a single call that went on all evening. Some were calling each band member for gossip, like bees collecting pollen. The more people they spoke to, with each little titbit passed on, the more excited they got.

Sue spoke to Ernie and he assured her that he had told Stuart everything, apart from their personal opinions and that it now would be investigated and out of his hands. He reassured her that they had no need to worry. The *bloodhounds of the law* were on it now. She was not convinced, however.

Bob called Adam and told him the story about the sheep and the missing animals and that Liz had almost confirmed their suspicions.

'I can't believe that this is actually happening in our village. I mean Bob, it is great and all that.

But it is a scary thing as well. It's alright when you hear of stuff happening to other people but honestly I don't want to come up against one myself.'

'Yeah, I get you. It's the only topic of conversation in our house and I love it. But there is no denying that I go to bed and worry most of the night that I will be attacked by a vampire in my bed.'

'That's natural. It's self-preservation, Bob. It would be hard though, if it was your Uncle, or someone you knew was normally nice, and you had to defend yourself. That first step will be a big one. You are attacking a person and don't have to fear the consequences.'

'Adam, if they attack you first then it is self-defence, whether they are human or not. Don't hold back. It'll be you or them. It's as simple as that.'

Colin sat in his house in silence and darkness. He was waiting for the crunch of his wife's, footsteps on the snowy drive. She was the local florist. Colin had been waiting for her to shut up shop for the night. Tired of feasting on cats he now decided to take the next step. His need to turn Wendy, came from the depths of his soul. He ached for her, and could no longer hold back. After satisfying his initial madness, he was now in control. Before.....well he probably would have killed her in his blood lust. Tonight, he was only going to have a small, sweet taste of her, as he wanted a companion to sit in this house with him forever. Colin didn't like the idea of being on his own or constantly part of the larger group.

Firstly smelling the flowers she worked with, he soon heard her on the path. He stood and moved to the door, straightening his shirt and pulling his collar straight with both hands. She was having trouble getting the key into the door in the dark. It then found it's way, clicked and the door opened a crack.

'Colin? Why, are there no lights on?' She called out.

'Take my hand,' he said. She jumped as the words were so close to where she stood. He took her hand and pulled her through the door. 'Is this a surprise?' She asked excitedly.

She never got a reply. He was on her in a moment. Colin tried to make it as painless as possible, as she was such a small lady and he knew that she had a really low pain threshold. He was quick and gentle. She soon was lying in his arms, as he stroked her hair.

'There, there,' he said gently and kissed her. They embraced. All was now well. Colin could move forward happily.

Stephen was in The Grange. He was itching to go out. That day a few of them had brought Mark back early in the morning and now he was one of them too. He was plenty of fun so Stephen and Michael were pleased that he was now one of their gang. The Master had had a long talk to Mark. They weren't present. Mark had wandered off as soon as it was dark and The Master had not stopped him. This was unusual. How would he be controlled? If he wasn't there, they couldn't mate around with them. Stephen was bored. The devil makes work for idle hands.

Stephen wanted to visit a girl from their Band, who he had very much fancied before he was turned and still found he did after. He was pestering Michael all the time to go out and The Master was hunting, so he kept on, until he finally wore Michael down. The Master had said that Michael was in charge of Stephen, so Stephen forced him to go out, by saying he would go anyway without him. Stephen did not feel the cold anymore but Michael certainly did. He was wrapped up warm and in fact had popped Stephen's coat on top of his own, as he did not need it. They walked out into the snow. Stephen had not said where they were going, just *out*. Her house was not very far from The Grange.

'You know, you were right when you told me you can get any girl you want.'

'I'm always right. Why the surprise?' Michael looked at him and raised his eyebrows but Stephen ignored him.

'The girl I want is Amy.'

'What are you planning to do with her. Turn her?'

'Eventually, yes.'

'So what are you doing first?'

'What do you think?' He said. 'Do you realise that I can make girls do what I like now? They enter a receptive state and I just have to think about what I want them to do and they do it automatically. This is the best feeling and I thank you for bringing this to me. You were right, my dreams really do come true and I feel so powerful.'

'Do you have any regrets, Stephen?' Michael asked very interested in the answer.

'None at all. I do not miss anything.'

'I am just wondering about, when it's my turn, you know.'

'No, I do not miss one thing about my old drab and stupid life. I was doing nothing with it, so The Master did the right think to take it.'

They arrived at Amy's house and tried to look through the gaps in the curtains. They could see her, but no one else. The television was very loud. Michael noticed that they were leaving footprints everywhere but hoped that these would be blown away by the snow. When they walked around the back Michael tried the door but it was locked. Stephen took the handle and pressed down and in with a great deal of force. The door swung open, the handle broken and Michael stepped inside. He turned to Stephen.

'Come in.' Michael said. Stephen went into the kitchen, which was dark and smelled of stir-fry and he shut the door behind them. Michael could hear that Amy was in the living room still watching the television. He looked back at Stephen and he nodded to say go ahead. Michael's heart was beating so loudly and he could hear it inside his head. He swung open the door and Amy stood up fast, turning towards them. Stephen was behind Michael and was trying to get in front of him so he could get Amy to look into his eyes and compel her to do his bidding. But Michael seemed to be the one wanting to call all the shots as usual, as he was supposed to be in charge of Stephen. So in he went. Of course she started shouting at them.

'What are you doing in my house!? I am in my bloody pyjamas.' She strode up to Michael as if to slap his face. 'What the hell do you think you are doing!? Who the hell do you think you are!? If this is anything about Band, you don't just walk into someone's house!' She then noticed that Stephen was in the doorway. 'What are you doing here, as well?' She stopped. Her next words stopping short halfway up her dry throat. She started to fear about what was going on and thought *I am going to get attacked here. What are they after?* She looked again at Stephen and she knew. Amy started to scream and Stephen flew over and put his hands around her throat in an instant, cutting the first scream off in mid-cry. He squeezed, so hard, then he heard a crack and he let go. She fell to the floor. Instantly dead.

'What have you done? You can't do anything with her now,' said Michael.

'I don't know. Maybe you can still,' said Stephen sadly. He looked down at Amy, with her lilac pyjamas covered in owls and her fluffy white slippers and her lovely blonde hair covering her face.

'And what if you can't? What are we going to tell The Master? We can't say that you bungled it up again.'

'We'll just say it was her own fault,' Stephen said.

'Oh yes,' said Michael sarcastically, 'we'll just say she strangled herself shall we, and The Master will believe that surely, Stephen!'

Stephen looked at Michael and said nothing. He stood there blankly and shrugged. When Michael realised he wasn't going to come up with a good excuse, he resigned himself to the fact that he would have to sort it, again. Then Stephen moved towards Amy.

'I will have to see what I can do about it, maybe I can make something happen.' He picked up Amy, like she was just a rag doll, in his arms. 'She's really soft and warm. I'll take her upstairs. Just clean up any signs of us Michael. I won't be long.'

Michael sat down on the sofa and thought about how he had been given a difficult job looking after Stephen and that he would be glad when he was turned or when Stephen was trained up. Michael was sure he wasn't going to be this much trouble, when he was finally turned. It wasn't long before Stephen was back down.

'Er....I tried to turn her but she was having none of it,' He sat down next to Michael. 'You will have to ring The Master to sort this one out, Michael.'

'You do know that you have got me in a lot of trouble now, Stephen. He might not turn me for this. This is not my fault and make sure you tell The Master. I was supposed to be looking after you and you went off half-cocked.'

'You were in my way. I couldn't catch her eye to do my hypnotism thingy.'

Michael realised Stephen might be right there. However, Stephen was still more to blame and he wasn't going to take the rap for this one.

'I am going to say I tried to warn you.'

'Don't worry, I am going to say that she strangled herself,' he said knowingly, nodding his head.

'Well you are a bloody idiot, then,' said Michael under his breath and picked up his phone to call Norman.

17 – Tea Towel

The first caroling job always happened in the middle of November. Ernie liked to get ahead of the game and said if the shops could do Christmas from September they certainly could do it from November. He had never had a complaint yet. They walked the streets of Friarmere playing a selection of carols, in cul-de-sacs, lanes, and in the middle of the village. They did it in groups of ten. One party doing a particular part of Friarmere one day, and another ten doing the places the original group didn't get round to a couple of days later. The idea of this was so people didn't get tired or too cold. The percussionists had nothing to do on these nights, so went round with committee members knocking on people's doors asking for donations to their local Band. It had been snowing earlier on in the day but now it was clear and bright. Ernie had promised that if it was too snowy their job would get cancelled but as he knew it would be fine that evening, it was an empty promise.

They would start at the bottom of the village and wind their way up through the streets, one by one up the hill. As they got higher, towards the moors, it got significantly colder.

Wee Renee had offered to provide some mulled wine and mince pies at the end of the job at her house, so they were all looking forward to this treat. She also said that she had plenty of information to impart about the current bad situation they were in. They were just gathered together waiting for the last couple of people when Laura came up with a tin to shake at passers-by.

'Hey, I just saw Keith,' she said.

'Did he speak to you?'

'No, Ernie.'

'What did you say? Are you sure that it was Keith?' Ernie asked. It had been a while since he had seen him and if did see him, he would be giving him a piece of his mind.

'If it wasn't him he has a double, who also wears a police uniform. Him and Stuart had their truncheons out as well. Ernie, didn't you say that you had spoken to the police the other day.'

'Yes, I made sure I spoke to Stuart and not to Keith though.'

'You never usually see them together do you?' asked Tony.

'Are you saying they are the same person, Tony,' Wee Renee said, 'I never considered that possibility.'

'No. I'm just saying you never see them together, Wee Renee,' Tony replied bemused. Laura laughed.

'You are right, Tony, you don't. But tonight I have. I don't think they are friends usually. I know Keith better than Stuart, and I would say in all honesty, who would want to be friends with Keith, if you didn't have to. But one thing was, the look on Keith and Stuart's face, it gave me the willies. I thought Keith said he was ill and wasn't at work. Well he is obviously one of them, isn't he?' Laura rambled on. 'He can forget saying he is ill now. He has been lying to you, Ernie. The worst thing is, Stuart looked exactly the same as him. They were pale and looked like they were on an angry mission. It also explains why I haven't heard anything back from Stuart about Teresa going missing.'

'I think there is a strong possibility, that we will have bugger all help from the police then,' said Ernie matter-of-factly.

'What were they doing?' asked Gary.

'They were walking into the park. I had just come past the gates to the park and know that there is a gang of teenagers having a snowball fight.'

'God help them,' said Gary, 'Let's get going, Ernie. Push on up. The quicker we start, the quicker we will be finished and further away from them two.'

They started trudging upwards. The non-players knocked on the doors. The band would stop every so often and play a carol. First came *Good King Wenceslas*, next *O' Come All Ye Faithful*. They would rotate their way through the Christmas Carol book. All the way around each one picking their favourite or doing requests. If a person would make a request, they would generally get themselves outside with their family, and stand next to the band to listen and give a little applause after.

This happened less tonight. And what was also apparent was that on a standard caroling night, they would get someone not answering their door, maybe one in every ten doors. Today was quite different, as only about one out of ten doors actually opened. Some people's houses looked dark. Other villagers looked through the windows, shut their curtains and would not answer the door. Previous to this, they knew that they never had this many people not wanting to part with their cash. There was always the odd one every year, usually the same culprits, they found. But as there were so many tonight who would not open their doors, they thought that they were not the only ones who were cottoning on to the goings on in Friarmere.

As they walked around they chatted about this, the cold, and Christmas.

'What about this concert? Do you think we should cancel it?' asked Gary.

'There's not a cat in hell's chance of that, Gary,' Pat said, 'you know Ernie never cancels a concert. He never misses a chance to make cash for the band.'

'You are right there. It's not getting cancelled. I am sure everything will be tickety-boo by then,' said Ernie to Pat.

Stuart and Keith had been busy in the park. Of course they knew that when they walked in through the gates, that the kids would start throwing snowballs at them and this would give them ample opportunity to vent their anger out on the teenagers. During what looked like the defence of their honour, Keith was far more vicious than Stuart. This really was an attack on the teenagers, not as the boys knew it. It was amazing how hard you could hit a body with a ball of snow. It helped that there was a stone inside each snowball. Their eyes were made for the game, as there was no lighting in the park. They both thoroughly enjoyed it and had a wild old time there. Those lads would be telling no tales on them.

Stuart and Keith had been given a mission tonight. They knew from the weather reports and from The Master that an enormous amount of snow was coming tomorrow at some point. So what they had to do, needed to be done before that. They were to go to the top of the Moors in their police car with a bag of tools including wire cutters. The Master had given them specific technical instructions on how to take out the mobile phone masts. This was the most important action of any vampire that night and Norman had entrusted it to these two policemen. By all accounts tomorrow, they would have to do it by foot with no transport, if they waited. The snow would put pay to the roads and also maybe to the train lines. But they had instructions for that too.

Wee Renee's house was small and cosy, but as she would say, just enough for her wee soul. When they entered tonight, the usual smells of lavender, bleach and herbs, had been overtaken by the smell of mulled wine and mince pies. Everyone had a bit of a shock as they walked into her living room when they saw that one wall had been taken over by some kind of a CSI police crime board.

'Wee Renee! I'm impressed!' exclaimed Gary.

'Aye, I've been busy,' she said gleefully and winked at him.

They all walked up to it and started reading all the pieces of paper that she had printed off about vampires or missing animals and things going on in the village. There were lengths of red wool pinned between each one, going this way and that. On the small amount of wall that was left by the window, there was a map covered in pins. Around the pins there were three pieces of red tinsel that Wee Renee had pinned into a triangle shape. There was a note and arrow to the tinsel triangle which said *'very important.'*

'What's this tinsel triangle?' Gary said, pointed and tapping the wall.

'It signifies the Melden Triangle.' She replied in awe.

'What?' Ernie asked.

'You've heard of the Bermuda Triangle haven't you?' They all nodded. 'Aye, well this is the same thing. The Melden Triangle. All the weird happenings have occurred in that triangle. Not just over the past couple of weeks but for years. People going missing, never to be seen again, the wolves, wee faeries sighted and strange lights up above. You can see it cuts into the top of Friarmere, at its highest point, and covers Melden and Moorston. That's why I didn't do the band job at The Grange. *That* is situated within the Triangle.'

'There are a lot of pins in that triangle, Wee

Renee.' Tony said frowning.

'Aye, there is, and that's why I didn't go. I was right not to wasn't I?'

'You can't argue with that. Everyone check out the map.' Ernie said.

When they turned around to the other wall, they noticed the prolific amount of crosses, she had put up. She saw the looks on their faces and said

'My theory is don't die of ignorance. This is the central hub of all the information we have gathered. They would love to get in here and know how much we are tracking them. I have tried to find out as much as I can about vampires too. We don't want to go about this unprepared.'

Lynn was reading some of the printouts that Wee Renee had pinned up. Renee had highlighted, what Lynn thought, were all the gruesome bits and the ways to kill them. She was still not ready to accept the reality and her palms were sweating. She was in shock at the horror of it. Lynn seemed to not be able to breathe, all of sudden feeling hot inside, with her coat on. She pulled away at her coat and her vision was getting blurred. Pat was laughing.

'You've never mentioned that you had been up to this, Rene,' Pat said in between laughs.

'Ernie, I feel a bit faint,' Lynn said quietly and flopped down in the chair.

'It might have been the walk around in the cold,' said Laura, concerned.

'It's more likely this room and it's hitting her square on. You know Lynn can't even look at blood or have an injection,' Gary said. The rest of the group nodded in agreement. They thought it was the shock of Wee Renee's CSI room as well. Ernie was not in a panic and told them she often went like this. He went into the kitchen and came back with one of Wee Renee's tea towels. Laura noticed it was a souvenir one from Gretna Green, and started wafting it over Lynn's face. Lynn sat there, dazily, her curls wafting this way and that. She was obviously used to this treatment.

'Carry on regardless,' Ernie said. He stopped, looked at the tea towel, read it, then said, 'Very nice.' He continued wafting.

Wee Renee carried on relaying what she had found out about the area. Apparently a bag of cats' heads had been found, which they all had rather not known about, particularly Sue. Ernie carried on talking loudly and wafting and then laid the tea towel down over Lynn's face. She seemed quite happy to sit with it like that.

'Me and Rene have been thinking that it is not safe to sleep on your own anymore,' Pat said.

'Now that is what I am talking about, right up my alley,' said Gary with a cheeky grin, 'I think I'm going to like this next bit.'

'No you dirty bugger.' Pat laughed throatily. 'What I meant to say was we need to be stopping in groups. Taking it in turns at each others' houses or something, but we don't want to be picked off one by one.'

'I am sorry about that,' said Lynn said, taking the tea towel off her face. 'Wee Renee, I know you have put out the mulled wine but actually, after all this, I think I would like to have a nice cup of tea.' Everyone agreed.

'That's no problem. I'll soon sup all the mulled wine in a day or so. I might even cook a brisket in it,' she said happily. 'I'll go and put the kettle on. Then I'll get out a scrapbook I've made up of pictures I've found. I've got a picture of that bag, and the bits of sheep. All important evidence. You know. And just a few wee ideas for killing them. Beheadings and stuff. Does everyone want tea, or do some want coffee?' They looked up at her with wide eyes, swallowing in dry throats.

'I hope you are all hungry.' She got up and started to walk into the kitchen. 'I've made five dozen mince pies!' Lynn put the tea towel back over her face.

Sandra was sitting outside Tracy's house that evening in her car and she knew that Simon was inside. He said he had been going out on a caroling job but she knew he hadn't, as she had seen the band out caroling and he wasn't with them. He didn't realise that she would be going out tonight and would discover another lie he had told. She had been watching him closely, especially since her unexpected meeting with Keith. He hadn't even bothered to take his instrument out with him. That is how careless he was getting. It was about nine-thirty when Simon left Tracy's house. Shutting the front door like it was his own and parading down the front path, smirking. She would wipe that off his face, he could be sure of that. He threw up his car keys and whistled catching them, without a care in the world. Once he had driven off, Sandra quickly got out and went up the path to Tracy's front door. She could still smell Simon here and that made her even more determined to make him pay. She rang the bell and heard Tracy's feet on the laminate floor.

'What have you forgotten now?' Tracy shouted from inside, giggling as she swung the door open to Sandra. She looked so shocked and it was obvious she didn't know who Sandra was.

'Oh, hello. Can I help you?' Tracy asked.

'He hasn't forgotten anything. Only neglecting to tell you that he is married.' Tracy stood with her mouth open, a blush instantly rising to her cheeks. 'Should I come in and we'll talk about this?' Tracy was still shocked, then seemed to hear Sandra's words.

'Yes, yes of course.' She stood aside, pushed the front door open and in came Sandra. No more words were said as Sandra strangled them off with her bite.

Stuart and Keith got to work in more ways than one. Silent and contemptuously, they worked together. It was a lot easier than they imagined. By midnight, when the snow started to fall again, Friarmere was cut off from the world.

That night, the villagers of Friarmere lay warm in their beds and the snow began to blanket them. For some of them, this would be the last night they would ever see. In silence and muted glory, Christine prowled the streets, hungry. She walks like a queen. A queen of the snow and the dark, in her red lipstick and her red dress, snow sticking to it, up to her knees. She looks for food. She looks for love. She finds neither – there is no trace of her after. A dark cloud passing through the streets one by one. If she finds you, she will eat you.

18 - Cats

Mark had been told to carry on with his job of delivering milk, as it was the ideal job for scouting out new victims, for himself or The Master. The Master counted on the villagers having a false sense of security, just before dawn. They had slept, had their night terrors, made it through the night and now it was morning and everything was safe until tonight.

After last night Lynn Cooper had had very little sleep. She had given up trying at four am and had come downstairs to watch a cookery show she had recorded. She got up off the sofa when she heard the milk float coming down the lane. Maybe it would be the last time she would get a delivery for a while, as the snow was getting thicker. She often went to say hello to Mark, if she was awake. She thought it must be a very lonely job he had. He always seemed glad to see her too, and gave her a friendly smile. Lynn thought she needed it this morning after all the happenings of the last few days. Normality. When she knew that it was the ten-piece band that were coming down with the mystery illness, she was so happy that he had not visited The Grange that night. He was one of her favourite members of the band.

She heard him stop and heard his feet crunch on the snow, milk bottles clinking. She opened the door. *Wow, that is cold,* she thought.

'Morning, Mark,' she said cheerfully. He was very surprised to see the warm invitation from Lynn.

'Could I have a word, Lynn?' he said in the darkness. Which was even darker as they had a carport, which made it exceptionally black, cutting out a lot of the street light. She could imagine what this was about, and opened the door for him. He came in slowly, his eyes quickly checking around the kitchen and into the living room. She looked alone. Lynn shut the door behind him. Shutting the cold morning out. Trying to recover some heat, she pulled her dressing gown closer round herself.

'Are you well?' she asked.

'I feel exceptionally well.' He turned towards her and their eyes met. She was instantly lost. She was peaceful and she never felt a thing as he turned her into one of The Master's own.

When Ernie got up two hours later, Lynn was dressed and sitting with the curtains closed saying she still had a headache. She had a load of washing on, including her nightwear that she said she had sweated through. He never had one moments doubt about it.

'What's for breakfast?' he asked.

This is how Friarmere woke up that morning. The snow was deep and getting thicker all the time, soft and silent large flakes came down, cycling and whirling to the ground. The trees bent lower with the weight of this beauty. Inches upon inches of it fell as the hours went by.

You could not tell where Friarmere ended or begun. There was no definition between roads, pavements, gardens and houses. From above it was a large white mottled area. Nothing moved. There were no cars out and about, no buses. No more food would get delivered, only what was already stuck in the shops. No more trains. Friarmere would have to look after itself. The villagers were quite used to times like this and so often had freezers full of food. Long life milk and bread. They had experienced snow like this before, and were prepared. However this time, the people of Friarmere felt scared and isolated. It was not because of the snow. Many of them knew, or suspected, that they were being picked off. No-one would help them. They knew that some of their neighbours were not answering, or could not answer their doors. How many people were lying behind those doors and closed curtains, dead. Or maybe worse. They did not want to call on neighbours, in case that person was lying in wait for them. Then they would also be the ones not answering their doors. Their natural impulses caused made them hide away. Hide from the unknown and threatening. You could not fight what you could not see. So hide, until everything is back to normal. Some houses were empty because other people had come to the realisation about all this early and had got out to stay with relatives in the pretence of an early Christmas break, or shopping.

The sky was dark, even in the day. The large flakes blocking out the light, the snowflakes themselves came out of angry grey clouds. This weather had played into The Master's hands. His new children of Friarmere were watching their next or first victims from deep inside the shadows of their houses. How absolutely wonderful.

It snowed all day. As the afternoon starts to turn into evening, the villagers' fear increased along with the dark shadows. As night falls, the snow also still falls, covering all footprints. There is no sign of the prowling death in this virgin snow. There is no outward sign that anything is wrong in Friarmere. It is not for anyone to know. It is a secret.

Keith and Stuart were had an important job to do for The Master. They were to visit Tony, Sue and Bob. The two of them had done a good job the previous night and The Master thought that they made the ideal predators. Keith's ferocity and Stuart's control being their assets. They walked up the road to Sue and Tony's house, in silence and anticipation.

Sue and Tony's cats were not impressed with the snow. Needless to say, Sue was horrified when she had heard about the cats heads in the bag. She hadn't looked at the picture. When she got back she was pleased to see that they were safe and she was determined that they were going to stay that way. She was only letting them out for a very brief moment to go outside if they wanted to, then she was calling them in straight away. Most of the time they were happy to use the litter tray, as they were all not fond of four cold paws. Tonight though, it was as if they knew that their owners were under attack, as they had run off from Sue and had hidden themselves underneath the shrubs at the front of the house.

As the two men stepped onto the property, the cats revealed themselves. They were close to the ground, growling, spitting and hissing at the two vampires. They stepped back, for a moment shocked, at the suddenness of the attack. However, three cats were not a problem to them. Keith reached forward towards the first one, but just then a slight movement caught his eye. He had noticed the old lady that lived next door to Sue and Tony. The two vampires had been distracted by the cats and had not heard her door open. She was just staring at the two men who stood on the drive of her neighbours house. The bags of rubbish in her hands that she was taking to the bin, dropped.

Unfortunately they were not in police uniform and Keith had fed earlier so his clothes were in a state of disarray. She was utterly flabbergasted. To see two men on her next-door neighbours drive, with three cats hissing at them and one of them with a shirt covered in blood! What she also noticed was that they were only wearing shirts. She stood with her mouth open wondering what was going on. Stuart knew that it was only a matter of time before she started screaming and was just about to go to her and put his hand over her mouth, but as quickly as Stuart could think about it, Keith ran past him to the old woman, grabbing her head and twisting it, breaking her neck. Stuart joined him and they dragged her body back into her own house. They lay her in the hall on her black and white tiles, then went back outside and made a quick getaway. Sue Tony, and Bob would have to wait for another night but at least they had put an obstacle out of the way towards this deed. The Master would not be too vexed with them.

Sue's cats watched the two monsters disappear down the road towards the village. They waited until all was clear and then one by one they went into the warm house, through the catflap for some treats.

The Thompsons were under strict instructions. The Master had told them that someone from the band was a danger to them. A threat. And this person was also working in a position where he could tell a few tales. He had spoken to them at length about it and they agreed. So they were dispatched to kill him. The Master knew that they were perfectly capable of this. As he explained to them, previous to tonight, if he asked them to chat to someone, they killed them. If he asked them to turn someone, they killed them. Whatever he asked them to do, he seemed to get the same outcome. So sending them, would make sure he got the desired result.

Of course Michael could have gone at any time, as he was still human. But as Stephen was not, they had to wait until it was completely dark before they went to visit the threat. There was a short time, when he was shutting up shop, where he could be found alone. They had taken Adrian with them, a recent but willingly turned vampire, who had drank most of the wine, on the night Maurice and brought it into band. Michael thought they should help him out on his first kill, as he had always been impressed with his tuba playing and he thought it was time he paid Adrian back. They would probably have taken Mark too if he had been about as he was so funny, but they hadn't seen him since The Master had turned him and had been told that Mark's job was to turn people whilst delivering their milk. They didn't tell The Master they were taking Adrian. But they thought this foe might be formidable so it was probably best to go three, against one.

Ian was in the back of his Butcher's shop, looking at his stock for the next day. He was resigned to the fact that he may not get another delivery for a while, when he heard his door go.

'I'll be with you in a minute,' he shouted from the back. Walking out of his large fridge, he shut the door. As he turned around from the door, the three attackers were already there. All his fellow bandsmen. There was no question what they wanted and Ian quickly reached out for a large meat cleaver at the side of him that was currently embedded in a piece of pork, ready to cut into chops. He swung the knife in front of him, making quick arcs, that whistled through the air. They moved forward and back, like a macabre barn dance. Ian lunging forward, the two vampires and Michael jumping back. They would lunge at him, trying to get around the side and he would turn and sweep his knife down again.

Adrian, being a young vampire and still a little foolhardy, decided he had had enough. He felt strong and this was boring him. He never liked to play with his food, even as a child. Crouching lower, he ran at the butcher. Before his hands touched the man, Ian was already moving his large cleaver in a crossward motion, which hit home. He hit the side of Adrian's head, across the bottom of the ear, then straight through the cheek, parting the teeth. The meat cleaver was long and it had cut all the way through the back of Adrian's head too. It became embedded, close to the centre of Adrian's head. Ian wiggled it but the weight of the vampire, which he was now holding up, by the cleaver, meant he stood no chance of getting it out quickly.

Suddenly his back felt hot and he thought he had maybe pulled a muscle between his shoulder blades.

'Got you,' said Micheal.

Ian slowly turned, his legs and feet felt like heavy weights that he was dragging in a circle. He felt drunk, and very tired. Ian looked up at the knife, poised above him in Michael's hands, and could see three inches of blood on it. He briefly thought, *how did that get there* and furrowed his brow. Then he wondered no more and collapsed to the floor.

Indeed, this man had used his skill and weapons with great effect. He would never know it, but he was the first to slay a vampire. 'What are we going to do now?' asked Stephen, looking down at the two of them dead on the floor.

'Make sure he's dead first,' said Michael. Stephen took the knife straight out Michael's hand, bent over and slit Ian from the middle of his rib-cage to his pelvis. He then put his hands inside, pulling out a good portion of Ian's organs and intestines and stabbed around at them with the knife. Then he plunged the knife into Ian's chest and stood up.

'Done,' he said triumphantly.

'You don't do things by halves these days, do you?' said Michael.

'No. What next?'

'Right. Well…..' Michael rubbed his chin, his eyes surveyed the ceiling desperately after inspiration. 'The Master doesn't know we bought Aidy, and we will be right up the creek if he knows we messed up again and he lost one of his guy's. So I am thinking that we don't tell him and hide him.'

'Where?'

'Here, in the shop. There is no reason for The Master to come down here. We did our job. In the end we were victorious in our mission, because of me anyway.' He raised his head high, to show how very important he was. Stephen knew he would bring this up again and again. 'Grab his feet, we'll shove him up the back. No-one will ever know.'

19 - Butcher

Ernie had arranged that this Saturday's pub meet, was to take place at lunch, in as broad a daylight as they could manage. Lynn had stopped at home because she said it was too cold to go out, and she was still very nervous about the situation. Apart from that, she didn't really feel in the mood for discussing it that day. Ernie reluctantly agreed that she could stay at home as she felt that she was perfectly safe because it was broad daylight and they didn't come out in the day. Or not that she knew of. And he couldn't argue with that reasoning. He would be back well before dark. It was still snowing, but lighter at least. Nearly icing sugar. But Friarmere, even in the day, was not sweet.

The band started to congregate in the pub. Ernie, Freddie, Laura, Andy and Liz, Danny, Gary, Tony and his family, all came in out of the cold one by one. Taking off their coats, scarves and gloves. Relishing the burning hot fires that were warming their toes and fingers. Bob was standing too close to the fire and his cheeks were getting very rosy. He stared into the flames, transfixed. His mother came behind him and put her hand on his shoulder.

'Come, and sit down. You are miles away.'

'Yeah. Just thinking about stuff,' he said.

Sue's heart ached as she thought about how hard it was for *them* to go through this, but how her young son had to go through this as well. She wanted to protect him and physically, she would. But neither her, nor Tony could protect his mind from the horrors they were going through.

The final two people to arrive were Wee Renee and Pat who both had string shopping bags with a carrier bag inside. As they came through into the pub from the foyer, an eye-watering cloud of aroma swept over their friends. They emanated an overwhelming smell of garlic, which told exactly what they had been doing and why they were late. The others were bemused at what was going on, but knew it wouldn't be long before all was revealed.

They went straight to the bar and ordered their lunches, as they could see that some people had already got theirs. Wee Renee ordered a prawn sandwich saying that she could not face meat and Pat ordered a large macaroni cheese meal. Bob thought it sounded nice too, and so did the rest of the family, so Sue went up and made another three orders of that for them.

Ernie cleared his throat. 'Before we start, I have been thinking and I think we still shouldn't cancel the concert.' There was a large amount of muttering and general disagreement with this from the rest of the group.

'You're playing with fire!' explained Pat.

'I'm not!' Ernie said adamant. 'And it's not just about the money, before you say anything Pat. It's about the fact that they are trying to interrupt our lives and we are not going to let them. Those kids look forward to their concert with us. To *their* Christmas. If we choose to cancel then it's us messing with normality, instead of whatever's out there. I don't think anything should change. We are prepared for what might happen. Whether the kids are there or whether they are at home, we are all sitting ducks essentially now. What I think is at some point this village will get back to normal and so I am going to try and carry on. It might actually be over by the night of the concert. If their teachers cancel it then that is up to them, but I am not going to do it on the kids. For all we know it could just mainly be band members and nothing will happen at that concert. They will probably expect us to cancel it. It could be the last place they expect us to be. I think it is a good reason anyway.'

'It's a reason. I don't know if it's a good one, though,' said Gary, laughing to himself.

There was silence for a while as the barmaid brought over their meals. Wee Renee was tucking in quite heartily, and when she had finished, she looked at Pat, who indicated with her eyebrow that Wee Renee should start speaking and let her finish her macaroni cheese.

'Right then,' Wee Renee said and every one looked towards her. 'Haven't we been busy last night and this morning?' she said to Pat, who swallowed her mouthful of food with a gulp.

'Yes and we stink,' she said, and put another mouthful in.

'Yesterday,' Wee Renee continued, 'we went round to every shop in this village that could, or may, have sold garlic and bought a few wee cloves of it.'

'How many do you have?' asked Laura.

'Five hundred and thirty one!' Wee Renee said happily. They all looked around at each other and laughed.

'I don't think we need that many,' moaned Ernie.

'The fact is, we might do and I don't want *him* buying them, to get rid of them. Or someone buying them up and wasting them on a bolognese, so that we can't have them. Put it that way.' She winked and looked at Danny.

'Don't look at me. I won't be the culprit I've been warned off that by Barry!'

'I don't know when we might next get our hands on some more, with the snow and everything,' said Wee Renee.

'I think all the people are twigging on. I had to nearly fight someone in the co-op, for the last bulb of garlic.' Pat said as she concentrated on scooping the last of the macaroni cheese out of the serving bowl. The rest of the band could quite see this happening, and knew with Pat being what they called, *a big bride*, would win.

'So what are we going to do with them?' asked Sue. 'Have you got any good ideas?'

Wee Renee pointed upwards and giggled. 'I have got one under my bobble hat, right now!'

'Weird,' said Bob

'No, not really. Consider this. You can carry it round all the time and it's close enough to your neck that if they get near, it would repel them. Hands free protection.' She gave a slow blink of explanation as she said it.

'Okay, not weird,' Bob chuckled.

'You're not wrong there,' said Tony, 'I take it you have got some with you.'

'Me and Pat have peeled about 200 of the cloves between last night and this morning!'

'Sounds like a fun sleepover,' said Bob.

'It was,' said Pat honestly. 'We had a Basil Rathbone marathon and ate a whole three wheels of Scottish Shortbread.'

Wee Renee opened her string bag, with a smile, which was lined with a co-op carrier bag. Inside they could see lots of clear food bags with garlic cloves in them.

'Ten cloves in each bag. Ten bags,' Wee Renee exclaimed proudly.

'I have ten bags too,' Pat said, pointing to her string bag, with her fork. 'Rene thought it would be best to split it.'

'In case a wee mugger was about, and took one of the bags!' she said with wide eyes.

'You had Pat with you!' said Gary. 'Maybe a gang of muggers could take her, But, not a wee one!' They all laughed, even Pat.

'I'd fancy my chances against a gang actually, Gary!' Pat said.

'I think that's my cue for the toilet,' Gary said, hoisting his jeans up, and making his way to the gents.

'Could I have one, please?' Bob asked suddenly. Pat got a bag of ten cloves out, opened the food bag and placed it in the middle of the table, the open end towards him.

'Don't say, I never give you anything.' Pat gave him a long look.

'Thanks.' He took a clove out of the bag, sniffed it, rolled his eyes and then popped it under his wooly hat. They all began to take one, including Sue who put hers under her sequined beret, hoping that it wouldn't take the colour out of the sequins. Liz who was not wearing a hat, took one, smelled it, grimaced and then put it inside a bobble that was holding her hair back.

'This only works, when you are out,' Andy remarked. 'If they break in at night, you won't have it on you.'

'Why not?' asked Wee Renee, obviously not understanding him.

'Well, you won't have your hat on in the house, or in bed.'

'Oh, right. My wee mother gave me a bit of advice the night before my wedding. I was a maiden, you know!' She looked around for a response but nearly everyone looked down at their drink apart from Bob, who sat staring at her with his mouth open. 'Yes, she said, Wee Irene, always keep your mystery. Make sure you always keep something on in bed. Just one thing. So he would have a wee bit left to the imagination.' She laughed. 'So I left my hat on. He wasn't impressed!' She had painted a very vivid picture and Laura, Liz and Sue laughed in particular.

'Just keep your bloody hat on, Andy,' said Pat.

Gary came back from the toilet, rubbing his hands dry.

'What have I missed?' he asked.

'A right gem,' said Ernie. He could see everyone fiddling with their hats.

'Is it garlic time at the OK Corall?' he asked. 'Damn, I have just washed my hands.'

'You are not getting out of it,' said Danny, 'I am not having my mate chewed up!'

'Alright,' Wee Renee said, 'I will stick it in your baseball cap.' She took a clove then tried to lift the cap up. 'It's a bit tight. How am I supposed to get this in. How do you wear it like that? I am surprised you haven't got a headache all the time.'

'You do have a massive red line on your head, when you take it off.' Danny added knowledgeably. She sat looking at the clove and then at Gary's head.

'Just thumb it in, Wee Renee. I don't care,' he shrugged.

'Oh, right you are,' She pushed her thumb behind the clove, so it moved under the tight baseball cap.

'We are all protected now,' Pat said. Quite clearly relieved.

'Yes, I tell you what. I for one will say that the beast will not penetrate me!' Wee Renee said, her finger in the air. They all looked around with their mouths open. Wee Renee looked at them back. She quite clearly didn't know why they were so shocked.

'You lot have got very dirty minds,' Pat said shaking her head.

Wee Renee suddenly realised what they were thinking. 'No, I meant penetrate with their teeth.

Not their penis!' she whispered, looking at the group.

'Wahay! Penis!' laughed Bob.

'Anyway, if they start on that track, they are in for a big shock!' Wee Renee said. They gaped at her. Freddie took a sip of his drink and looked round at the others. With a big breath he said,

'Go, on. I'll buy it. Why?'

'I've got another one down my wee long johns. Never underestimate the element of surprise.' Sue looked at down at the open food bags on the table, full of cloves of garlic. She then picked up one of the cloves of garlic and dropped it down the waistband of her skirt and tights, pinging the elastic several times, so the clove until it worked itself down. The men looked round at each other. They all picked one up and in unison, dropped it down the front of trousers. With a smile Bob took another one then dropped it down the back of his trousers too.

'Watch out where you put them actually, mine is really chafing,' Pat said looking at her lap. Everyone looked down at Pats brown leggings. 'It's worth it though. You can never be too sure.'

'Now we have made sure that we aren't going to get any interest of any kind from vampires of any sexual orientation, can we carry on,' Danny uttered.

'Yes, let's face it. Who gets there genitalia out in this weather anyway?' asked Pat.

'I do!' said Tony proudly. 'So speak for yourself.' Sue blushed.

'Hey, too much information,' Bob said frowning, 'Listen guys I know I am the only kid here but I have got a bit of a theory about where this has all started from. I have been talking it through with my friend, Adam and I think I might have the answer.'

'Okay, we'll give it a whirl. Carry on Bob,' Gary said, sitting back in his chair, ready to listen.

'Right well, picture this. An old dark house, on the moors. Someone who is a recluse living there, not really mixing with the rest of the village. No-one knows them. No-one knows *anything* about them, only what *he* tells them, which could be a pack of lies. He gets a group of people and all of a sudden all of those people are ill. Then the next stage is that they drop out of circulation and get visited by someone or something. They become vampires and not part of our band anymore. Do you see where I am going with this?'

'Norman Morgan from The Grange!' said Ernie 'Yes it certainly fits the bill. But I can't see why all the village wasn't infected, when he got them up there.' They all stopped for a moment and wondered about this. Liz caught her breath. She had worked it out.

'He gave us different food in the changing room, separate from the other guests. He told us we were to eat that. The other must have been fine.'

'That would explain why there wasn't so many all at once. He would start it off slow, then he mean he would be able to turn them one by one, until he has enough to take over the village,' Bob said nodding in agreement.

'Sneaky wee bastard,' Wee Renee snapped.

'I haven't met this Norman,' said Danny, 'but surely if he is a foreigner, we might just be jumping to conclusions.'

'Okay, so what if he wasn't a foreigner?' said Bob. 'What if he was just an English man? Would we still think it was him? A stranger comes here and then weird things started to happen.'

They all agreed that they would still think the same thing. 'Has anyone seen him in the day. Has he been round the village. He supposedly had a party to get to know everyone. His hospitality and friendliness seem to have ended there. Everyone who went there only saw him in the dark. How did he contact you Ernie? Did you see him in the daytime?'

'No, lad. It was just over the phone. He paid Michael with a cheque, which he posted through my door the following evening.'

'So, no. Physically, the only people that had contact with him were the ones that were ill, and that was in the dark. What was he like, Liz?' Bob finished, looking at Liz.

'Very charming. I think he is European some way. Maybe Swiss, or something like that. He was a right flash Harry. He is just the type to do it, though. I really think you have hit the nail on the head, Bob. In fact, deep in my bowels, I know you have.'

'So what are we going to do about it, now?' asked Andy.

'Storm his house with a load of weapons in the daytime,' said Bob. 'My friend Adam will help us, as well. He has said he is really up for it.'

'What are we supposed to use? Wooden stakes and the like? Isn't that what you do? Or do you have to cut off the head from the body?' questioned Freddie, very interested in this subject.

'That's zombies. The heads,' said Bob, 'but I reckon it would still work especially if you booted the head away from the body.'

'You could always bash them in the teeth with a sledge hammer as well,' added Gary helpfully, 'then they couldn't bite you.' They all turned towards him, very impressed.

'That's not as stupid an idea, as you think,' said Pat, obviously thinking out loud.

'I didn't think it was stupid. I thought it was my best one.' He looked at Pat shocked, but continued. 'I am a handyman. Handy in many ways. I know what you could use but I don't have tools for everyone.'

'You know who will have tons of knives. Proper good ones and great big long pokey things?' asked Bob.

'Ian!' exclaimed Tony.

'Yeah, Ian. What about that? Where is he anyway?'

'He would've been here today, only he's got to open the shop,' said Ernie.

'He will probably have some really good ideas of how you could kill them, as well, being a butcher,' said Bob, excitedly.

'Yeah, he will be an asset to us. Well, if the mountain won't come to us, and all that….' said Gary, and stood up.

Ian's Butchers shop was only ten shops away from the pub. The group of friends finished their drinks, then put their scarves, gloves and coats back on. The two older ladies picked up their string bags and off they went. A few of them were quite fired up and once they were outside they started to charge up the street. There was laughter and a slight hope of triumph over adversity. The snow didn't matter, the struggles, the fear because they felt they had won already. What a strange collection of people they made. Old and young, smelling of garlic, determined and on a mission.

When they got to Ian's shop the blinds were down and the door was shut. The open sign was turned to closed.

'This is strange,' said Sue, 'Ian is usually open all hours.'

'Yes and you think he would be cashing in on everyone only being able to get their meat off him. And not being able to get out to the large supermarkets,' said Ernie.

'Trust you to think of that,' said Pat.

'It's just good business sense,' said Ernie. They had started to walk off when Andy decided to try the door, which opened into the dark.

'Shit!' he said.

'Oh God!' said Pat. They all looked round at each other. 'We will have to go in.' Reluctantly they all agreed. Andy went first, as his hand was on the knob, with Gary, Danny and Tony right behind him.

'Ian!' they shouted. The noise came back to

them from the tiled floors and walls of the butcher shop. Echoing, its emptiness. There was no one behind the counter but there was meat on the refrigerated cabinets.

'Quick everybody come in. There's no one here,' said Ernie quietly and they all shuffled in behind him, very quickly, covered in snow, and shut the door behind them. As they shut the door, they shut out the majority of the daylight. There was quite clearly no one in this part of the shop. Danny cleared his throat, and took a brief glance at the open doorway that led to the rear of the shop.

'We are going to have to go further, aren't we?' said Danny. He walked a bit further and poked his head through the doorway. It was incredibly dark.

'It smells weird.' Said Andy.

'It's a butchers, it is full of dead creatures. Don't tell me you have never noticed?' Liz replied.

Danny fished in his pockets and pulled out his mobile phone, switching on the light to shine into the back room. Andy moved beside him and switched on his too. They both moved forward. Liz following right behind Andy, clutching hold of his shoulders, ready to pull him back in an instant from any danger.

'Are you sensing anything?' Liz asked quietly.

'No, nothing,' he said, 'There seems to be no presence in here at all.'

'Well, that's alright then,' said Ernie, 'Lets be on our way.'

'Shit…shit… shit….. what! What the hell!' Danny jumped backwards towards the small congregation behind him. 'Don't look, don't look!' But of course everyone did. Andy shone his torch into the room, as did Danny. Above them Ian was hanging by a hook in his own refrigerator. From the looks of it he had quite clearly been dead a while and blood had dripped down onto the floor, in a pool below him. It now was a congealed brownish black goo. It was clear he had been ripped open and in this light, there were many shiny, pink, white and red shapes tumbling out of his stomach onto the floor. This looked like it had had been done with a knife that was now stuck in his chest. Another hook was deeply embedded in Ian's abdomen for some reason. His internal organs clearly had bite marks too. In fact chunks had been taken out. The bite marks definitely had two prominent punctures in them. They were speechless for a long time. 'I've seen my first dead body,' said Bob.

'It's my first dead body too,' said his mother kindly, putting her arm round him.

'Shine your torch on to this blood down here,' said Liz. She stooped down and Andy came over with his phone to shine a light on it. 'Round the edges,' she said, 'it looks weird.' Gary came beside them both and looked too. 'It looks like something has been licking round the edges.' He pointed at the edges and they all could see it now he had told them what it was. You could see definite impressions of a tongue in the blood.

Luckily the light was so bad in there that no one could see very much. Out of the corner of Liz's eye she saw the light pick a faint impression behind, and to the right of Ian.

'Are those feet, sticking out on the floor inside that cupboard thing there? Is someone inside that?' Liz stepped back, but indicated with her head where to look. No one else could see anything.

'Has Andy been feeding you carrots? I can't see a thing?' Ernie said under his breath.

'Oh, it's this vampire thingy, and I have better hearing too, so watch what you say to me.'

'Noted!' said Freddie.

Gary picked up one of the big meat cleaver's that lay on a rack in the back of Ian's shop.

He put both hands on the handle and weighed it up. Swinging it a couple of times. He walked two steps in front of everyone. The two men with lights on their phones, one step behind him.

'Go. You are outnumbered.'

They all started shouting, each picking up something from Ian's butchers rack, even Bob. Gary moved forward suddenly, kicked one of the shoes and then jumped back. The group stood in silence. Nothing happened. He looked quickly back at the lot of them, his eyes darting this way and that down at their hands, then back to the shoe, in case it moved. Then he looked at Bob and said, 'Lend me that, lad.' Bob passed him the weapon he had chosen, which was a long silver sharpening rod. Gary took the rod and immediately poked it hard into the ankle of the foot. The figure still did not move. He whacked it on the leg really hard, and a dull crack echoed through the shop. 'It's as dead as a door nail,' he said confidently, handing back the rod to Bob. He breathed a sigh of relief.

'That doesn't mean it won't jump up and run after us!' said Bob.

'Clever lad. You take after my side,' Tony said.

'Enough of this, lets go for it. Come on lads, if we don't do something soon, I will need to shave again,' Danny said this whilst giving his phone to Laura. 'Point it at him.' She did.

Danny, Andy, Tony and Gary walked forward and grabbed the figure by the ankles. They sharply pulled it out six feet into the open and it was revealed to be Adrian. He was one of their tuba players, who they had never suspected was a vampire. But quite obviously, had been turned by Norman.

'Aidy, No!' exclaimed Tony. Adrian had been one of his best friends.

'Ian made short work of him, make no mistake,' said Freddie, who seemed very impressed. There was a meat cleaver embedded in his cheek and it had gone nearly straight through to the other side parting his upper and lower sets of teeth so his head was on a pivot from his left cheek.

'Shit!' said Danny, 'Shit it *is* Aidy. Look at his teeth. Aidy's teeth were nothing like this. I mean, where have his other ones gone? This is the first one we have seen. If nothing else it confirms that

we now know we are dealing with vampires?'
Gary was stooping down looking at his head
closely.

'Look at the state of him as well! He isn't just
dead,' Gary remarked, 'He isn't human anymore.
Look at him, the insides of him are already
green. Now look at Ian, who has got chopped up
at the exact same time. He isn't anywhere near
it. The insides of him looks like they're already
bad. Plus they are really dry. Where's all his
blood?'

They all looked between Adrian and Ian. Ian
and Adrian. Bob walked up and poked Ian gently
with his rod a couple of times.

'Sorry Ian, mate,' he said. He then walked
over to Adrian and poked him in the same
places. 'Someone do what I have just done and
tell me what you think, so I know it isn't me.'

'I will!' said Freddie, very willingly. It was if he
had been waiting to be asked.

He poked Ian, a little harder than Bob about
ten times and nodded, as if memorising the feel
of it. He then walked over and poked Adrian in
the same way. Even with the first poke his head
darted up, surprised and looked straight at Bob.

'Well, bugger me!' he said surprised. He
carried on poking away and with the fifth poke,
he pierced the hand of Adrian, and stopped.

'What is it, are you getting a wee fetid smell? I
certainly am.' Wee Renee twitched her nostrils.

'That's probably me, to be fair Rene. You
know my IBS flares up when I get scared.'

'Oh aye, Pat. I forgot.'

'No he's kind of really soft inside, but kind of empty, with a thin skin,' Freddie said. He knew there was an easier explanation, but he couldn't quite put his finger on it.

'An inflatable paddling pool on it's way down!' said Bob.

'That's it! Excellent work lad.'

'Thank you, I'm here all week.' He smiled at them. 'Ian, was like poking a person, or a piece of meat. Yeah, it's soft, but then, the rod stops, and you would have to put in a lot of force to pierce the skin and the fat and muscles underneath. But Aidy was like a really thin piece of plastic or nylon with air underneath. But it isn't air. It just looks like soft powder.'

'We know now we are not dealing with normal people and can fight them with whatever we want to. Surely this is 100% proof now. What I don't understand is, how they got to him? He wasn't one of the original ten piece band,' said Danny

'No, he wasn't. It doesn't fit,' said Ernie, but then as afterthought said, 'But he did drink some of that wine that Maurice bought over, last week.'

'Who else drank some?' asked Sue.

'I don't know. Someone had a small glass when I was in the looking the back door. Because, when I came back Adrian said, who is for some more, there is only one glass gone out of this bottle. And I said it is only you, so he tipped into a big squash glass and drank it straight down. He burped, then said, *waste not, want not,* to me, then walked out the door.'

'Well it is him who has been wasted now,' said Gary.

'Yes, Ian definitely could be proud of himself. He defended himself well and took one down. But who got him after he had killed Aidy?' asked Tony.

'More than one person I would say. Lets face it, Ian wasn't the smallest man you would ever meet, and he was handy with them knives,' Gary remarked.

'And they had to lift him right up, to get him on that hook. I know I couldn't do it,' said Danny.

'I don't think three or four people could do it together. I would say Ian was over twenty stone.' Gary was weighing him up in this mind. 'Mmmm.....I wonder how many there are, all in all, and how many tried to come and overpower Ian.

'Well thanks to Ian there is one less,' Bob declared.

'Yeah and thanks to Ian we have got a load of weapons and we also know that it doesn't have to be wooden stakes,' remarked Tony.

'I am not being funny or anything,' Wee Renee said, 'but number one, it is going to get dark in a couple of hours and I would like to be locked away in my house by then. And number two, there is a load of meat that will go bad here if we don't take it home. It has been refrigerated but won't last forever. So who's for filling their freezer.' A few of them agreed and they took some carrier bags from behind Ian's shop counter. They all agreed that he wouldn't mind and took as much meat as they could carry and as many bags full of weapons. As they shut the door behind them, they looked sadly at the closed sign, all ready to go their separate ways.

'I think, it was probably how he would have wanted to go,' Wee Renee said in a peaceful way. They all looked at her in shock. She carried on by saying, 'In his own shop, with all his bits and bobs around him,' she said gently and walked away with Pat. The rest of them watched her go. That was Wee Renee all over.

'Strung up like a pig, and gutted! I doubt that very much,' said Ernie, shaking his head.

20 – Sausage Roll

When the morning dawned on Sunday, it was still snowing outside. It was as quiet as death. If you opened your door you could hear the snow settling. Each flake falling on layer after layer already accumulated.

Bob had woken up excited and also forlorn. Whilst the prospect of no school tomorrow was great, he also wanted to go to a party tonight and it looked like there was going to be no chance of that. Adam's Mum, Julie, was having a birthday party for herself and her friends at their house. These were always riotous affairs with lots of drink and party food that she cooked up in the afternoon, from the local freezer shop. She had told Adam that he could have a friend over, and he had chosen Bob. The plan would be that he could come over, have some food and keep Adam company in his room. They would play video games and have a laugh. Adam also thought they would manage to go down and sneak two cans of lager back upstairs. Generally they thought they would have a whale of a time, after which he could sleep over. However, with the current snow situation, and everything else of course, Sue had said the previous night that there wasn't a cat in hell's chance of him going there.

'What if the snow stopped?' he asked.

'It would have to stop and then all the snow would have to melt, before you got to go, Bob.

So, wish for a heat wave.' He had then tried his luck with his Father by putting on his most mournful expression.

'Dad could you take me in the Land Rover?' Tony looked round to check that they were alone.

'I am not going against your Mum it is more than my life's worth. Remember that when you are married son.' So that was it.

Sue couldn't have been more relieved that it was still snowing. After all, what was going on in Friarmere was worrying enough, if he was with her she knew he was safe. She looked out into the snow from her bedroom window at the house opposite. Hmmm, she hadn't seen Vincent's mother, Alice for a while. Maybe she should call in on her later. She might need some groceries from the village. Switching her thoughts back to Bob, she would not have allowed him to go to the party anyway, but would have had to think of another excuse. Of course she knew at the moment that most of the people infected were in the ten-piece band. After Aidy though, what did she know? Tony had tried to speak up for Bob about this party. Persuade Sue, that their son would be fine.

'Adam's mother isn't in the band, so he is perfectly safe.'

'You can never know what might go on and they are being very crafty. There is no way that one of us is splitting off, and getting picked off. You can't gamble with his life.' Whilst Tony did want to stick up for Bob, and let the lad have some fun, he did agree with her.

If he had really known how many predators were in his village there is no way he would even consider letting Bob out of his sight. There were now nineteen vampires in Friarmere. In their houses with the curtains closed. In their basements, attics and under beds, in someone else's house or safely tucked away in The Grange.

They had all decided last night not to tell anyone about what they had found in the Butcher's Shop. So Ian still hung there with Adrian's dead body lying nearby. Bob thought about this as he looked out at the snowflakes.

Both men there, so cold. Silent, with just the sound of the snow. Maybe not going to school for a week would be worth not going to the party tonight. All the other kids from his school on social media didn't know what would be happening next week. Whether the secondary school would be open, or not. They had all their fingers and toes crossed. One kid had said that the local primary school would be still opening, as their caretaker kept going in and stoking the boilers up. The headmaster had had too many parents who complained when school had to be called off because they had to go to work. With the primary kids too, mostly their distance was short and most of the children went there on foot. They could easily get though five minutes of walking through the snow to their classes, then play on the floor with sand, or whatever they did. There was no point guessing about tomorrow. Just wish for the snow to carry on if he couldn't go to the party. He thought again about Aidy and Ian, and if he was honest, he didn't want that happening to him at a party. It was getting to the stage where, it was just a fight to survive. Time to look after yourself and each other now.

Bob looked at up at the sky, then down to the ground. There were still no tracks in the road outside. He thought, *there is no chance I am going out tonight, this is set in for the day.* He said to his Mum that he was going to call Adam and let him know. He went upstairs to his room and tried him on his mobile phone. It wouldn't connect. It was showing no signal bars. He wondered if there was a lot of snow on one of the mobile phone signal towers. Bob wondered what he could do now. He couldn't let Adam know now. It was five minutes before he worked out that he could use the landline as it was so unusual. Luckily he had Adam's home number written down or else there would've been no chance of contact. He went back downstairs, picked up his cordless home phone and called Adam. When Adam's Mum Julie, had answered and realised it was Bob, she sighed and shouted upstairs for Adam. Bob heard footsteps, then heard Adam's Mum moaning at him. She said loudly, that if he tied the landline up all afternoon then her friends couldn't get through and tell her if they were coming or not.

'Have I got you in trouble mate?' Bob asked.

'No, she's just having kittens about this party and the snow.'

Bob told him about his current situation and his mother's decision.

'I would have been really shocked if you had been able to come anyway,' Adam said after he had explained, 'Lots of people won't be coming, I bet. It could even get to the stage where it gets cancelled. So don't worry. We are bound to have a party at Christmas at any time. You know how she is.' Adam thought his mother loved an excuse to get drunk. It told in her figure too, she had thin arms and legs but a great big belly. She said she was naturally apple shaped and couldn't do anything about it. Adam said she had a beer belly, which she didn't like one bit.

Bob told Adam that he had an update on *the pressing matter* they were mulling over. He told him in every detail about the garlic cloves, he had hidden everywhere, which Adam thought was hilarious. When Bob told him about the discovery of Adrian and Ian. He wasn't laughing. He could tell in Bob's voice how terrible it was, and was fascinated about the texture of the vampire. Bob must have been on the phone to Adam for about an hour, because at one pm, his mother shouted to him to come off the phone as lunch was ready. She had cooked a piece of beef from Ian's shop and they were having Yorkshire puddings, roast potatoes, vegetables and gravy. She had made an apple crumble for dessert with custard, so that cheered him up. The boys had decided that they would both play online this afternoon from two pm until the guests came which Adam thought would be about six tonight. Although his Mum said that people were already cancelling.

So that was the rest of the day sorted for Bob. Adam said at six he would get some food, before everyone else came and take his games console up to his room, so he could carry on playing from about six-thirty.

Just after dark Stephen made another visit to Ian's butcher shop. He had enjoyed the way Ian tasted. Very meaty and blood rich, from eating his own produce, for all these years. He had tasted the blood that pooled underneath Ian and also had had a few bites out of his juicy bits. He had only been back in there for about five minutes, enjoying his feast, when he heard the shop door open. Startled, he wondered who it was. He thought this probably wasn't going to be good for him, if he was found. Stephen backed away into the corner and was totally hidden in the shadows. The shop was naturally unlit and outside had been dark for at least half an hour. Ian didn't need to invest in radiators so it was deathly cold in there with it being a butchers shop, and below zero outside. He heard at least more than one set of feet walking into the shop. They stopped just inside the door, walked to the back of the shop and then stopped a short way away from him. They waited in for a moment. Stephen wondered what was about to happen to him.

'We saw you coming in here Stephen and we know you are here, because we can smell you are here.' Keith's voice came from above one of the sets of feet. Stephen, relieved that it was not a threat after all, came out to see that it was indeed Keith. Stuart stood beside him. They were both dressed in their police uniforms.

Their skin was so white with the cold and the fact that they were both dead that it was translucent. Stephen could see their veins showing through their skin. It looked like a mini map of the London Underground. Stephen thought that there would be no way that they would pass off as regular people anymore. And then wondered what he himself looked like. He decided to be sociable.

'Have you come in for a feed Keith? Could you smell it?'

'I couldn't no, not over the smell of the rest of the meat, but we were on patrol looking for lost little sheep, you might like to say and saw you coming into this shop. Is it good?'

'Yes,' said Stephen. He looked at Ian hungrily and then back at the two others. 'You are welcome to have as much as you like,' he said, gesturing towards Ian with his hand.

'I think not. We prefer it a little warmer and fresher than that,' said Stuart.

'It's still fresh, I just had some. It's lovely, try it. He's just maturing.'

'How did all this shit go down?' asked Keith as he looked down at Adrian.

'Adrian attacked Ian and Ian managed to get him a good one with that meat cleaver but then I came and managed to overpower him from the back.'

'What's with all the disembowelment?' Stuart asked a little crossly.

'Well, Michael was with me and said I had to make sure he wouldn't get back up again. And I had been wondering anyway, if people were the same inside as sheep.' Stuart looked at him for a long time. 'They're not.' Stephen said as if Stuart was waiting for an answer.

'I still aren't sure that makes sense. It's not civilized, even for us.'

'He can do whatever he likes to anyone now. We all can,' Keith angrily snapped at Stuart. As if to defy him he walked to the half frozen pool of blood, put his finger in and tasted it. He seemed to be processing with his mouth and his tongue clicked quickly on the roof of his mouth. He reached down with his hand and got some more on three fingers and put them in his mouth. 'That is good mate,' he said after finishing what was on his fingers. 'He was a tasty one. I can understand why The Master has decided to settle here.' Stephen nodded.

'What have you been up to these last few days?' asked Stephen.

'Oh, you know, following The Masters orders. Taking out the mobile phone masts, important stuff like that.'

'Right. Me and Michael, we've moved into The Grange. The Master wanted us close as we are his right hand men.' They seemed to be playing a little game of one-upmanship. 'So what have you been up to, Stuart?'

'Turning people on The Master's orders.

Making new ones of us.'

'What are you doing tonight. Do you want to go out, all three of us?'

'No,' said Stuart condescendingly, 'That wouldn't look good, would it? We are both in uniform and you aren't. It would look like we had arrested you!'

'Yeah, I forgot,' Stephen muttered downheartedly. In the war of *who was most important*, the two policemen had won.

'Anyway, we have got work to do again for The Master. No rest for the wicked. More important stuff so that we can cut off the village,' said Keith

'Yeah that is important. We don't want any interference,' agreed Stephen.

'Fear not, whilst me and Stuart are in control, everything will go swimmingly. So you just carry on with your work and we'll do ours. We will be off now and I'll leave you to your feed. Leave some for me. Ian is too good a dish to miss out on. I will be back later.'

Adam's Mum had been cooking all day. There were empty boxes of frozen party food all over the kitchen and she was laying plates and serviettes out on the sideboard. Adam had been instructed to have a wash and not be rude to any of her friends. He had taken the games console upstairs. She said that surprisingly few people had called her to cancel as she had checked her mobile and it had no calls on it and also the phone hadn't rang all afternoon. Adam said *rock on* and went upstairs. She followed him and put on her outfit, satin trousers and a sequined top. She felt great.

Julie was getting a little worried, but at six thirty, the doorbell rung for the first time. Screeching excitedly, she went to open it. Adam was in his bedroom. She said he could come down and have some of their food when some of the guests had had theirs. His door was slightly ajar, and muffled voices could be heard in greeting. He could hear people knocking snow off their boots and then the door shutting after them. After about four doorbell rings he thought he had given them plenty of chance and he crept downstairs.

His mother was preoccupied with all the people there. He got a paper plate and piled it high with food. Checking where his mother was again, he took a can of lager and shoved it down the back of his trousers waistband and pulled his sweater over it. He quickly and stealthily went back upstairs and thought if he was lucky, he might get away with doing that mission another two times tonight.

He had his headset on talking to Bob online, whilst they played their game. Every time he moved it a little away from his head, he could hear how raucous the party makers were. At eight o'clock he said to Bob that he was going down to get another plate full of food. He noticed that there were roughly about twenty-five people in his house. Adam only knew about ten of them. The others were from where his Mum worked. He didn't look anyone in the eye, as he didn't want a conversation to start up. Then his mother would discover him and his game would be up. There was still plenty of food left, but he noticed the booze stash had certainly been depleted. Of course the food was cold now. Filling another paper plate, this time he took a couple of mince pies and balanced them on top. Then his second can of lager went in his secret place and up the stairs he went again. It was getting quite rowdy down there and he thought it was a good job his Mum had invited both sets of neighbours round to the house. There certainly would have been a lot of complaining otherwise. When he was last down there he did not see his Mum, but he hadn't gone into the living room as he thought he might get told off. There seemed to be a lot of Steps songs on very loud and a couple of Spice Girls numbers that he recognised. A couple of women were singing loudly and tunelessly to these, and others were laughing at them. He didn't want to see how his mother was involved in this, but he bet she was dancing on the coffee table or being sick or something. He had witnessed both these things before at parties and he never wanted to have a repeat performance.

Just after ten o'clock he lost contact with Bob. The connection just went dead. He messed about with all the contacts, leads and plug. Frustrated, he thought that for the moment, there was no getting back online. He picked up the phone to call Bob but that was dead too. Maybe the snow had taken down the lines. So that put pay to him playing with Bob. He thought that he might as well play offline on his own for a bit. It might come back on. There was no chance he was getting to sleep, with all that racket still going on. He played for about another half an hour, but was getting bored without the banter from Bob. He took his headset off. It was surprisingly quiet, he thought that the guests must have gone home early, because of the snow. Usually these parties lasted all night. He opened his curtains a little and saw that it was still coming down heavily. Looking downwards from the front door, he could see several pairs of fresh footprints. He thought he would go down and see what was left of the food. Might not be able get that third can of lager if his mother wasn't distracted though.

Even from the top of the stairs, he noticed that the guests had laid waste to his house. There were cans, bottles, glasses, paper plates serviettes and bits of food everywhere. He imagined that this was what student accommodation was like, and in a couple of years, he would probably be one of the ones adding to his mess. He just knew he would definitely be blackmailed by his mother to help her clear all this up the following day. With him doing the majority, as she was in a delicate condition.

He went into the kitchen and there were indeed a few bits of food left. So he put them on a plate. He still didn't hear any noise so thought that he would check on his Mum. She probably had passed out asleep on the sofa and left the doors unlocked. He checked the back door and that indeed was unlocked. He put the bolt on and thought he would check on her before doing the front. He popped a mini sausage roll in his mouth then began to walk into the living room. There was a woman leaning over someone kissing them.

'Oh sorry,' he said quietly. Even more incomprehensible, as his mouth was full of pastry and sausage. He started to pivot on one foot to go out, his fluffy socks silent on the laminate floor. The woman looked up quickly and turned round to look at him. He had never seen her before and there was blood around her mouth and the person that he thought she was kissing on the sofa was his mother, Julie. His mother slowly rolled her head towards him. She had a look of ecstasy on her face. He saw this and his legs went to jelly and he thought, *oh god they are in my house.* He threw the plate of food at the two of them and ran up the stairs. His fluffy socks slipped on the stairs and he missed his footing. Adam felt like he was fighting his legs, they would not go as fast as he wanted them to. It seemed like it took forever to get up those stairs and into his room. He shut the door and started to put things behind it. Soon he saw that the door was being pushed from the other side, it was open enough, for the vampire to look through at him, her one unblinking eye visible through the gap.

He threw himself at the door and started pushing back. He heard voices and then stopped to listen. He heard his mothers voice. 'What do you want me to do Diane?'

'This can be your first. The Master wants to collect families and your son will help us get another family that The Master particularly wants above all others. You will do this now and I will help you.' Adam stood the other side of the door desperately wondering how he could defend himself against two vampires, one being his mother who he particularly didn't want to hurt. He tried to recall everything he had read, and seen. All he had talked about with Bob. It seemed inaccessible at the moment. Think. Think.

Adam quickly looked around the room while he had his hands against the door. They hadn't stormed the door yet, so he had a few moments to plan. He tried to think about what worked and what he had that he could use. A wooden stake, garlic and decapitation. His eyes darted at each item in his room and judged if it could be used. He had his console and TV, his homework and loads of clothes in his room. What could anyone do with that? Even the most inventive person could see that he had nothing. Then he did see something that he could use, the problem being he would have to let go of the door before he got to it. Plus he would be lucky to get both of them with it. As if they knew he had finished thinking, they both started pushing against the door again. He realised that he wouldn't be able to hold it much longer against the two of them. Letting go and in a world record attempt, he tried to get to his bedside table. They were in before he could do anything about it and he had only got as far as his desk. The vampire Diane got to him pretty quickly, he picked up his console and slammed it across the side of her head, which knocked her against the wall.

He stepped back a couple of paces and his mother was on him. Diane was in the corner but conscious.

'Show me. How do I do it?' Julie screamed angrily.

'I am trying to get up again,' Diane said through gritted teeth. She was tangled up with all of Adam's cables and chargers. Adam's Mum had been telling him for ages to tidy it. It had his belts in there, a goal net from football, his dressing gown belt and many other tangled items. 'Do it now Julie! Do it!' Adam got his bedside lamp, which had a wooden base, smashed the top off it and plunged it into his mother. It still had part of the plastic and metal bulb fitment on it. The lamp cut through her quite easily, making a two-inch channel from the front of her, straight out the back. It stuck firmly in her, the ridges of the turned wood getting trapped in her ribs. He tried to tell himself she was no longer his mother after all. Adam didn't know whether it hit her heart but it seemed to do the trick as she fell straight down like a sack of potatoes. No gasping, or turning to dust or reaching out to pull it out of herself. As it hit her she fell. Diane jumped up, free at last.

'You will pay for this, child.'

Adam put his hands over his face, he had no other weapons left. Closing his eyes, he tried to imagine he was with Bob and everything was fine. He wished it was summer and he was in the school playing fields, the sun on the pair of them, kicking a ball around at break. The best of times. He needed someone to help him. Feeling the pain in his neck, he knew no one was ever going to. His very last thought was that he needed Bob.

21 – Fruit

Monday morning was the same as the previous few days. Snow built on snow. It was murky and looked like it was set in for the day and it was forecast to snow for the foreseeable future. Wayne thought that he would get his post route out of the way as quickly as possible as it would only get worse the longer he left it. It was still not officially light, but how light it would get, he didn't know. It was getting him down now. He couldn't ever remember it snowing this much or for so long and wondered how long it would take to get back to normal. *Weeks* he thought.

He had walked through the village up amongst the houses, delivering the letters and parcels. Some of them had glass porches and he was concerned to see that the post from last week had not been taken inside. As he walked, he thought about various explanations for this. Maybe some people had gone away early for Christmas, or had got blocked off from the village. It was a worrying thought. The post he was delivering was actually a backlog that he was working through. There had been no fresh post for the last few days and he was hoping that this snow would do one soon because there would be an enormous amount of Christmas Cards building up for him somewhere to deal with. And what about all the people who ordered online for Christmas? Black Friday had meant that he had also had a lot more to deliver and he hadn't managed to do all that yet. Looking on the bright side, at least he was getting some way towards catching up. Even though, he didn't want to go out in the snow, he thought it was better to go out and get on with the job. If he stayed in, he would only end up watching another box set. He would thank himself in the future.

Another point that struck him was, where were all the snowmen? He usually saw at least ten on his rounds in the winter. Some kids managed to make one with about one inch of snow. But with inches and inches, even feet in some places where it had drifted, there were none. No snowmen in Friarmere. Weird. Come to think of it he hadn't seen kids sledging for a few days. He had seen kids out on the odd occasion last week, throwing snowballs, but not many since. He had seen a few small ones, bundled up, with their mothers off to school. Maybe kids didn't like playing in the snow anymore. They were too interested in going online, taking selfies and the like. He longed for the old days.

When he saw that he had two parcels and three letters for Christine Baker, he thought it was a good job it was early. She might still be in bed. Get it out of the way. Sneak up to her door, snipe the letters through, and with it a card saying you had to come to the post office to get your parcels. He had nothing for The Grange luckily, so her post would be the last one before he made the trek over to Lazy Farm. The snow came down straight, with big flakes. There wasn't a smidge of wind so at least it wasn't drifting today. The flakes made tiny quiet patter noises, which he liked. It might be only him left in the world. No birds, no cars, no sheep baahing, no trains. There weren't any other sounds apart from the settling of the snowflakes and his footsteps. When it was like this, no one else about, he quite enjoyed it and as he had been walking for a while, he was very warm, although it was way below zero degrees.

As he got about twenty feet away from Christine's house he saw that her curtains were open and she was standing in the window looking out into the dark. It wasn't yet seven am and he thought it would probably not be light, or approaching some kind of light until about eight at this rate. She moved out of the window and he knew that she was definitely making her way to the door. This was not how he had wanted it to happen. After he had just been feeling so good about the morning, his route was going to end up like this. But he had never been a lucky guy.

By the time he had walked up the short path to the front door, it was open and she was standing in the doorway. The dull light from a candle shone behind her, her legs were planted slightly apart and her arms were outstretching. She seemed to have some kind of nightdress on that was black, lacy and nearly completely transparent. *Oh why couldn't this snow make me snowblind.* This was not the most attractive thing that Christine could wear. It had tiny shoestring straps that cut into her shoulders. Wayne was pleased to see though, that it came with the matching panties. That would have sent him over the edge. As it was, there was nothing hiding her *low hanging fruits*. Wayne thought he might start complaining about it to head office, so they wouldn't make him deliver here every morning.

'Morning!' he said in a bright and cheery voice. He had all her post in one hand and held it out, with the other side of him turned away so as to quickly make his escape.

'Wayne, sweetie, you have got to come in. I am a state. I am having such a problem. You need to help me. I don't know who to ask,' she gasped out at him desperately. *You're a state all right* he thought. All his dreams of making an escape gone in a flash.

'What's wrong?' he said in a beaten voice.

'Come out of the snow, sweetie. You are getting cold and Chrissy might get a bit cold *too* standing here. So come inside and I will show you my problem. We can have that nice drinky that we spoke about. Maybe a nice hot toddy to keep you warm on the rest of your journey?'

'No, I can't do that Miss Baker, I would lose my job if they caught me.'

'I have told you it is Chrissy, to you. We are special friends, aren't we?' Wayne ignored this question and reluctantly stepped inside.

'That's better,' she said shutting the door behind him, 'Chrissy was getting a bit cold!'

'Maybe you should put your housecoat on then,' said Wayne. Hoping she would take his advice, 'Anyway, what do you want me to look at?'

She stared back at him confused, obviously not knowing what he was talking about, now that she had got him inside. He waited for her to tell him but she just cocked her head to one side and smiled.

'I thought you had a problem, you wanted me to look at.' Her eyes widened in realization.

'Oh yes, Oh yes, Wayne sweetie it is in here,' she said and trotted into the hall. As he followed her into the hall she stopped, waited for him to come through, then shut the kitchen door behind them both. He thought this was a bit strange, but imagined that she just trying to keep the heat in. They went through to the living room, which was cluttered with very dated furniture. She stopped and pointed to the corner of the room.

'It's down there, sweetie.' There was another door in her living room and she gestured towards it.

'What's in there?'

'My basement. I have a really bad flood and it is going to keep rising and I know that there is a way you can switch it off but it is just too high for Chrissy to reach.'

'So I'm going to get wringing wet?' He cried in astonishment.

'No, no. You'll see when you go down there. I just need a big tall strong man like you.' She opened the door and inside it was like looking into a pool of ink.

'Looks like I'll need my torch.' He bent his

head, to retrieve the torch from the back of his belt. When he looked up, a beautiful young woman stood in the doorway of the basement, smiling. Christine looked at him and raised her eyebrows up and down a couple of times, cheekily. He cleared his throat. 'To be honest I don't know where this is going, but I am seeing someone.'

'That's not a problem for me,' Christine said seductively, walking towards him. 'Is it a problem for you, Kate?

'Never has been before,' Kate replied. She stared at Wayne. He could not shift his gaze. Unbelievably lost in her. In her beauty. Wayne wanted to find out everything about her, to be hers, to *be* her even. Christine was behind him now and gave him a gentle push.

'Go on sweetie. Go to Kate.' He shuffled forward. There was a small part of him that could see this happening, like a movie. A small part that was still Wayne. *Wake up, run away it shouted.*

He reached the top of the stairs. Kate took hold of his jacket at the shoulders. Christine gave him one last shove and he disappeared into the inky black with Kate.

'Welcome to the fold, sweetie,' said Christine as she followed them both in and shut the door.

This was the last band practice before the concert on Wednesday. Ernie couldn't call anyone. The phone lines were out, the mobile phone network was down so, their communication network was well and truly blocked off. Ernie had left Lynn at home. She was not feeling well at all, and had stayed in their bedroom all day. Lynn had said there was no reason to go, as she didn't play an instrument and she didn't want to go through all that snow, getting freezing cold, catching her death, just to sit in band that night. Ernie would rather have had her at band feeling ill but safe, rather than at home, alone. But she had insisted, and after he left he stood outside until she had bolted herself in. That was all he could do. He couldn't drag her out of the house by her hair feeling terrible, just to sit in band all night. But it was doubly important for him to be there and kept in the loop about what he called *The Invasion*.

He had taken a long walk up to the Primary School today to speak to the headteacher. Mr Shufflebotham had insisted that the children were looking forward to it and with everything else going on, it would be good for them. He had some staff off as well as children, afflicted suddenly with this mystery bug. As he was now short staffed they had to call off a visit to the village Methodist Church Christmas Tree Festival, as the risk assessment had looked a nightmare. And a trip to the Christmas Pantomime in town had been cancelled, due to no transport. At least with the Christmas Concert it was up to the children's parents to get them there and back safely. Ernie walked away, knowing he had tried his best. Now he had to let it go, and realise that the concert was still on.

Before he got to Band, he had roughly worked

out that there would be probably fifteen players left to play the concert. *That really was a skeleton crew*, he laughed to himself. He couldn't find better words. Ernie would tell them that tonight. It might raise a titter. *Bugger only knows, they needed it at the moment.*

Freddie was down in the dumps because he could no longer contact his wife Brenda, who was visiting her sister Doris, in Melden. He had spoken to his wife two nights ago and she had ensured him that Doris was well and truly alive, but very ill in bed with an unknown illness. At her age that was worrying. She also said that the snow was just about as bad over the tops. Brenda had not got out much really, and her other two sisters had been bringing groceries for them both. She said too, that the weather was making sure that there was no one out and about.

Barry had felt a bit better than the other night, which Ernie was very relieved about. He needed his conductor for the concert, which was most definite. Mrs White conducted all the children and Barry would conduct the band. They needed it to be a harmonious and seamless process.

All fifteen of the players did not make it that night, but they had also told him previously, that if it was bad snow, they might not make it. The band room was close for some people, but others lived further, or weren't brilliant on their feet and didn't want to slip and break their legs. It was unthinkable for them to be lying in the snow, either freezing or being someone's takeaway dinner. Those that thought this way said they may skip band to ensure an appearance at the concert. On the other hand with no option to contact them, they might not be there for other sinister reasons.

Ernie was reassured that Barry was only going to practice the music for the concert and then finish, as everyone was concerned about getting home. They had travelled in groups, thinking that it would be safe to go home in the dark and through the snow. No one would take the chance of going alone, and being *chosen*. They were still stopping at each other's houses, and would do, until this was sorted. As Ernie reminded them, in his words.

'To be got by the short and curlies means you are also sacked from band.' To him this meant more than being bitten.

It was a short uneventful rehearsal. After band, they all left in their small groups. Freddie asked if Ernie, who was just locking the outside door, if he was okay to get home. Freddie had got Gary and Danny to come to stay at his house as he wanted to man the phone, just in case Brenda rang. Ernie's car was right by the door because as usual, he had been the first to arrive.

'Yes, I'm fine. You get off out of the cold. Lynn will have the kettle on.' Freddie drove off slowly. Ernie waved to him, listening to the muffled tyre sounds and compacting new snow. It had stopped snowing again. His hand was on the door handle of his car and he was still waving, when Lynn popped up from the other side of the car, next to the bushes.

'Boo!' she said loudly, 'Surprised?'

Ernie, knew straight away that this was no longer Lynn. She stood in her fleece jacket, twigs in her hair. Her eyes were blood red and he could see her new, very sharp vampire teeth. He wanted to say, *I told you I shouldn't have gone out.* But he didn't say it. He didn't think that Lynn would listen to his advice again, so there was no point. One small part of him was comforted knowing that he was right.

'Look who I have found? Two more people to play with.' He wasn't thinking clearly. His brain felt like soggy cabbage. He still had his mind on band.

'I don't suppose you mean you have you got me some fresh players for Wednesday?' he asked dazily but optimistically.

'No just recycled ones.' He heard his two back doors open and out of the car got Vicky and Jake. His eyes were wide open.

'Join us.' Lynn said flatly.

Jake and Vicky were already either side of him. He looked from one to the other. The similarities to his wife's condition were obvious. Then Lynn was at the front of him. He glanced up and started to put his hands up to defend himself. The three of them struck all at once, Ernie dropping to his knees as he took the weight of three people. He looked up the track and could still see Freddie's taillights, going oh so slowly. Ernie watch them get smaller and smaller, along with all hope for Friarmere Band.

22 - Teeth

The next day's snow was thick but at least falling snow had stopped. It was quiet. The village in stasis. Most roads were reduced to tracks. Two firm indentations, where tyres had gone before, but still perfect snow in the centre. So you had to get onto those tracks if you wanted to try and move around. You could not go out of the village anyway, as the village was situated in a deep valley. To get out any way meant going up over the hills. Even on the way up, car tyres could not grip the road on the steep inclines, so they kept slipping back. The higher you got up the road the snow became increasingly deeper, so the problem got worse. All these roads were now completely cut off.

At just after seven in the morning Mark was going around the village delivering milk, it was going to be his last delivery in the milk float. His float only just made it on the two tracks. Often he heard the snow dragging across the bottom of the vehicle and it would tilt alarmingly to one side or another. Along with dropping off, he was also planning to pick up.

Paula was running around her house trying to get herself sorted so she could set off for work. She was a large, fifty year old woman who plodded through life, just doing the bare minimum and looking forward to a big bar of chocolate and half a bottle of Malibu every night.

Today, she had been asked to attend a yearly review at work, which was an office in the village and she fully expected it not to go well. Paula needed to be there and ready at eight o'clock before work, so the boss could get this out of the way before everyone else got in to start their day.

Mark was looking through her window. She was going to be out for the rest of the day, so had opened the curtains. As it was dark outside but light inside, anyone could see what was going on inside. She was fully distracted in her haste and Mark waited outside her kitchen door with his back against the wall. He was really looking forward to this, he did every time, and couldn't imagine he would ever get sick of it.

The Master had indicated that they were to make less vampires, and start feeding or else there would be no one around to eat. If they were discreet, he felt it was now time that they could allow for feeding and leaving the corpse.

Mark had decided that Paula, would be the first of them. He had to wait another minute, staring at the side of the next house to hers. He heard a key rattle and she opened her door handle. A rectangle of light shone through onto the snow, first small then very large, until it was larger than the actual aperture. She appeared in the doorway, causing a shadow in that golden rectangle for a moment, huge, like a giant. Then her arm went up and she clicked off the light. All was dark, she started to step outside.

He quickly revealed himself, turned towards

her and pushed her back into the house. She wasn't expecting it and being quite a large lady, with a low centre of gravity, she easily fell over. She flopped backwards onto the floor, her handbag came open and all its contents were splayed over the kitchen floor. Her arms scrabbled about in its contents, knocking them helter-skelter around the kitchen, grasping for some kind of weapon. Her purse went flying across the floor, a lipstick, her sad white sandwiches with a pale cheese filling wrapped in cling film. He jumped on top of her with his full force expecting to bounce, as she had such a large stomach. But he didn't. What he did do was squash all the wind out of her, which only made it worse for Paula. Soon he was drinking his own pints of nourishment.

Later that day when Paula's cats came in expecting to find an empty house they found her lying there. A mess of her own blood, torn clothes and the contents of her handbag. The sandwiches would forever remain uneaten. These cats were unable to save their mistress. They would wait for two days and then decide that their owner would have to be their next dinner.

The primary school was still in session. The secondary school however, did not open. Lucky for Bob. The primary kids were all still practising for their concert, unlucky for them.

By mid-afternoon it had started snowing

again. The Master had asked for several of his new vampires to come and see him at The Grange. He was having a lovely get together and had a couple of dishes on the menu that they would enjoy. As he said to them, it was a *Meat and Greet!*

Diane was in attendance and Keith, along with a few of the others. After they had been there a short while and the initial niceties were over, The Master stood before them to give a little speech. Christine, Kate and Michael Thompson stood alongside him. His proud lieutenants.

'Welcome to my home, my children. The village is exactly where I want it, at this time. I want to stress a few points as we move further into our new lives. This will help and ensure that we thrive as a new community.' The vampires all listened carefully. To break a rule that The Master had set, would be terrible. 'Firstly, from now, you are not to turn children. I know some of you already have done. And what these small members of our community do, will have to be monitored as, in my experience, they are quite unpredictable and not suitable for turning.'

'What do we do with them, then? Eat them,' asked Diane.

'Eat them all, sweetie. Very tasty,' Christine said, excitedly clapping her hands.

'Also old people. Please, unless they are very influential in the community, they are not to be turned.'

'Waste them,' said Michael.

'Quite.' The Master knew Michael would have

to say something tonight, so he felt important. There it was. The Master continued his speech. 'Pass this message around to the others.' There was much nodding around the crowd and mumbling.

'Now, there is a Christmas Concert being held tomorrow. Some of you might know this as you are former members of Friarmere Band. Tomorrow we are going to have a feast!' A lot of applause followed and Michael stood with his hands behind his back, nodding his thanks, as if he had arranged it all.

'What are the arrangements?' asked Keith.

'I am just getting to that!' Norman said haughtily. 'I want all of us that played in the band to attend how they would normally. They will be our people on the inside. There will also be a few others in attendance. I will be there to start off proceedings.'

'We're all coming, don't worry,' said Michael reassuringly to the crowd. The Master glared at him then cleared his throat.

'This is where the balance of power shifts to us, my friends. It will be a wonderful evening and one that Friarmere will never forget.'

The Woodalls, Peter and Janet had not been asked to go to the Grange. They were on the prowl tonight in the falling snow for any victim they could find. Both very hungry, encouraging each other to make their first kill. They made quite a formidable team, the pair of them. Both tall and quite heavy set. If anyone got in their way, they would stand no chance.

The person that did end up getting in their way was someone they knew very well. She was just on her way out to meet some friends again. Sophie was walking down her street, concentrating on her feet, so that she didn't slip. She didn't let rumours around the village stop her going out. Vampires! Monsters! It was a load of rubbish. She was sick of small village mentality. Probably made up by a bunch of old people, so that kids didn't go out and they could have the pubs to themselves. Well, Sophie knew better than them. Nothing was going to stop her. It was boring staying in with her mother who now kept to her room most of the time, or disappeared out without telling her. Besides that, having a few beers, kept the cold out.

When she saw them walking towards her in the snow, she knew straight away with their height and size, that it could be none other than the Woody's.

'Hello, I thought it was you two out and about. Are you a bit better?' she asked Peter.

'Hello, yes I am feeling far more sprightly now,' said Peter. As they drew closer under the lamplight, Sophie knew that something was wrong with them. Their eyes were red and Janet already had her teeth bared, which looked very different and sharp. Sophie was instantly worried.

'Take us home. We were just on our way to talk to your Mum.'

'She's out,' Sophie said quickly.

'We insist on coming home and waiting for her then,' said Peter, 'We know she's out, and where she's been. So that's why we know she is on her way back. We insist.' They both grabbed an arm of Sophie's and, pinching it, marched her back up to her front door. She was so in shock, that she did not do anything about it, until she got close to the door when she realised all the rumours were true and she had been pigheaded and ignorant all along. She started to struggle and cry out but Janet put her hand over Sophie's mouth and the falling snow muffled any other sounds remaining.

As Sophie had left the door on the catch because her mother was due back soon, they just pushed it open and forced their way in, shutting the door behind them. The Woodalls sat her down, stood before her and quite frankly told her all about what had happened to them in the last couple of weeks. They also told her what her mother was, and who the new friends were that she was visiting tonight. 'You've got the choice, of whether you want us to carry on and turn you, and be like us. Which, I can highly recommend. Or to die, as our food source. It's as simple as that. At some point you will be one or the other in Friarmere. And no one is getting out of this village, you can be sure of that. This is The Masters central hub. We turn people and have time to change the whole village. By the time the snow is gone. There will be enough of us to turn the country. Great Britain will be ours.'

Sophie shocked them with her response.

'If you put it like that then it is a no-brainer.' She knew something was different about her mother, but she had been hiding herself away a lot. And Sophie went out the rest of the time. Something had not been right at band, and now, she had met the two Woody's. The penny had dropped for Sophie. It was really happening here. It didn't bother her as long as she could still see her friends, or at least some of them. Her mother and the Woody's seemed quite happy. She would get to live forever and stay young. Now she had all the facts, she was eager for it to happen.

'I want to be turned but I would prefer if my mother did it.'

'Oh no,' said Peter, shaking his head, 'That is not one of the choices, I gave you. After all, we must feed tonight. You just have the choice on the outcome, not how it starts.'

'Okay, try to not make it hurt that much then,' she said and pulled her long brown hair away from her neck. This action was too much for Janet, whose mouth had been watering through the whole of the conversation. They both pounced on her, satisfied their needs and then turning the willing Sophie to one of the undead. Within five minutes of agreeing, she was one of them.

Diane burst through the door. She could smell the blood from outside.

'I did not wish for her to be turned!' she

screamed, 'How dare you!'

'We did give her the choice. And she chose happily,' said Peter. Sophie nodded at her mother. 'Sooner or later you would not have been able to protect her. Just like tonight. She would have just ended up someone's meal, then discarded. We gave her the choice, as a fellow bandsman.' Diane after a few moments knew they were right.

'I have been surviving without human blood. Until recently,' she added quietly.

'That's your decision. We are loving this new life. I love the taste of human blood. We are taking Sophie out now, to find some more, if you want to come.' They did not wait for her answer. The three got up and walked out of the door. She followed them into the night. Into the swirling snow.

Lynn Cooper was certainly having a new lease of life. Ernie had not had not taken well to the change and was having to stay in the house, she thought that this was due to him having a very strong sense of what was right and what was wrong before he had *become*. Lynn had felt great, however and was roaming the streets. Niggles of pain she had suffered before, due to age, had disappeared. Tiredness had gone too. It was wonderful. Earlier, she had been at The Grange as well, and had listened to the advice of The Master. She absolutely loved this new part of herself and had taken to it with gusto. Even though Ernie wasn't adapting as well as her now, she knew he would come round, when he started appreciating the advantages, as she had.

The Master had given her specific instructions about the person to turn next. He could tell she would be a good and obedient vampire and a faithful servant to him. He had instructed her to turn someone that was already infected from his blood, and marked forever. She knew of others but until tonight had not known of this other person. If she had put her mind to it, she would have worked it out. Gliding effortlessly through the snow, she did not feel the cold but just a thrilling exhilaration coursing through her body. She could quite see how some of the others had got themselves in a pickle. The feelings and urges were quite overwhelming. It would be very easy to get caught up in the excitement of it all and to make mistakes. She wouldn't be caught out.

Lynn knocked loudly on the door. Barry opened it happily. He was eating a cornish pastie.

'Hiya Lynn, I'm just getting my appetite back.'

'Good. I want to talk to you about that. Can I come in.'

'Yes, come in. Do you want a brew?' She walked in and he shut the door.

'Yes please. I'd love a brew'

That night, a tremendous amount of snow came down. The inches could be seen going up and up. Along with this, the vampires made sure the village was blocked off. The people left were just going to end up one thing or another. At two in the morning, the wind began to blow a little stronger and shift the snow this way and that, painting all the walls white, drifting the snow into twenty feet high walls. If there was anything the vampires had missed, the snow took care of it.

23 – Cheese Knife

On the morning of the school concert, Friarmere woke to the worst snow it had ever seen in its several hundred years of existence. As it was still snowing by ten, the primary school finally decided to send their pupils home. It really was no use to be in, as a lot of people had not come in today. Staff and pupils.

Mrs White presumed they all must be sick or had colds and this was very worrying but she didn't want to panic the children and parents so had said that the concert was still on tonight. She understood if some children couldn't make it, or their parents decided to keep them away. All the pupils were very eager to do the concert as they had been practicing these songs since the Harvest Festival. They also got to dress up in their best clothes, instead of school uniform. Every year, after singing, they got a special reward too. Mr Shufflebotham would buy a chocolate Santa for each of them. Whilst shaking their hands and saying Merry Christmas to them on their way out, he would give them their gift.

Ernie Cooper had called Mrs White the previous week about arrangements, telling her that the Civic Hall would be open from three that afternoon. From that time the band would be putting out all their instruments and music stands. The committee would dress the place up for Christmas. Mrs White advised Mr

Shufflebotham that she was going to stay at school for about another hour then go back home to get her head down for a couple of hours and get ready. About three thirty she would then make her own way down to the Civic Hall to make all the preparations for the children, arriving there just before it got dark and set everything up. There were a few jobs to do. Putting all the song sheets on the audience's seats that she had printed out. Laying the chairs out for the choir. Plus, putting out all the prizes for the raffle. It all took a surprisingly long time to do alone. She thought she might as well stay there and eat her tea instead of going back out into the cold. Probably a flask of soup and a sandwich. A paperback book was in her bag, which she thought she might get half an hour to read.

The band had been preparing for this day. Not only musically but in other ways. They knew that there would be a lynch mob there tonight and they would just be sitting ducks. Luckily they had liberated quite a few weapons from Ian's Butchers Shop. There were also other things that Gary had brought along and as usual Wee Renee had a few ideas of her own. They had some knives and some axes. It was clear from the death of Adrian in the butcher shop that it did not necessarily have to be a stake through the heart. Severe damage to the brain or head would also do the trick.

They were meeting at the band room at twelve noon. Pat and Wee Renee had put some sandwiches together and Sue was providing some cakes. Laura would bring the tea and coffee for them as she had abundance at home, the coffee van being off the roads, in this snow.

They were going to have a brief meeting about what they could do tonight and share out their weapons. Sue had no idea how many people would turn up to the meeting, the concert or to watch them play. She was worried, scared and also excited and couldn't choose which was the greater emotion. Opening the band room door carefully, peeking behind every door she hoped that Ernie and Lynn would be there soon. She could not contact them over the phone or mobile network now and their house was on the opposite side of Friarmere. Her priority now was to look after Bob and Tony.

Freddie arrived. Quite down in the dumps because he could not contact Brenda, who was still looking after her sister. He was getting really worried, but in another way, knew that she was best out of all this and was probably much safer being over the hill. She would also have two sisters to help her, and their families. He was just wishing for the best possible outcome tonight and had brought with him a walking stick that had a six inch silver plating round the bottom and then a big rubber bung stuck on the end of it.

'What are you doing with that. Have you been using it, now that Maurice doesn't need it?' asked Sue.

'It's not Maurice's, I will have you know,' he

said. 'This is my old Papa's. I have customised it. I will show you later.' And he winked. She realised he was trying to keep cheerful for everyone else.

Tony and Bob finally came into the bandroom. They had arrived with Sue, but had been messing about in the back of his Land Rover. It had only just made it there. The snow was unfathomable. In Tony's pocket was the gun that he was so proud of, although Sue told him that he shouldn't fire it anywhere in that place, with the kids about. He said he was not having something like that and not being able to defend their family, so she couldn't really disagree with that. Liz and Andy turned up. They had got a knife that Andy held out in his hands all the time, which he had taken from Ian shop. Liz said she had some other items from the shop, like skewers and hooks that she had got in her instrument case and was feeling slightly stronger again. She was hopeful for what they could do as a gang.

Gary was picking up Danny and they arrived soon after.

'How's she doing in this snow?' he asked Tony.

'Struggling but just about managing courageously. Hopefully it will stay off now.'

'I wouldn't bank on it,' said Danny, 'I have just heard the weather forecast on the radio and it said more snow tonight.' Gary shook his head.

'As if we haven't got enough to cope with,' he said miserably.

They had a few fold up tables in the back of the bandroom. Sue had put them out, pushing them together and putting seats all the way around the edge. It ended up being a big dinner table or conference table, which they would need both of today.

'I can't stop that long. Maybe an hour.' Gary informed them, 'I have got stuff to do. The weight of all the snow has been on the bushes and they have pushed down my back fence, so I feel like I have no defences. I want to work on that and get that looking a bit better at least.'

'You might not even have to worry about that at all, if tonight goes down as I think it will,' said Andy. He was looking very downhearted about it all.

'We have got each other and we are quite a formidable team,' said Gary, 'Don't you get negative about it all. We will be brilliant, you just watch. They have underestimated Friarmere Band, if they think they can take all of us. That gang of bullies have taken enough of us already. Anyway I have promised I would do a bit of work up at the school, as well. They need some work on the boiler. Hopefully I can get it going and the kids can get back in tomorrow. So I will have to join you tonight. I will be coming straight from work.'

A couple of the others arrived and settled themselves in, with various bags, their uniforms and instruments.

The final two people that came were Pat and Wee Renee. They had just come from Pat's house, thus coming the shortest distance to the band room, so had made it on foot quite easily. Wee Renee had a twinkle in her eye and was obviously excited about all of this. Pat had a grim look on her face and her jaw was jutting out. She certainly looked determined and no one wanted to tackle her.

Sue had been making tea and coffee, putting cakes on plates and lining them up on the big table. The heating had now taken full effect and the band room was lovely and warm. They all took their coats and boots off. Liz put out some vegetarian food and Pat and Wee Renee laid out some of the sandwiches they had made. Which were extensive as Pat always catered for herself when she was counting out numbers of people, so everyone had a portion that was about three times bigger than they needed.

'No Ernie or Lynn then,' said Freddie, which was the elephant in the room, 'That's very strange.'

'What isn't strange these days,' said Danny.

'I can't get my head round it. I don't want it to be true at all but, to be honest, I hope if they have been got at, that they haven't been changed into one of *them*,' said Freddie, 'because that means that I would be next, being their friend and the only senior committee member left. Between them and Maurice, I'm already dead meat.'

'It doesn't necessarily mean that,' said Sue. They might not pick us off by seniority on committee.'

'No. You're right Sue, I'm just being daft. I am worried about becoming uncontrollable and going after Brenda and Our Doris.'

'It isn't going to come to that, we'll make sure of that Freddie,' said Gary.

'I see no one's doubting that they are one of the undead, then?' asked Wee Renee.

'He'd be here especially at a meeting of the clan Rene. I've never been so sure of anything in my life,' Pat said firmly. The rest of the party firmly nodded.

'Ah well. Best get on with having our sandwiches and lets have a nice tea and cake, then we will clear all this off and lay out what we have on the table,' Wee Renee said resignedly, instantly tucking into an egg and cress sandwich.

They ate their sandwiches and talked about other matters like the snow and Christmas. To be exact, what was the right time to put up your Christmas Tree. This was the one matter Wee Renee and Pat disagreed about. Pat said the 21st December, whilst Wee Renee had already had hers up since the last Sunday in November. Trying to focus on the normality of life whilst they ate, so it would not put them off their food.

'I like this, on these sandwiches here, Pat,' said Bob, 'What is it?'

'Braun,' she said pointedly.

'What's that?' Sue and Wee Renee looked at each other and Sue quickly shook her head vigorously.

'It's a type of wee Pate, you know. Like beef paste,' said Renee changing the subject. 'You're a good boy. Wee Renee has bought you a treat. I'll let you have it, if you eat all your Pate sandwiches,' she laughed gently. Sue glared at the others and they carried on eating their sandwiches. Everyone, afterwards avoiding the braun apart from Bob and Pat.

Wee Renee had bought Bob a king size Yorkie bar and she dropped it into the hood of his sweatshirt as she walked past to go to the toilet, feeling sorry that a lad of his age should have this burden on his shoulders. On the other hand, she also thought that it would be the making of him. She was pleased that her two daughters were both in Scotland and were well away from all this.

They finished their meal and the women picked up the empties and gathered all uneaten food. There was more uneaten food than eaten by far and whether this was because Pat had been too overgenerous or whether they didn't really have appetites, they didn't know. But there were plates and plates full of food left which Sue put clingfilm back over and put in the fridge.

'So,' Gary said, 'let's get out all our stuff.' There was five minutes of clattering, banging and thumping, whilst people laid out what they had brought in front of them. Some people only had one thing. Some people had many. Gary looked at what was on the table, then around at the group.

Tony waited until the end, then with a flourish got out his gun and gently put it on the table. It was an old handgun, blackish and battered.

'It's an old Enfield? Can I take a look at it?' asked Freddie.

'Yes, yes. Take a good look at the beauty.'

Freddie picked it up and looked at it through the bottom part of his glasses. He stroked the barrel and looked at all the nicks in the metal.

'It's an old war hero, this. Who's was it?'

'My grandad's, he told them he had lost it. He thought the family might need it at some point. I don't think he realised how much we would. Just seventy years in the future.'

'Can I look at it, Dad.' Asked Bob.

'No!' said Sue.

'I think we should carry as much as we can and share stuff,' Gary said as he looked around at peoples piles, 'What in God's name is that?' He pointed towards something in Pat's pile.

'It's a Walker's toffee hammer that I got one Christmas. I thought if I had used up everything, then it is better than nothing.'

'I might disagree with that, Pat,' he replied, bemused.

'Look, if I put a lot of force behind it, I could probably crack open the odd skull or two.' She picked it up and swung it down hard. It whistled through the air. 'Or at least an eye socket.' He watched her in full flight.

'There is no arguing with the fact that you could do that Pat, so fair enough.'

'Never mind you questioning her about that, which I agree, is a bit pathetic. What's that thing there?' Danny pointed to a kind of knife-like hook that was not that large, in front of Gary, in his pile.

'Ha ha! That is my secret weapon. It is my weed whacker.'

'What do you use that for?' asked Bob.

'You know the block paving, like what is on your mum and dad's drive? This will get all the weeds out from in between them, in the summertime. You have to have one in your arsenal when you are going out to do a bit of gardening. I just thought the hook part would be quite useful.'

'I know where you're going with that. Great minds think alike,' Wee Renee said shrilly. They looked at her pile but she did not have a weed whacker on there.

'What are you talking about,' asked Tony. She reached into the back pocket of her jeans and pulled out a cheese knife, with a wooden handle, which she slapped on the table.

'This will be great. I have been thinking along the same lines as Gary. Look at the hook on this. Plunge it in and rip out their gizzards. Or you could stick it into their eyes and pluck them out, dangling down on their cords, that should do it.'

'There are no words, are there!' Freddie laughed. Mildly shocked, but also amused at the vivid picture Wee Renee was painting.

'But it's a cheese knife!' exclaimed Andy 'It's a bloody cheese knife!'

'Yes,' said Wee Renee, 'and I might have you know that this has cut some very hard cheeses in the past. Don't you worry about this!'

'I thought I was shitting it before,' said Andy, 'but now obviously I feel fine, when I know I am behind you two. One with a toffee hammer and one with a cheese knife. You do know what we are dealing with don't you?' He was starting to sound a slightly hysterical. 'These aren't some little fairies or people with a strong opinion. These are monsters, you know. Great big tall monsters, who want to eat us!'

'Andy, don't you worry. I was just trying to think out of the box. And they aren't any taller now they are dead, than they were alive.' said Wee Renee. Andy looked back at her. She could tell he wasn't convinced. 'I also have this. She fiddled in her backpack, chuckling.

'I had forgotten about this.' She carried on looking.

'I know what you're on about, Rene,' Pat said and she looked at Andy, 'You'll like this.'

Then, Wee Renee pursed her lips. Suddenly, and with a great deal of force, she pulled it out. It clattered down on the table.

'A machete!' Andy shouted. 'So you remembered the cheese knife but you didn't remember the machete?'

'Well, Gary reminded me about the cheese knife, or else I would have probably forgotten about that as well.'

'So we are okay as long as we keep shouting out your different weapons, eh Wee Renee and you can keep remembering where you put them,' Danny laughed, 'Other than that you will sit there with your cornet in your hand, thinking *what should I do?*'

'You just wait until you are my age, you cheeky monkey,' she said, 'You know I am constantly having a senior moment and Pat is worse than me!'

'Speak for yourself,' said Pat lightheartedly, 'I am fine and everything I have brought I have remembered to take out and put on this bloody table. You will be pleased to hear that me and Rene had another lovely sleepover, and we peeled another load of fresh garlic. So that is in the string bags, as usual.'

'Okay, so can we share all this stuff out?' Gary picked up about five things from his pile of about twenty weapons. 'There is plenty there for other people if they haven't got much stuff so let's make use of it all. It is no use being here left in the band room.'

'Yes, but we do have to think about how we are going to conceal all this,' said Sue, 'I mean we can't just go sitting there, playing O' Come All Ye Faithful, whilst being tooled up with machetes and guns. I mean it's not exactly a festive look.'

'We can take as much as we like really,' Bob said thoughtfully, 'We can put it behind the drum kit.'

'Yes and the timps,' said Laura, 'We could have Gary's big holdall full of stuff.

'Yeah, we'll rush behind the percussion, get the weapons and that's where we'll make a stand,' Danny said happily.

'We can always have a few wee things on us to defend ourselves,' Wee Renee said, 'Bob, I have seen you eyeing my cheese knife, you can have this you know, if you want it.'

'Are you sure?' He said, obviously impressed by the capabilities of the cheese knife, as she had described it.

'Oh aye. I have got plenty of stuff.' She handed over the knife. He took it and looked at it appraisingly.

'This is great. I fancy taking a few gizzards out, as you say. Get them back for Ian. Is that what was dangling out of him?'

Sue thought she would change the subject. 'I think we should aim to get there at about threeish at the latest because of it going dark,' said Sue, 'With all these weapons and the instruments we might have to make two journeys, although I'm hoping not. Is that timing okay with you all?' They nodded. 'Gary, please try and come before dark. I will be so worried until you get there.'

'That is not a problem for me,' said Gary, 'I am hoping for just half an hour on each of these jobs. What doesn't get done, I will have to leave. It is too important to be off the streets before dark. Don't worry I will be standing side-by-side with you all tonight.' He made his way out of the door and they all looked in down in silence at the table covered in weapons.

The Master was sitting in his house. He was excited about that night, knowing his preparations over the last few weeks would ensure that this would go along swimmingly. There was no way that having so many of his vampires inside the band, in the audience, and outside could fail. He would make sure that everything and everyone had a right good old Winter Feast. He was up early that day comparatively for a vampire at two in the afternoon, still daylight hours. The others would not be awake for a couple of hours but he was up and wanted to greet them all as they awoke. Michael had made sure that all the curtains were closed. Norman always got Michael to see to this, and he had done it every day, since he had asked him, to be fair. That at least, was something he was good for. He would only be making a brief visitation to the concert tonight. It would be festive to pick up just a few children for him, and Kate. Then they would be on their way back to The Grange, out of harm's way. He was sure that, even though they would be victorious tonight, there would be a few casualties and he was not prepared to sacrifice himself, or Kate for this. No use tempting fate.

24 - Concert

The band got there well before dark and they were setting up the percussion and the music stands. Mrs White arrived shortly after and Sue contemplated whether she should talk to her in confidence. She tossed it around in her head for half an hour, deciding that Mrs White, being a logical and intelligent woman, would not believe what she heard and would think Sue either mad or that it was a pile of mumbo jumbo.

There was an undressed Christmas Tree in the foyer which was brought in every year, from Ernie's garden. He had potted it up five years ago, and had luckily driven it over the previous week. The band and Mrs White had brought Christmas decorations for the tree, the foyer and the main hall, to make it even more festive. Tony thought they shouldn't bother with this, as he wasn't interested in Christmas decorations anyway on a general day to day basis, and even more so this year. Sue had reminded him that they were fighting for their own lives, freedom and the right to behave like they wanted to. So they should carry on regardless and not let all this change things.

Gary arrived about five minutes before it went dark. He had indeed come straight from work and still was wearing his tool belt. He advised them that had been talking to the school caretaker who said that many of the kids were ill.

Struck down with a mystery illness. The others were downhearted at this news and shook their heads.

'Kids. Biting kids,' said Sue quietly, 'They are cowards. I can't believe it!'

'I can't believe it either,' Danny angrily announced, 'Because this means we have a bigger job than we thought we had.' Wee Renee shook her head, looking into his eyes. She knew what he was thinking.

'Yes, it's bad enough to try kill an adult that might be coming at you. But to kill a wee kiddie, that would be horrific!' she uttered.

'It doesn't bother me,' said Bob matter-of-factly, 'If they are kids or if they are adults they are just vampires and nothing else. The kid is gone from inside that thing. Don't forget that, or else you will be a goner. There will be a little ankle biter, biting your ankles.' The group knew he was right and started to square this point to themselves. It was a sobering thought, but one that now he had brought up, might stop them from hesitating out of guilt and save their lives.

'From the mouths of babes,' Wee Renee said, 'You are a very sensible lad.' Sue and Tony were so proud of him.

They looked at Mrs White who was quite happily putting out song sheets for the Christmas Carols onto all the chairs and benches.

'She must have some idea,' said Laura, 'I mean with all those kids off school, she lives in the village, she must know there is something wrong.'

'Maybe she does, and is in denial,' said Danny.

'A bit like you then, before you saw Aidy and Ian,' said Tony, 'Until you see it with your own eyes, you don't want to believe it. To believe it would mean, you are gullible or that nightmares are true and they are after you when you are awake. You have to deal with it. Mentally and physically. And you are putting it off until you really have no choice. Once you have made the full connection, well……it's just something that you have to see for yourself, I think. And she hasn't.'

At six o'clock they started to change into their band uniforms. Wee Renee gave them all a couple of cloves of garlic. A few of them had Christmas Tinsel around their heads and they put their cloves of garlic in those. They put one in their jacket pockets and their trouser pockets. They had taped some weapons underneath their chairs and some of them actually had them attached to their instruments. Pat had taped a large knife to the other side of her tenor horn so that nothing could be seen and a couple of all them managed to do this including Danny with his baritone. Gary stressed that they should have the blade facing downward in-case they got pushed from the back on to their own weapon. Wee Renee crossly fiddled with her cornet and a flick knife for at least ten minutes before giving up and putting it in her cleavage. Bob watched the whole of this scene wide-eyed. He thought she was great.

Soon the seats were all ready, and each person had one, which they had *tooled up*. Any remaining weapons, they put in Gary's holdall, and hid it behind Laura's first timpani. They had just put out the right number of seats for the players, there were no extras. Suddenly they heard the back door, which was the stage entrance, slam open. They all stopped breathing for a moment, silently listening. Hearts beating loudly.

'Please tell me someone remembered to lock that back door,' said Pat, through gritted teeth, 'Perhaps something has dropped off a shelf.' Laura hopefully uttered.

They all looked around at each other, hardly breathing, knowing it was the back door. Their worst fears were realised when the sounds of quite a few footsteps could be heard coming slowly up the stairs. Their eyes quickly moved around, Mrs White obliviously finished putting the last of the raffle prizes out and strode into one of the side rooms. The footsteps got louder. Liz could feel a scream rising in her throat.

Ernie stood at the front with Lynn at his side. 'Isn't this a band concert? It doesn't look like a full band to me!' He had the rest of the players behind him fully dressed in their uniforms with their instruments in their hands, looking at them all menacingly. 'We've come to play,' said Ernie cheerfully, 'We're all going to play together tonight.'

'Yes,' Lynn joined in beside him, 'Get some

more chairs. There is not enough for all of us. You are making us not feel welcome!'

They stared aghast. No one said a word apart from Gary.

'Oh bollocks!' he whispered, swallowing.

Jake and Vicky, Diane and Sophie, the two Woodalls, Vincent who was no longer wearing his dentures, Colin and Darren both smiled at them. Finally at the back, standing tall and proud, there was Keith and Stephen. Keith did indeed look ferocious. Stephen finally had become a powerful predator, far from the cuddly, likeable man they had once known. Then there was one more set of footsteps coming up the stairs, one by one. Freddie feared so much that this would be Maurice and that he would have to fight and kill him. This was the worst case scenario for him. But it was not Maurice. It was Barry, who guiltily stood there on his own.

'Sorry guys,' he said to the group, walking round the side of the group of vampires and sitting down in one of the chairs for the audience, which were currently absent. An apologetic smile on his face. They were doomed.

'Is that the full band?' whispered Danny to Gary.

'No, not everyone. As far as I can see there is still Mark and Maurice missing but that's about it,' he replied to Danny. After a moment, he said, 'Everyone stay on your chairs and just let them put their chairs in between us. Just move your chair out of the way.' They all thumped their chairs along until there was enough space for each new player. As if this was a sign, the new group went to the back room to get chairs, to put in between.

'Why don't they just storm us?' asked Laura.

'Because they are waiting for the big feast, aren't they?' answered Bob, 'This isn't about just us. This is about the several hundred people that are coming to watch us. All the kids and parents they want to eat.' Gary nodded. He spoke quietly but everyone heard.

'Don't you move out of them chairs for anything. Say we are not going in the back room. They might turn us there and then. We won't walk out from the back when the audience is seated, we will just stay here and act like that is part of the performance. In fact get your carolling books out. We can start playing when the audience comes. Do not go into the back room, no matter who tries to make you.'

Woody walked around to the percussion section. It was a very tense atmosphere, that could be cut with a knife.

'By all means go on the drum kit, if you like tonight, Woody,' offered Bob, looking at Laura in wide-eyed terror. He glanced at Laura's timps.

'No, Barry has said to me that, as I haven't been at rehearsals, I'm on sleighbells all night,' Woody replied flatly.

Laura felt her shoulders relax. The last thing she wanted him to do was to say he wanted the timp seat, where all the weapons were hidden. Good old Bob had worked it out and offered up the drum kit seat. She was highly amused though, that even as a vampire, Barry had musical standards and wasn't going to let Woody bungle up the concert by sight reading.

The vampires all sat down and then realised what they could smell. And what they were sitting right next to.

'There's garlic everywhere!' exclaimed Sophie wrinkling her nose in disgust.

'Yeah and it isn't my bolognese either, before you start,' announced Danny. The living band members all laughed.

'You stink,' Vicky said under her breath to Pat.

'That's rich!' Pat defensively squawked. 'Do you think we smell as bad as you all do? You are rotten and smell like the grave, you dirty bugger. I've seen inside one of you, and you're green. Green, yes! I wouldn't use that horn after you for a million quid!' The rest of her group laughed loudly.

'Well said, Pat,' said Wee Renee, 'They smell like poopoo.' Even more laughter erupted.

Ernie and Lynn had moved to the back of the hall. Unaffected by Pat and Wee Renee's comments they calmly waited for the laughter to stop.

'Are we ready to open the doors, everyone?' The calmness in which Ernie said the words was chilling. They could not shake off the feeling that, they were going to lose. It had never crossed the minds of the vampires that they might not win. They were all fully confident of success. The realisation dawned on them, that this had all been a big mistake. A huge trap. *Was it really worth carrying on normal life, just for life to end so soon?*

A sudden gust of cold air hit them as Ernie opened the doors in the foyer. They heard Ernie say 'Hello, hello. You're a bit late.' In walked Michael Thompson, Norman Morgan and the lady that had been at the party, Kate, less than a month ago. A further wave of dread swept over them. The main man was here, the original monster. The one that had defiled their band. They heard someone else's footsteps clatter in the foyer.

'Wait for Chrissy.' In walked Christine Baker, in what they imagined was her Christmas Outfit. It was unbelievably tight and glittery for such a large lady. She also was wearing thigh length boots.

Liz didn't even notice her, she was fully in a panic now and thought that Norman was there just for her. The final one he hadn't managed to turn. She could hear the blood rushing in her ears. Her breath was quiet and light. Liz felt like she was barely breathing at all. She felt herself watching him walk up the aisle, even though she didn't want to believe he was there. As if he knew, he looked back at her and kept his gaze fixed as he made his way right up to front seats, where all of them could see him. She was lost, she knew it.

'Don't look in his eyes.' Wee Renee whispered to her.

Before anything else could happen they

started to hear children's voices from a distance and the rest of the audience started to enter. Children that were in the choir came in with their parents and then sat on seats to the right of the band in orderly lines, Mrs White directing them to each particular place. Mr Shufflebotham arrived in his best suit very pleased with himself and sat next to Mrs White.

As the audience continued to file in, the group of heroes realised that it was hard for the vampires not to reveal their intentions as they came in. They smiled at each other with a knowing look and they were noticeably pale. If you knew what you were looking for, it was very easy to see who was, and wasn't one. There certainly were some children that had been turned. Some looked very gaunt, their small eyes were animated and darting about hungry. They all still attended with their parents, some who had succumbed to their young ones advances at one point, it was clear. Christine stood up and turned, looking at the main doors and started waving towards the back of the hall.

'Wayne, sweetie! Here, here, I have saved you a seat!' She beckoned with her hand. When the postman looked towards her from the back of the hall, he definitely looked like he wasn't enjoying his new-found death. He looked like a zombie, or someone who was on very heavy drugs and being manipulated. Wayne dragged his feet forward; not knowing what he was doing, not caring. He walked slowly up to the front, weaving clumsily between kids and parents as they decided where they were going to sit. Dropping himself down in the seat, blinking, he sat next to Christine. Keith's wife Yvonne came in. She was quite obviously one of Keith victims and she made her way through the crowd to sit next to Karen who was Colin's wife. She had been got at as well.

Simon, who unfortunately was always too busy looking at himself in the mirror, found himself noticing the truth finally from his vantage point at the front, in the harsh lighting. He saw, horrifically, that his wife Sandra and his mistress Tracy came in together linking arms. They stared at their lover, their eyes telling him everything he needed to know about them. His two children came in behind Sandra and she took them to the back to sit with Mrs White. It was quite apparent, that she had remade them her own children.

'In the Bleak Midwinter,' Gary said to the band and everyone, even the vampires and Barry, started to prepare for the carol. They started to play. Barry was conducting, a very strange group, indeed. They were so busy playing and looking out to the audience that they did not notice that someone was coming from behind them, out of the stage door. It was Stuart who was also the Civic Hall caretaker. He waited until they finished their carol then cleared his throat.

'Everything to your satisfaction?' he asked and smiled wide, His back to the audience, he showed his new teeth, quite happily. They had obviously known that he was one too after Laura had seen him the previous week, with Keith, but had forgotten. Again, another wave of defeat swept over them, as they were so vastly outnumbered.

Sue watched from the side, not being a player. She counted the number of people in the band that they would have to kill, including Barry. There were twelve vampires in the band so if they all got one each that would be fine. They did still slightly outnumber the vampires, including her. However, she could also count about twenty or thirty more at least in the audience, and the children with Mrs White.

Ernie slammed the two front doors, which shocked vampires and non-vampires with its boom, and then walked into the main hall. He walked to the front, as always to start the concert and welcome the audience.

'Welcome everyone. To all the audience from Friarmere Primary, and all village guests. I am heartened to see that so many have made it here through this weather. I have shut out the cold out now, so let us have a great concert. Shall we start, Barry?'

Bob's stomach turned over.. it was going to happen. Barry lifted up his baton and they started to play.

25 - Gun

As it was, they didn't even get through the first Carol. Norman stood up right in the middle of it. The band watched him, terrified as to what he was going to do. Liz didn't even have enough breath to play her cornet, but just held it to her lips. Kate followed him, then Christine and Michael. It was as if this was the signal to start. They stood up and started walking to the door, back down the aisle, the rest of the audience wondering what these four people were doing.

As they reached the back row, Norman took two children firmly by their upper arms and pulled them through the doors. Micheal Thompson turned back towards the band, and bowed low to them. Andy thought that Norman wasn't as clever as he thought, giving Michael even a little bit of power. All this went on as the band still played. Just then, Christine turned around shocked and looked back to the front.

'Oh no! Wayne, sweetie is still there!' She quickly clacked her way back up to the front, with everyone watching her open mouthed, 'Come on, come on. Drinky!' He got up slowly, still appearing to be drugged and started to walk out, but by then Norman, Kate and Michael had shut the doors and barred them from the outside.

The band vampires put down their instruments and regarded the people seated at the side of them. The children who were vampires beamed at the thought of the fun they would have. They each had their first victim in their sights. One of the children tip-toed over to Mrs White, sat on her lap, as if to be comforted, nuzzled their head, into her neck and bit down.

'Go!' shouted Gary. There was a lot of movement in the audience. Some people just ran to the back of the doors, with their children, but they could not get out. They had seen the child bite down on Mrs White and had felt for a while, that the atmosphere was electric with the coming attractions. Pat took the knife off the back of her horn, unobserved, as Vicky was turning to Andy. Vicky was thinking this was her lucky day. This wasn't happening on Pat's watch and she plunged the knife in the back of Vicky's neck. It came straight through the other side. Pat put both hands on the knife and moved it up and down, making a three inch gash with her knife. The metal made a grating sound on Vicky's neck bones, and the vibration went up Pat's arm. A strange blackish green fluid, which quickly turned to dry powder, dribbled off the tip of the knife onto Andy uniform. She shook once then collapsed on the floor.

'One down,' said Pat, setting her jaw again. Tony did not have his eye on Keith so he did not see Keith push Roger's chair over, on to the carpet. Roger was struggling with his instrument, on top of him, flapping about on the floor. Keith rose from his seat, and straightened his collar and tie, before casually kneeling down and biting into Roger's neck. His back pulsated as he drank. Then he twisted his head to one side and drew quickly up, fully tearing a piece out of Roger's throat, after draining his life away. Tony was watching Barry. Currently not attacking anyone, he seemed almost sad at the prospect of it all and when Tony ran at him, with one of Ian's long knives, his two hands on the handle and hacked him straight across the neck, he did not even try to defend himself.

Graham on B-flat tuba, the biggest of the instruments, was very unfortunate to have a vampire either side of him. His instrument was in the way of him leaning over and getting his weapon out from under his chair. He then remembered that he had also put one down the back of his jacket by the collar. Now he didn't know which to go for, but was a little too late as both vampires already with their instruments down, began to advance on him from either side. He managed to get his knife out quickly from down his collar and in one moment as he drew it out, he slashed Vincent across the cheek which did not bleed at all he noticed, but just made a black slash. Bob was behind him however and drove a sharpened drumstick through the chest of Colin. This did not kill him, Bob was shocked to see. Maybe he had not got the heart or maybe wood did not work at all. However, there was an unholy scream from Colin, who began to beat at the area where the drumstick was embedded. He didn't try to remove it however. It was strange to see that it did not kill him, but he could not touch it. He seemed to think the best thing was to run away, maybe to plunge himself into the snow. Bob thought *does it burn?* He ran out of the main room to the exit. Bashing himself constantly into the doors, his skin and face starting to break up.

One fact interested Bob. He had noticed that it was very easy to plunge that drumstick into Colin. They seemed kind of soft, even before they were truly dead. Again, it reminded him of something inflatable. Graham could still not reach his weapon under his chair so he thrashed around at Vincent to try and keep him at bay. He moved backwards and his hand latched on to his tuba mouthpiece. He twisted the mouthpiece out of the instrument. Using the full length of his arm he punched it into Vincent's eye, the spigot of the mouthpiece going deep into the vampire's head. A black slimy substance started to run languidly out of the mouthpiece that was now firmly wedged into the eye socket and Vincent screamed and fell to the floor. That looked like that was it, for him. Vincent started to crawl away and Graham watched him go, finally free of the two of them. It was because of that, that he did not see Colin's wife Wendy, behind him. He did however, feel her stab him in the back with some scissors that she held. She pushed him down onto the floor, her strength greater than his. Graham's head fell on the carpet. The rough nylon was coarse on his face. Wendy was only five foot two and he was six foot four, now she was above him. He tried to raise himself and managed to get his body up into a *push up* position. The pain was crippling. She picked up his tuba like it was a bunch of tulips, lifted it up over her head, and back down onto the scissors, further pushing them through into Graham's body. They came out at a point just above his heart the other side and he looked down at it for one brief second before falling back onto the floor.

'Kids! Food!' she shouted. A few of the children who were not attacking scrambled up over the chairs and instruments, like rats and started to feed on the freshly dead Graham.

Laura had been really excited and had been sharpening her sticks for three days with a penknife. Between her and Bob she had an idea that they had maybe one-hundred wooden stakes between them. She hated the fact that she was doing this to expensive sticks but they wouldn't mean anything to her if she was dead. When Bob did not kill with his first drumstick she knew that they could only be used as a kind of a pokey thing and not a form of instant death weapon, which made her even angrier. Laura had effectively ruined all her sticks. Now she really did want revenge.

She noticed that Keith's wife, Yvonne, was making her way painstakingly to the front. She was indeed a strong vampire. Maybe Keith had given her his inner strength too. She seemed very powerful and was tossing parents and children, left, right and centre on her way to get to Keith. Laura wanted to prevent this from happening, as the two of them working as a duo would be pretty formidable. She was quite a distance away, but she noticed Gary was halfway between Keith and Yvonne. She shouted over to Gary, gesturing over to Yvonne.

'Stop her, Gary.' Gary was doing pretty well and had already taken out four vampires. He had put his flugelhorn case underneath his seat and inside it he had his tool belt. He had quickly put this on, and it had all his best weapons on it. He had a battery operated nail gun and this was proving to be a brilliant deterrent. It did not fully kill them but it certainly stunned than enough and you could be quite far away to use it. Now it was himself, Bob, Tony and Danny that were moving forward getting each predator. As they moved forward, four onto one it only took a few seconds for each, as they chopped and hacked and nail gunned their way through the attack.

Sue had heard Laura's shout, looked across and knew what she was trying to prevent. She could see that Yvonne was moving forwards towards Keith. In between were quite a few vampires and also the group of four trying to save them all. Gary had his eye on Yvonne. She was about three vampires away from them. Yvonne looked like she was going to move out to the side to avoid the four hero's. Sue moved forward and went under Tony's seat. She had been determined for him not to use this gun, but by god, if Yvonne was going to touch her boy she would be using it in a heartbeat.

She pulled it out, ripped the tape off, and walked a few steps towards Yvonne, checking out the status of the situation. Yvonne was still fixed on Keith, who was dealing with a few parents quite strictly at the moment so did not see her. However, with his improved sense of hearing he did hear the click of the gun as Sue walked a few more steps without fear to Yvonne. She put it to her head and pulled the trigger.

The boom scared everyone, who could not mistake it for anything else. Yvonne fell to the floor, flat on her back. Unsure whether she would get up again, Gary walked over to her, wiggled the nail gun into her slightly open mouth and pressed the trigger. Yvonne screamed, but not very well as he had attached her tongue to the back of her head. He put his foot on her chest and she clutched at his leg, her eyes, watering and bloodshot were full of hatred. Placing the nail gun back in her mouth, he pressed the trigger three more times. The scream cut off and her head was now securely attached to the floorboards. The grip around Gary's leg loosened and then her arms dropped to her sides. Her eyes forever would be fixed on Gary. The vampires scattered and Gary, Bob, Danny, Tony and Sue, were quite free in the centre. Keith lifted his head upwards, yelling out his frustration from the bottom of his stomach. It was a guttural inhuman sound with no words, which shocked the crowd once more.

The army of five, split outwards. Danny scanned the crowd for Stephen Thompson. He had not targeted Danny, who he was sitting beside in band, which was very fortunate for

Danny, as he had been busy watching Norman walk out the door. He spied Stephen, trying to drag some small children out of the back door for himself. Danny could see that he had already laid waste to a couple of kids by his condition. The front of his face and his shirt were drenched with the children's blood. He ran after him.

After Andy and Pat had finished dealing with Vicky they decided to move over and help on the cornet section. The only three that were not vampires were Liz, Simon and Wee Renee. Pat looked over at them with a steely gaze. They would hurt Wee Renee over her dead body, if that is what it took. Andy was going to save his beloved Liz. She had fought all this time and he wasn't going to let all that be for nothing. Jake had his eye on Liz and she was hitting him up the head with her instrument case, which was full of weapons, so was heavy and noisy. He just kept on coming back at her. Andy came behind him. His weapon was from Ian's shop. He imagined it was for chopping meat, but it was a cross between a machete and an axe. Andy brought it back, aiming at Jake and then it whistled forwards with a *thwack* across Jakes upper arms. It cut straight through half his arm and partway through the bone. If Andy could aim it right, he could take that right off in the next chop. This he did, which made him extremely happy. The vampire didn't seem to notice. Then he did the same on Jake's neck. The first whack, made Jake swivel round at him, his head, cocked to one side. The green black blood ran down from the top of where his arm used to be, staining the side of his uniform. Jake's mouth opened and shut mechanically, getting slower and slower, like a wind up toy, coming to a stop. Andy had to hit him from a different direction to take off his head, but he managed after three tries.

Wee Renee had decided to take on Sophie *and* Janet Woodall. She had her machete in one hand and the long metal knife sharpener she had taken from Ian's shop the other day, in the other. Her eyes switched quickly in between each of them as they advanced. She stepped back, as they moved forward. Wee Renee knew it wouldn't be long though before she would have to attack as they had nearly backed her into a corner. Laura saw this going on and picked up her sharpened sticks. Sue still had the smoking gun in her hands and they both strode confidently over to this ambush.

'I think you'll find someone behind you bitches,' Pat shouted at them. Janet and Sophie turned around to see Andy, Laura, Sue and Pat behind them, each holding their weapons. This was the distraction Wee Renee needed and she was determined to get both of them. She shoved the rod shaped sharpener, between her knees for a moment. Took her machete in both hands and slammed it straight through the back of Janet. The vampire was quite a few inches taller than her and she cut diagonally crossways under the ribs, the machete getting stuck, but Janet did fall to the floor. Wee Renee leaned over her wiggling the machete out, then hit her again, at an angle in the abdomen making a V shape. The large triangle of flesh slipped down, the black insides exposed. Something in there was pumping the matter out quite freely, over the carpet. Other tubes, just trickled Janet's issue out gently. She seemed to deflate, her eyes sinking into her head. Janet's hands twitched. Pat kicked her in the open V of her body. This seemed to rupture something and an almighty flood of more liquid substance flooded out. Pat looked down at her black lace up shoes. 'Ruined,' She said.

Sophie watched all this with utter amazement, facing the new threats. Her back was to Wee Renee, then she started to snarl knowing her time was close too.

Wee Renee, grabbed the sharpening rod, which was still between her thighs. She jumped high into the air and with a war cry, she brought the rod straight down through the top of the vampire's head. Sophie dropped. Wee Renee put her foot on Sophie's head to hold it, whilst she yanked the rod back out. She jumped up and down, pushing on the head and trying to wriggle it out but it wasn't budging. She then picked up the machete again.

'I enjoyed that. It was a wee bit exciting wasn't it? Next!' They went back into the crowd.

Always the coward, Simon had decided he was going to try and get out of the fire exit door.

He thought he could easily find somewhere safe. Wait until it had all blown over and everything was back to normal. Simon was a lover not a fighter. What he didn't consider, was that his wife Sandra and his mistress Tracy, had been watching his every move. They were waiting for him close to the door with open arms. His two children were behind them, hungrily waiting for the spoils.

26 – Timpani Mallet

'I bet you've always dreamed of this,' said Sandra.

'He told me plenty of times how he wanted two women at the same time,' said Tracy.

'You got your wish,' said Sandra, 'But it is on our terms now!' She smiled. It did not reach her eyes.

'Girls, we can all make this work,' he said.

'I don't think so. In fact, me and Tracy have been getting along just fine without you.' They closed the distance between him and them. He was thinking frantically about what he could say to save his bacon.

'Listen girls I kept you two happy before, why do you think I can't now?'

'That's a matter of debate,' Sandra informed him venomously, 'I certainly wasn't happy.' Tracy tilted her head to one side thinking.

'I wasn't too bad. But I know that you aren't enough man for us both, now. We need more. Sandra and I have come to an understanding.' They moved forward towards him, they were only four feet away now

'Look, I will do anything,' He pleaded, 'We can be a big family. Me, you two, and the two kids. It will be great.'

'No, I'm sorry. The two kids only need us. We trust each other. We have got to know and like each other well and we don't want to share.' He had been looking at Sandra all the time she spoke, as she walked forward whilst talking.

When she finished, he looked round for Tracy and saw that she had quickly moved behind him.

'Oh shit,' he said, rolling his eyes.

'Ah yes, you can still be useful in one way, Simon.' Sandra said, a wry smile on her face.

'Girls….come on,' he pleaded.

One woman bit down at the front and one at the back of his neck. He was not going to be turned. They had argued with The Master about this. They needed their sweet revenge, and The Master had finally agreed. Norman would get them to repay the favour at some point. Simon's two children watched with glee as their mother and their new Auntie Tracy killed their father. They clapped her hands. *Again! Again!* They said. Sandra turned to them, so pleased with their reaction.

'Come on kids, there is plenty for everyone.'

Danny had blocked Stephen's exit. They were in the back corridor of the building. The rear exit to the car park was behind Danny, the door to the main concert hall behind Stephen. Danny was determined that Stephen was not going to escape with the two children. They cried and stared at Stephen, pulling away from him, while he held their arms tightly.

'Let them go, Steve,' said Danny.

'No, I want them.'

'No, you don't. Be a man and let just the big boys play.'

'They're my dinner. The Master said we were to feast tonight and these are mine.'

'Come on Steve, there is plenty more where

that come from. Lets have a chat, man to man. He considered this and Danny's words worked somehow as he let both children go. They ran back towards the hall screaming, away from him.

'Fair enough,' said Stephen angrily, 'If you think yours are big enough. Come and have a go. I know you always thought you were better than me. You got all the girls and had the principal baritone seat. But now we'll see who's best.' Danny threw his head back and laughed loudly.

'Are you that sad? Are you still bitter about all that shit? I was better, and I am still better, and you being a bloodsucker, isn't going to change that, mate.'

Shaun had seen Danny, Stephen and the two kids go through the doors, but he was the other side of the room. By the time he had got to the doors, the two kids came running out at him.

'Go find your Mams,' he told them gravely. He poked his head through the door gingerly. No one was hiding around the other side. He looked forward and could just about see two people moving in the back. The noise was so loud behind him that he could not hear what was being said.

Shaun turned around to see where the two kids had gone. They seemed to not be able to see their mums and were terrified. They ran over to Mr Shufflebotham for help, who seemed to be in shock and had a few children clinging onto him like a life raft. Shaun didn't know whether to help Danny or help Mr Shufflebotham, or maybe even help his dad who, at the moment, was fighting a lady out of the audience who was snapping at his arm with her teeth. He was hitting her around the head with his euphonium, which was definitely changing her face shape. Soon her mouth wouldn't be able to snap anymore. Shaun decided after seeing Stephen that it would probably be Danny that needed his help the most. He walked towards the darkness, it was colder in here, just looking back once, he saw Diane biting down on Mr Shufflebotham. The kids scattering like ants, when hot water is poured on them. Mr Shufflebotham dropped to his knees and put his hands together, obviously a religious man in prayer.

Now that he had fully committed to whom he would help, he quietly went down the stairs in the back corridor. He arrived to see Stephen just about to strike at Danny. Danny had a curved knife and also a chopper, which he had taken from the shop and was hacking away towards Stephen with a lot of power behind the strokes but Stephen was extremely quick. It was so dark here and Stephen seemed to be thriving in these conditions. Danny seemed to be struggling though, his eyes wide, trying to pick out the vampires movements in the lightless corridor. Shaun had a new idea. He had picked up one of Laura's timpani sticks earlier and it was stuffed down the waistband of his trousers. He took his cigarette lighter out of his pocket, setting the fluffy white end on fire. This gave Danny the extra light he needed to avoid Stephen. The vampire turned around to see what the increased light source was and saw Shaun.

'Two against one, Stephen. Those odds work better for us,' Shaun said.

With lightning speed, Stephen ran at Shaun in anger and knocked him over. Now an experienced killer, he bit down on his neck instantly, not giving him a chance to retaliate. Shaun flailed about with the lit timpani stick poking it at Stephen, trying to stab him with it. All this happened before Danny could get to them. It caught Stephens nylon band jacket and started to burn, the flames quickly licking up the side of his face. Stephen stopped and screamed, his hands trying to touch his face. He ran out, past Danny through the back entrance into the snow, plunging his head and neck into the mountains of soft white flakes. Danny ran over to Shaun, who was shaking, his eyes wide. One hand was on his neck and the other still held the flaming stick. Blood was flowing out of him very, very quickly. It was obvious that this was the end for him.

'Thanks mate, you saved my life.. thank you,' Danny said, choking back unexpected tears. Shaun clutched his arm.

'I don't want them to eat me and I don't want them to turn me. Go and help everyone else now, quick.' He looked at the timpani stick for a moment and Danny knew what he was about to do. He dropped it on his own uniform. The nylon quickly caught fire and spread over Shaun's body. Shaun was already very close to dying. He shook a couple of times and he was gone.

'Sleep well, mate,' Danny said as he ran back into the crowd of people.

Danny thought that after Shaun had saved *him*, the least he could do was to see if he could aid Shaun's dad, Geoff. He could see that Geoff had put pay to quite a few attackers, and was making his way back to where they all had made a stand on the stage. There was the odd one coming up attacking them and they were managing to keep them off. Geoff walked backwards and had to keep watching as there were bodies all over the floor that he had to keep stepping over.

As he stepped over one of them, their hand grabbed his leg really fast, pulling it from beneath him. As he was stepping up, he had one leg in the air and he had all his weight on this one leg, so he toppled over backwards clutching hold of his euphonium.

'Oh hell!' he yelled, all of a sudden lying on the floor and looking up at the ceiling. Geoff had quite badly banged his head and the room was spinning. He felt a heavy weight on his legs that crept up his body. The weight was Peter Woodall. He reached up to Geoff's waist from where he was at his knees, and pulled at his shirt, trying to get closer to Geoff's neck. Geoff kicked upwards and outwards, wriggling, trying to pull away as fast as he could. He tried to hit Peter with his instrument, but from this angle he only managed to knock at him a bit. Peter slowly inched his way up Geoff's body. Now his head was near the top of Geoff's legs. His weight was immense. When he got to his shirt he pulled it out and, in a flash, bit into his stomach. Geoff was so completely shocked at this, he just looked down at Woody. He stopped trying to hit him. Now he was infected. It was the end. Woody continued to crawl upwards.

Danny rushed over as fast as he could. Peter looked up at Danny as if to say, *you are too late* and then with his fists clenched he punched them into Geoff's chest. He opened the hole a little looking in, then seeming to find what he was after, he quickly grabbed at his prize, ripping out his heart and taking a bite.

'Mmmmm… ,' he said licking his lips, 'Too late Danny!' Danny stood aghast then turned around to help the others as Peter put his head into the pool of blood that was flowing freely out of Geoff's chest.

Gary and Freddie were now being the most productive. Gary had a large knife in one hand, nearly as big as Wee Renee's machete. He was moving forward, chopping away fiercely at anything that came near him. In the other hand, sure enough, he was using the weed whacker to shove into eyes or stomachs. He then twisted the whacker when it was inside to hook body parts with loops, ripping them through and out.

Freddie had taken the rubber bung off the end of his walking stick. It revealed a fine pointed, solid silver casing to the stick, which he had sharpened. He was using this to batter them, but more effectively, as a sword by piercing the vampires in the chest, neck, eye or straight in the mouth and out through the neck. He was really cutting a sway through the vampires for an older guy. *That's impressive,* Danny thought, *he must have been really something when he was a young man.*

Bob, Wee Renee, Pat and Sue had formed a tag team and were ganging up on particular vampires picking them off again. Bob had made good use of Wee Renee's excellent cheese knife and a set of sharpened sticks. Wee Renee was armed with the Machete and the flick knife, the long knife sharpener was still embedded in Sophie's head. Pat had an axe and a lump hammer. The toffee hammer unused, in the inside pocket of her band jacket. Sue had the gun, which she hadn't fired again. She looked behind them, to cover their backs.

Laura approached Danny. Even though the band were doing really well, not many other people were surviving. For every one they killed another two were being made.

'I think it's time we left,' she said regretfully, 'There is little else to be done here. If we stay, it is only a matter of time before we get turned or killed.'

'Yes, there's not hardly anyone else here to save, and most of us are still okay. We will be able to get through the back,' He glanced over at the back door, 'We just need to watch out for Stephen, he is out there. I haven't been watching the door, constantly, there could be others who have escaped.'

'There's still probably more in here, than out there, whatever has happened. We could take a couple, if they are out there. Find something to bar the door with,' Laura added.

She saw Keith was in the process of turning Mrs White into one of their flock.

'Yeah, lets get everyone. Get us all out. This is not a good place to be right now. We have done enough for one night.' They passed the message round one by one, to start moving back. Carefully and still fighting, they moved to the back doors.

Wee Renee was extremely cross with Pat, because they had to make a detour back to the stage. Pat said that there was no way she was leaving her Round Stamp Horn for them to have. Wee Renee said that if Pat wasn't careful, that horn would be all she had to remember her by. Gary also agreed with Pat, saying that his Flugel had been given to him by his Dad, and over his dead body would he leave it. Liz picked up her cornet too, and said she had been bought it when she was six and she was taking it, thinking there was no chance they could return for anything.

They got to the rear entrance door of the hall. Quickly looking back and checking, that they had not left anyone alive back there. They shut the interior door to the hall and wedged a chair under the handle. With their torches on their phones, they ran down the dark corridor, past Shaun who had stopped burning. After the fight, they were so hot they were quite pleased about going out into the freezing cold snow, to cool down. Gary and Danny checked outside the stage door and indicated that the coast was clear. Stephen must have gone off somewhere, licking his wounds. They closed the door and through the two hoops that usually held a padlock Danny found a sturdy broken branch and shoved it through.

'That should hold them, at least until we can get away,' he said hopefully. They hastily made their way into the night as best they could. It wasn't too far to the band room and that is where they had planned to go. They had left more weapons there.

'Thank god they are trapped,' said Wee Renee, 'We wouldn't stand a chance if they were on the loose.'

'I suppose they can do what they want in there now. Probably too busy to think about us,' Laura uttered shuddering, 'Making their new mates.'

Stuart walked out from the darkness of the trees, as they made their escape. He had not wished to be involved in this feast tonight. Stuart liked to do his feeding in private. Deciding, however, that this was still a lot of fun to watch, he strolled over to the door sniggering, yanked the tree branch out of the two hasps and flung the door open to the night.

27 - Plan

The little army of friends started to walk through the streets in the deep snow. They had their weapons out quite boldly as they knew no policeman was going to stop them in their village. Occasionally they would see the odd shadow looking out at them from an alley, archway or deep doorway. The vampires retreated back into the darkness, hiding, to wait instead for an unsuspecting drunk or late night dog walker. They did not approach or attack the group, as the eleven of them with their weapons ready and poised, were quite a formidable team.

Freddie was leading at the front. Gary walked backwards at the rear. Danny and Tony at either side forming four corners to protect the women and Bob in the middle. It had stopped snowing for the moment and even vampires left footprints, so they were not being covered up by a fresh fall of snow. They could see where the odd few that had got out, had disappeared to. Pointing them out to each other, they made a mental note for the next day. Unless one had doubled back to them, they knew exactly where they all were, apart from the one that watched them from the roof. The most dangerous one.

They didn't speak one word on their way to the band room. They were listening for any sign of attack. The crunch of snow, running feet, doors opening. Noises could still be heard through the night air from their battle. The vampires' cries of joy as they made another beast, who themselves, screamed up into the night as they rose. They saw a couple of people looking out of their windows at them sadly, just out of interest. Regular, healthy people, not vampires. They didn't seem shocked, they didn't seem like they were afraid of them. Just afraid for themselves. Their eyes darted up the street, watching. Then they would shut the curtains to ward away the sight of the gang, maybe being attacked. And the fact that, what they couldn't see, they wouldn't have to help.

No one had mentioned where they were going. It was already set. The natural place to retreat to was the band room. They could all be together, it locked, they had weapons there, food and refreshments were available. They could go there, tend to any injuries, recover, rest for the night and decide what should be done next. As they got further away from the cries and guttural sounds coming from the Civic Hall, the night became so quiet. They could hear snow falling in chunks from the roofs, with a heavy muted thud. Friarmere was beautiful and silent to the outsider. The streetlights glinted off the snow. It was white and twinkling and so perfect. It was as if they were in a land of shimmering glitter. Christmas was on it's way and the village was preparing itself to be magical. Unfortunately, they knew that behind the stunning fairyland the reality was blood, rot, death and danger.

As they walked past the pub, which was still open, Freddie all of a sudden, became very tired.

'Shall we stop for a bit and get our breath?' he asked hopefully. A couple of the older ones agreed with him. The majority didn't though.

'I think that's a bad idea. We should get back while the going is good. We can settle down in the band room. We can't expect the pub to take us in there, and lock the doors if we have an ambush. It's not fair on the other punters. Lets stick to the plan,' said Gary, making the final decision.

'Damn it,' hissed Norman as he wriggled flat like a snake, across the roofs of Friarmere.

They carried on. Because they were listening, struggling in the bad walking conditions and looking in every doorway and down every street, it took them nearly an hour to get to the band room. It was quite cold in there, even though they had only left it about five to six hours earlier. Luckily, it did have central heating and Sue rushed in to override the timer switch and get it going. As soon as they had all filed in and shut the door, it was immediately warmer than being outside. The heating clicked on quickly and they knew that from past experiences here, that they would soon be warm, as it wasn't an enormous room to heat and there were now eleven people in it. It was wonderful to smell the bandroom. They associated the scent in here with fun, friendship and safety.

Wee Renee, Laura and Pat started to fill the kettle, put the cups out and take out food from the fridge. There were lots and lots of sandwiches and cakes left, so they would be able to hold up a while here, no worries. There were also still several weapons remaining on the table, that they really had not been able to carry earlier. Some people had lost some, or left them embedded in a vampire, so were happy to be able to replenish their arsenal.

Liz looked very tired and was struggling. She generally didn't have much energy and with all the anxiety from seeing The Master, the fight and the walk back through the snow, she was exhausted. Her legs were shaking, she said she had pains in her chest and she couldn't get warm.

'It's stress,' diagnosed Pat. Freddie also sat down for a while, he was shaking and as white as a ghost.

'I know how you feel, Liz. I don't know if I am on my arse, or my elbow.' He seemed to have trouble breathing too. They all had a steaming pot of tea made for them. Wee Renee insisted that everyone took sugar in their tea for shock. In the calm atmosphere of the band room they sat for a while. Gazing down at the floor miles away, or contemplating their fingers. Putting their hands around the cups of tea to warm them and taking deep breaths. They were exhausted shocked and empty. A thousand thoughts and pictures ran through their heads. They had each left a part of themselves there that they would never get back. The first person to break the hush was Andy.

'That was so much worse than I thought it was going to be,' he said quietly with a sigh.

'They knew we were coming,' said Gary, 'Their plans were better than ours. We thought we knew best and have now lost people in our ignorance and arrogance. We didn't think that there were so many, and that they were so ferocious.'

'Kids as well,' Laura muttered, through a few tears, 'The kids. I couldn't believe it.'

'Er… does anyone want a sandwich?' Sue asked hopefully. No-one wanted one and only Bob ate a cake. Wee Renee got up to make another pot of tea. All of them needed it.

'The question is, what shall we do next?' said Gary trying to move on from his thoughts.

'If we make it through the night,' said Pat grimly.

'We *will* make it through the night!' Wee Renee announced loudly from the behind the steam of the kettle, 'Think positive! If we can make it with them all in the same room as us, that siege that we just experienced, then we can make it in here. We have our own territory to protect now. A wee fort. We have just got to get through tonight.'

'Then what?' asked Laura

'We will just have to get some help, won't we?' Freddie said matter-of-factly. 'It's clear this problem is too much for us now. It needs an army.'

'Split the group. The stronger ones will just have to get out of this village, through the snow and find some place that will give us some help and bring them back to the ones that will struggle to make it,' Tony shrugged.

'No way are we splitting this group up,' said Wee Renee adamantly. 'We will all make it together. I don't think splitting our resources, whether they are weapons or people will do either group any good. So we all go together and we go at the pace of the slowest person.' Collectively the whole group looked at Liz, who guiltily looked down.

'The good thing is, we all get on,' said Sue cheerfully, 'Can you imagine doing this and arguing between ourselves?'

'Yes, I agree. A lot of the bad seeds have gone. A lot I would have butted heads with,' Pat said under breath with a sniff. They all knew she meant Keith and Vicky. Secretly if you had asked any person in that room, they would have agreed with Pat. They did miss some people thought. Particularly, Freddie missed Maurice.

Lost in their thoughts again for a minute, Danny covered his mouth with his hand, then rubbed it on his stubble. He did that when he was nervous.

'Did you see what Woody did to Geoff?' he asked, obviously still in shock about the whole matter. A couple of them nodded and looked down at their cups again, morosely.

'What?' asked Laura

'He just punched into his chest, took out his heart and bit into it,' said Danny flatly. Liz started crying and Andy put his arm around her. She was panicking and was close to becoming hysterical.

'This is too much for me. I can't take it. My brain won't take it anymore,' she sobbed into her hand, her hair hanging over her face.

'It can take it and it will!' said Wee Renee firmly, 'Liz, we are going to defeat all this.'

Sue banged her cup down in desperation.

'How can we defeat something like that, tonight? We will definitely need extra help. More police. The army. We can't stay here and fight that kind of stuff. We are just people. Musicians. Just regular people that shouldn't have to fight for our village, or anything else,' Sue said quickly. The panic was starting to become infectious. Gary knew he had to step in at this point.

'Whoa there. What we need to do is protect ourselves primarily and we have a responsibility to make sure that this does not get out into the rest of the country. We can save everyone by just being messengers. It's as simple as that.' They nodded at Gary. That seemed easy enough. The atmosphere started to calm. He checked everyone's face and could feel the tension ebbing away from them. 'So do we have a plan then? That we go out, all of us, when we are feeling a little stronger, in the daylight. We try and make it out of the valley to another village and get help?'

'Yes,' they muttered, some of them, quite enthusiastically.

'Do you think you can manage that, Liz?' asked Laura.

'Yes,' she replied bravely. 'With all of you, yes, I can manage it.' They could see she felt better after her few tears and was encouraged by the new plan. 'What good can we do here? We can't stay here for the rest of our lives. The food will run out and they can come and get us anytime. Any band member will know where we would be. The thing is, we could see their footprints, but I just kept thinking that they would be able to see ours too. I really don't want to be here. It's dangerous.'

'We will wait for daylight then,' stated Tony.

'I suggest,' said Wee Renee with her finger in the air, 'That even if we can't now, we think about eating as much as we can.' Pat took this as her cue and started to eat a couple of thick slices of battenburg cake. She broke the cake into it's squares and ate first the yellow, then the pink, then the yellow again, then pink. Before she had swallowed that piece, she picked up another. Bob picked one up too and started to copy her. Sue was happy that watching Pat had tempted him to eat. Wee Renee watched before continuing. 'We don't know how long the journey will take. What we don't eat we will put in our backpacks. We can parcel up some of those sandwiches. But we need to eat before we set off and get some strength. We also need some sleep. Who is up for having alternate watches?' All the men said they would. With the additions of Bob, Pat and Wee Renee there would be plenty to cover the shifts. Each set of two had to do a couple of hours each. They all thought it would be very easy to stay awake as most felt like they would never sleep again. The one exception was Liz, who said she wanted to go to sleep as quickly as she could and shut it all out.

The room was lovely and warm now and they rolled their coats up to use them as pillows. They lay down in a couple of rows. Danny and Gary said that they would take first watch and then Pat and Wee Renee were up next. As soon as it was light, if they got that far, they would have another hot drink, some food and then set off as soon as possible, so they could use the daylight most effectively.

Outside, as the friends dreamed, wept, and cried out in their nightmares, Norman and Michael watched. The band room with its lights on was like a beacon in the dark.

'They were a lot more prepared than I thought they would be. Much irreparable damage has been made to some wonderful vampires. It vexes me so. I underestimated them. I won't do it again.'

'Don't worry Master. They are sitting ducks now. We will get everyone. There's still a few hours of darkness left. Lets get the others over here and get them girls, er, all of the band, tonight. Get it over with. Then you are fully victorious.'

'No, no. They won't get very far. We have made sure of that. My children need the shade of their beds after this great battle, to replenish their strength. There are many nights we can come and get them, whilst they grow weaker, day by day. They are isolated now. I need to regroup my forces. See how many of my flock, I have left. I may be recruiting a couple more villagers, who are hiding behind their front doors and then we will come for them again. What are they going to do? They can't contact anyone else and they won't be able to get out of this place. This snow has made it so easy. It is like a higher force has been watching over me these last few days. Besides that I have a few problems in other places to deal with and Kate is trying to sort something out herself. It is always one thing and then another for me. Michael, we have made losses tonight.'

'You still have me,' interjected Michael, but Norman ignored him.

'However, we have made more gains. We have more small children who have joined our cause, who will no doubt change their families. The more they do this, the more we will be protected.'

'The more the merrier!' Michael interrupted again.

'Your brother is still thriving and so are a lot of my recently made disciples, that are becoming very important to me. There are a couple of things to tie up but I see tonight, relatively, as a win for me.'

28 - Bus

The next morning the sun came out quickly and gleamed off the snow, unbelievably dazzling. It was a pure, clear morning. Beautiful crystalline trees and pure white snow, greeted the eleven friends. Nothing had happened in the night and some people had got a good few hours sleep and felt refreshed. Their spirits were up and they were all surprisingly hungry in the morning. The group heartily ate quite a lot of the sandwiches and cakes. Some of them had two or three cups of tea or coffee. The friends felt strong, as the ordeal was nearly over, *wasn't it?*

At one point, they could delay it no longer and were ready to go for it. The general feeling was excitement, a new day and fresh hope. They put their boots back on. Some were concealing weapons on the inside of their coats. Other items were too big, like Pat's lump hammer, so they carried them in their hands.

A couple of them had still insisted on taking their instruments, in the vain hope that life would get back to normal. Liz looked quite a bit better, rosier cheeks and definitely more cheery and they were all very thankful about this. Even just for the reason that their pace would be a little quicker the healthier she was.

Gary, although he didn't voice it, was a little worried that they had not been attacked in the night, but very thankful. After last night, he thought that their enemy already had planned something a bit cleverer than them at every turn. Norman Morgan was always one step ahead of them. Now they had a new plan, he wondered if they were walking into another trap. Gary just knew that it wasn't going to be plain sailing. This guy was too wily for that.

He had imagined that monsters had less intelligence than them and would just attack blindly. Surely a living tissue brain, worked better than a dead green one. Maybe some of them weren't thinking straight and were worried about other members of their family. Gary thought that he had no distractions and had been outsmarted. Of course he was no brain surgeon. A couple of members of the band were extremely clever, like Freddie, but then he thought of course, Freddie was worried about Brenda over in Melden. Bob was a bright lad, but worried about his friend, Adam, who he had had no communication with for a few days now.

They all walked out of the band room and Sue locked the door. There was food left in the fridge and they could still retreat back here. They were hoping that by tonight, they would have a police force on the way back here with them. Maybe a couple of hours walk in the snow towards the next village, or even the worse case scenario, the one after that. They could then find a phone or shelter and get help someway.

They started to walk towards the main road that ran from Friarmere into the next village over the hill, and then on towards Manchester. It was a wonderful sunny day. This was a good sign. They got to the main road, gathering in a group and surveyed the village. All was silent, there were no tyre tracks on the road. No-one had come along here for the last few hours, no tracks whatsoever. Pristine snow, stretched either side of them.

They turned left and now were enjoying the walk; with the sun on the snow it was warm. Bob kicked his way through the snow making long tracks. Mini snowballs cascaded across the flat top of the fallen snow. Choosing to try and distract them, Wee Renee told them a tale about a woman who had not had the use of her bowels for ten years, which doctors had given up on. She was healed by a Reiki practitioner in four weeks. Wee Renee also said she was witness to them healing a blind lady. She reached into her coat, and out of her sweater pulled a chunk of brown rock, on a piece of cord.

'What's that?' asked Bob fascinated.

'Petrified wood, lad.'

'What does that do?'

'It calms fears and gives me clear thoughts.'

'Wow, you are the calmest person in a crisis, I have ever met. It's bloody good stuff!' said Bob very impressed. A few of them laughed including Wee Renee.

'Aye lad. Some things that are weird, are wonderful, not terrible. But it just shows you, there is more than meets the eye about this world. We are just starting to work that out, aren't we, eh?'

By now it was around ten o'clock. When they got close to the edge of the village, Sue was the first to notice it. At first she thought it was her eyes and she couldn't work out what she was looking at. She rubbed them, the sun on the snow was blinding, and tried to focus in on the white. What it looked like was an enormous amount of snow. As the road rose naturally out of Friarmere towards the hills, they were automatically looking upbank. It just seemed to go very much higher upwards, in a short distance. Bob saw his mother trying to focus on what was before them and he followed her gaze.

'Is it a ski slope?' Bob asked, his mouth lifted up one side in confusion.

They all stared towards it. With no shadows or colours, it looked so strange. The group were dumbfounded. Pat caught up with the group, quite breathless. She set her feet widely apart and examined the mystery from top to bottom.

'Well, flap me sideways. It's a wall. They have built a bloody wall.' Pat said incredulously.

They moved a little closer. Now they had been told what it was, they could see it. It was like a Magic Eye Painting. They could see it had some kind of framework inside, covered in snow. The framework was across the road and the snow had been deliberately piled, to cover any gaps. Then lucky for the vampires, the weather had worked for them, and huge drifts sloped up the sides of the structure. It had a strange flat top though.

'What is that inside?' Freddie asked in wonder. They regarded the huge wall. There was something familiar that they couldn't quite put their fingers on. Freddie had a sudden thought. He turned around to the others.

'Bob, Danny, Andy? Throw some snowballs at the top of the structure.' The three of them started to make snowballs and pelt them at the wall. Laura and Tony joined in. This was the most fun they had had for weeks. Then, a chunk of snow cracked and broke from the rest, but did not fall. They all aimed for that spot. Soon a couple of them hit near the spot and knocked the chunk of snow down, which dropped down six feet, joining the drift beneath it. Underneath it was bright red.

'It's a double decker bus!' they all exclaimed. Indeed, now they could see how they had done it. A double decker bus had been completely parked crossways on the road and snow piled up at the sides and the front of it. The snow had fallen since, and drifted, making a wall over twenty feet high, with absolutely no way around it. The drifts meant that the wall was about thirty feet thick.

They gazed, stunned and feeling beaten. This small group of eleven people, against a horde of intelligent monsters. They felt so small. The size of this wall, represented the size of their problem. The friends were stuck here.

'Eh, never mind that way,' Freddie said, 'There are more ways than that to get out of this village. We will just go in the opposite direction. We won't go towards Manchester, we will go towards Yorkshire.' He kept his voice light, not wanting them to hear the worry in his voice.

'Not to be negative,' said Gary, 'But do you think they will have only blocked this way out?'

'We will have to check. What are we supposed to do?' Freddie replied, and wanted the women to not panic, especially Liz. 'Just try this way and then give up?'

'No, don't get me wrong, Freddie, I agree with you,' said Gary, 'They are always one step ahead of us. So, I think we have to prepare ourselves and start thinking outside the box.'

It took them about two hours to get to the other side of the village, through the snow. In the summer it was a half hour walk. On the Yorkshire side of the village there was a viaduct bridge. Again, a double decker bus had been carefully parked underneath. This and the drifting snow had helped make this into a solid wall, even higher than the other one.

Liz started crying and said that she was getting tired. She did look dark under her eyes and her rosy cheeks had disappeared. So had the sun, with their good moods. It was just a plain cold day now.

'Shall we go back to the band room, to have a rest and a think?' Andy pleaded.

'As much as I am sympathising with you Liz, I think that would be very silly. What is going to happen tomorrow? We will have less food. And will probably have to make a stand in the band room against a lot more vampires than last night. You know how much you wanted to get out this morning. Imagine feeling worse tonight. We will still have to find a way out, we can't get through them walls,' Wee Renee said gently, 'now we are out here, let's just try and go for it.'

They all agreed, including, reluctantly Liz and Andy. Downhearted and wracking their brains for ideas, they started to walk back towards the centre of the village. When they had walked for about half an hour, they went over the rise that took them to the lowest part of the village, which was its core. They could see a man standing in the middle of the road looking towards them. Just standing alone, in the middle of the empty road, looking towards them. It was obvious he was waiting for them and they all pulled out their weapons ready for another fight.

'Are you ready?' Gary asked them as they trudged to their fate.

'Wait a minute,' Wee Renee reasoned, 'It can't be a vampire because he's out in the daylight. It must be a friend, someone wanting to join our group. Needing our help. Safety in numbers and all that.'

'Not necessarily,' said Liz, sadly, 'It might be someone like me.' Instantly they knew she was right about this. They again wondered what they would have to deal with now. This one wasn't going to be easy. When they were about a hundred feet away, their eyes stinging with the cold, a couple of them recognised who it was. Freddie was the first to name him.

'It's Michael Thompson!'

As they got closer, he smiled at them. Some of them looked around at the sides of the road to see if there was some kind of half vampire ambush about to occur. But there was not one other person there, just Michael. They kept around twenty feet away from him.

'Afternoon,' he said genially, 'Out for a nice stroll are you? On a little band outing, and not invited me?'

'Judas!' spat Liz. He laughed loudly before answering her. He was the most confident they had ever seen him. Michael had a load of new friends, part of a powerful gang. Hanging around with a pack of vampires meant he could act how he liked.

'Yes I am a Judas. But it is better like this than how I was, and how you are still. Who is in a better position here? You or me? I can assure you *I* aren't at the bottom of this food chain.'

'What do you want?' asked Gary

'Yeah just get it over with,' said Danny angrily.

'Just to tell you, that it is no use trying to get out of this village. We will find you in due course. No-one here is getting out alive. You are not fetching help and you won't be saving anyone. So I just thought as a friend or an ex- friend, I would put you in the picture.'

'All right then,' shouted Freddie, 'You can bugger off now back up to The Grange. I suppose that's where all the monsters are?'

'Yes, that is exactly where I am going, and you can go back to the band room. Tonight, me and The Master will be outside watching you once again, laughing.'

'You've said your piece. Sling your hook, back to your Master. And keep away from the band room. You don't belong there,' Wee Renee, poked her finger at him, with every word.

'We will see you later. Count on it,' he laughed and began to walk away up the hill. He carried on laughing loudly, obviously put on for their benefit.

'Nothing he said was funny,' Bob commented, 'Why is he laughing like that?'

'Because he is an evil minion, of course, son,' Tony said smiling.

'He's a bag of shit, he is. Always was and always will be,' Pat sniffed. They watched him walk past the track to band room, where they had originally come from.

'Why did you tell him that we were going back there, Rene?

'So they would try there first,' Wee Renee solemnly looked at her friend.

'I get it, now Rene. It buys us some extra time tonight.' Wee Renee nodded and Pat hugged her, a very rare event. They walked to the place where Michael had been standing - he was already halfway up the street that led away from the centre of the village. It would take him straight up to the top of Friarmere and to The Grange.

'I am going to kill him,' said Liz flatly and they all looked at her and said nothing.

Freddie looked to the left of him and saw that the pub was open. He could see through the window from where they stood, it was empty. The fire glowed red through the window, so inviting.

'Come on,' he said, rubbing his hands and making his way towards the door, without waiting to their comments. 'Let's make a plan. In here! Come on.' He said insistently. It seemed a brilliant idea and they all went in, and were glad to get in and relax.

The barmaid sat on a stool behind the bar. She was reading a book about wolves, that she had borrowed from the library. When she heard the footsteps, her eyes darted to the door, and she held her breath, ready for danger.

'Oh, thank heavens, normal people,' she said, letting her breath out, her shoulders relaxing, 'I can't believe it, you are all fine!' She was visibly happy to see them. They all congregated in front of the bar, smiling back at her.

'What are you even doing open?' Freddie exclaimed.

'I thought some people might need a place to come. I will be shut at dark and these are massive doors. They won't get in. I am quite safe in the day. I will put a light on upstairs tonight, but I am off to my friend's house. Safety in numbers, you know.'

'Well I am glad you did. Do you know that they've blocked off the main road either side through the village?'

'I know. I suspect that they are the ones that have taken the phones out as well.'

'Yes that isn't the snow, I imagine,' said Tony.

'What can I get for you lot?'

'Mmm....we don't have much money.' Gary muttered, embarrassed.

'I wouldn't take any of your money. And I don't have everything from the usual menu. Today this pub is for the community. It is a house after all, a public house. Go sit down by the fire, I'll come over.'

Happy to do just that, they all sat down in their usual places. She came from behind the bar, with a pen and pencil.

'I can maybe rustle you up some hot soup with some bread? Would you like that?' It was just what they needed. 'What do you want to drink, something hot? Hot chocolate for you Bob?'

'Yes please,' he said at once. His eyes lit up.

'For everyone else? Tea, coffee, beer, whisky?' Everyone asked if it was okay, if they had hot chocolate too. Wee Renee asked if it was okay if she had *a wee dram of whisky* to settle her nerves, and a hot chocolate. The barmaid laughed and said, 'Of course.' She went off into the kitchen and they all heard her clattering about in there. In between they could hear the crack and snap of the logs, on the fire. If only they could pause this moment.

'We can't be here too long,' Wee Renee informed them, bursting their bubble, 'It is too easy to get comfy here. Warming our toes, as the hours tick by, whilst he sharpens his knives up at The Grange.'

'I know,' Gary said, nodding.

'His knives? He doesn't need them. Don't you mean his teeth.' Liz said.

'Aye. His dirty infectious teeth.' Wee Renee replied.

'Maybe we could hole up in one of our own houses,' offered Sue.

'I don't think it would take them long to find us, that way,' said Danny.

'Besides that, Ernie and Lynn know where we all live, they have all our addresses for the registration cards. Think about it too, these houses around here have big picture windows that would easily be smashed. They are low and the vampires could just walk through them. We would be eaten up in a couple of days,' Freddie informed them.

'Okay,' said Bob, 'I know this is probably a bad idea and you will think I am a very silly boy for saying it but what if we go along the top road by Lazy Farm?'

'That means going past The Grange,' said Liz, quite horrified.

'It means going right through the middle of the Melden Triangle. All the wee beasties could get us out in the open, I need to make that clear. Think of my tinsel triangle. Just picture it!'

'Bloody hell, Wee Renee, as if we haven't got enough on our plates, we have to think of your tinsel triangle. Anyway back to the plan, Bob.'

'Sorry Wee Renee, that is the only way out now, but maybe if we can get past and they are somewhere else or we are really careful then we can manage it.'

'You know wherever we go, we are leaving footprints,' Laura added.

'And that Liz is exhausted!' said Andy'

'I have an idea about that as well,' said Bob, 'We could go up to our house. I have a sledge we could put Liz on, then we could all take turns pulling hair along.' They all thought this was a revelation.

'That is not as stupid an idea as you think, son,' Tony said pleased.

'I didn't think it was a stupid idea,' said Sue crossly.

'I think that is a bloody brilliant idea,' commented Pat, 'You don't have more than one, do you?

'We have three actually?'

'What do you need three for?' asked Freddie.

'Because we all go out on one. We all go up to the farmer's top field, and come down on our sledges.'

'I get it now, so we could have up to three sledges. One with Liz on, and two with…..maybe provisions on!'

'What I am thinking as well,' said Sue excitedly, 'Is that if we pull the sledges at the back, then it might cover-up footprints, as we drag it over them.'

'It would cover them but it is still a track. They will probably still know, but maybe they won't be able to see how many of us there are,' said Gary.

'Yes that's a good idea,' Wee Renee clapped her hands.

'Can I just bring us down to earth?' Laura shook her head, 'We have nowhere to go tonight. The band room is definitely out of bounds and they know we also meet here. So we only have about three hours of daylight left.'

'I know what we can do!' shouted up Bob, 'The sledging! The farmer's top field? We can go through the estate, using the public footpath, cut through Lazy Farm. And go nowhere near The Grange!' They were ecstatic.

The barmaid returned with the first tray of soup and rolls. She came back again with another tray. Then the hot chocolates. She then went around the back of the bar and came back with five separate measures of whisky. Wee Renee picked her glass up, flicked the glass back at her lips and knocked her *wee dram* back. The waitress asked if she was welcome to sit with them and they were very happy that she did. She sat down with them.

'Do you fancy coming with us?' Freddie asked.

'We're going up the public footpath, up through the farm. Escaping,' Bob told her.

She looked shocked and rushed back to the bar, picking up her book. She turned it around. 'Wolves?' Bob whispered.

'I got it from the library after Tommy was in. It's not as silly as you think. Some people had them in private zoos. They are here in England. Packs have escaped in the past! Now they are running wild around Tommy's farm!' She looked at them all, wide eyed, 'I will stay here and hold the fort. Someone else might want to use the pub this afternoon or tomorrow. I am still holding out for good outcome.'

The group ate their soup and drank their hot chocolate whilst they went over the plan. They would walk up to Sue and Tony's house, and get the sledges. Once they got them they could put Liz on one of them. They would fill the other sledges with drink and food that could be easily eaten. On top of this, blankets. Bob had had another idea, about where they could stay overnight and they thought that this was great, but they had not seen it themselves. He ensured them it would work.

Freddie loved this idea, as this road they would be taking, meant going over the tops of the Pennines. The first village they would get to would be Melden, and he could check on Brenda. They all knew that no matter what, this journey was going to take hours and hours and they needed some place to hide when it was dark, away from the vampires. Bob's idea, might just work.

29 - Sledge

After they had left the pub and attempted a brisk walk up the high street, which was now getting quite slippy, they were not relishing the uphill journey to Sue's house. The group arrived at Sue and Tony's house just after two, leaving less than one and a half hours of daylight left. On the way up, chatting, everyone had been assigned their own little jobs in Sue's house, as they needed to use the time they had left, very effectively.

They knew they were in for quite an uncomfortable night outdoors, so as Wee Renee lived just a little further on than Sue, they would be briefly calling at her house as well.

The women rushed into Sue's house, going through the food cupboards and bedding. Between Sue and Wee Renee, they could provide each of them with either a blanket, quilt or sleeping bag. These were to be lashed to a sledge or in a backpack. Wee Renee said she was going to fashion hers into a *wee walking cape* for herself. Bob's job was to sort the three sledges out and put them out onto the drive in the snow.

Sue had been very worried about her cats and had laid all of their dried food into several bowls. She estimated that, if need be, they could last about six weeks on that, as there were sacks full. She left the cat flap open, thinking that they could make an escape, if the vampires came to attack. Although not happy, that was the best she could do for them. She told them she would return.

Bob had run upstairs to pick up his Swiss Army Knife. Yesterday he had felt it was pretty small and useless against the vampires. He hadn't bothered to take it to the concert and was glad, as he might have lost it. Today it was going to come in pretty useful indeed.

The men went outside into the back garden, down the path to the shed and went through Tony's tools. Tony had found a new washing line, and taken down the current one. This was to be used later. Gary already had his tool belt on, which still contained a hammer. He took some nails from the shed and a couple of other items. Hooks, ground pegs and wire. Tony and Danny took the tarpaulins off all the garden furniture that had been covered up for the winter. They folded these as small as they could and put them in a backpack, which would be carried by Tony.

Liz got on to one of the sledges and felt very, very guilty. She didn't really want to catch anyone's eye, so stared at her knees. Food was packed around her in bags, then her blanket put on top of her. As she wasn't walking she would soon get cold, but with one of the quilts on her, she should be able to manage. Gary had found a bungee cord in the shed and he fastened it around Liz, the sledge and the quilt, to form a large oval parcel.

They moved off to their next stop. Liz skittering along at the back on the sledge. Bob and Wee Renee ran in, whilst the others waited outside. Wee Renee ran upstairs, taking all of her quilts. Bob, started taking the crosses off the walls. She picked up her last few cloves of garlic from the fridge, and locked the door.

Bob and Wee Renee shared the cloves and the crosses out between the group. Wee Renee was adamant that Bob was to wear one, which Sue agreed to. Even though they had rushed and couldn't have possibly done it any quicker, they were shocked to see that it was nearly four o'clock and that it would be dark in less than fifteen minutes.

They had just got out of Sue and Wee Renee's street, which led straight onto the road that ended up at The Grange. They turned left, which would take them up the hill and away from Friarmere. When the first signs of darkness were coming, they tried to walk as fast as they could. They were still undecided as to whether they would chance going past The Grange, even when they had waited for it to be empty, or away from the Grange, and up on the public footpath, through the field, where the wolves had eaten the flock of sheep.

They knew that not only the Grange at the bottom of the country lane would be extremely dangerous, but after last night knew that Christine's house at the top of the lane would also be a no-go area. They carried on walking up-bank and were not making much progress with the depth of the snow, up here was much deeper. The wind was picking up a little, making it more difficult to drag the three sledges behind them. Gary looked up into the sky and sniffed.

'I can smell snow coming.'

'That can be good and bad, for us,' commented Pat, 'We can only do our best in these conditions, whatever our best is.' Within fifteen minutes it was truly dark and they felt vulnerable on the street. From where they were, The Grange was still high enough to be seen above them, and so was Christine's house. Their eyes were trained on The Grange above them as they walked bravely upwards towards it.

Lights started to appear in The Grange windows, and then there were some definite figures moving around inside. Christine's house was still dark and looked unoccupied, but within a few seconds, they could see she had flung the door open, the shadow of her large figure looking out into the night. They all stopped walking and waited to see what was going to happen next.

'Hide,' said Gary quickly.

They ran down the drive of the next house that they could see. It looked dark and deserted, or maybe there was another one of those things lying in there. Looking left and right, up to the windows, in the bushes, the group ran around to the back of the house and into the garden. It was a patio luckily, no problems with soggy grass, but of course it was still deep with snow.

'Get that big tarp out of your bag, Tony, quick,' Gary said in a frantic whisper. They pulled their sledges into the centre, gathering around the edge, forming a circle. Wee Renee, gestured with her hand to signal them all to kneel down. Tony quickly opened up the tarpaulin, and pulled it over the group. All anyone could see from the outside was a big pile of garden furniture, protected for the winter. They were absolutely silent.

'I can see onto the road though this eyelet hole, I will tell you when it is clear. Don't speak until I do,' Tony whispered. For at least ten to fifteen minutes they heard absolutely nothing. It seemed a lot longer, but Wee Renee kept checking her watch and showing the others. It was getting quite warm under the tarpaulin, with their hot breath. They had also been walking off and on, for a few hours and were generally quite warm which, considering they were kneeling in a couple of feet of freezing snow, they were immensely pleased about.

The friends were about fifty feet from the street and Tony was a little worried that he would not hear them pass. He could only see this side of the road. If they walked on the other pavement, he wouldn't see them. *What if they came out when they either hadn't got there, or be waiting ages and lose time?* He was starting to panic. He felt like he had been here all night. Just as he was about to try and go and look up and down the street, he heard the voice of Michael Thompson.

'Most of you need to stay with us, tonight, you know where we are going. The Master does not care if a few of you need to get some energy on the way. I have noticed some of you have already had to peel off and get some light refreshments. I understand,' he laughed, 'Don't worry we aren't going to do anything for a couple of hours, so you can catch up with us,' he shouted. 'Plenty of time to let them stew in their own juice.'

Tony thought that it sounded like Norman wasn't there. So where was he?

Tony had to wait another five minutes for all their voices to pass, then another two for good measure.

'Wait here,' he whispered. He got out of the tarpaulin, still keeping low, and walked down the drive against the wall of the house. Gary looked around the corner. He looked left, he looked right. He could not see anybody from this position. It certainly looked like they had passed. Creeping a little further down the drive, being very careful he looked up towards The Grange. The lights were still on however, he could see no one coming down the road. He thought that they should make a run for it now. Hastily travelling to the back garden again he whispered.

'Right everyone, lets try and get a bit further along. They have gone.' Standing up and stretching, they threw off their disguise. Four people helped to quickly fold up the tarpaulin and stuff it back into Tony's bag. It all took two minutes.

Very warily, they dragged the sledges back down the drive, Tony checking before them. Gary went out onto the road looked up and down it, left to right and front to back. He beckoned with his hand saying *it is all clear* in a loud whisper. Taking their positions again, they started off back up the hill. This mass exodus of the vampires seemed to have decided their route for them. None of them felt like tackling wild dogs or wolves tonight.

After only about three minutes walking, they were passing a house that belonged to Mary, an old lady that was a very big fan of Friarmere Band. The light was on and they could see inside her living room. It looked inviting and cosy. Mary was just about to shut her curtains. She was smiling and they could see she was talking to someone else in the room that they could not see.

'Let's get Mary. She can go on another sledge,' said Sue quietly, 'We can't leave her.' Sue turned to go down her path. Wee Renee grabbed her arm fiercely and pulled her back behind the hedge. She put her finger over her lips and pointed to the window.

Mary's hands were on either curtain to pull them, still talking. Behind her off the sofa rose, Ernie and Lynn Cooper. As she drew her curtains, they were both only one step behind her. The curtains shut. Something pressed both curtains flat in the middle, onto the windows, there was pressure, then the curtain popped out of its curtain rings in two places. Wee Renee turned Sue towards her, her hands on either arm.

'No, don't think about it. It is too late to meddle there. I know this sounds selfish, but that is what you have got to do now. Think of your own family.' The Coopers were too busy attacking Mary to see the eleven people walking past her front window, and up the hill.

They had to walk for over an hour before they got to the top. Every minute seemed like an eternity and they thought at any time that they were going to be discovered.

Maurice had fought all of his compulsions not to go to the Civic Hall the previous night. He had wanted to be with the band and even wanted to fight on their side. The reality was that, in the presence of the other vampires and in the company of The Master, he would have had no choice but to fight against his friends and this was the last thing he wanted to do. He still had not killed and would continue to resist with all his might.

He knew his friends were in the gravest trouble. The night-time was here now and he wondered how many of his friends were left, being especially worried about his best friend Freddie. He opened his front door to look into the night and was astounded to see Diane walking down his road quite happily in an evening dress and bare feet through the snow. She came to a gradual stop at his garden gate. They observed each other for a long time, trying to read each other.

'That is a nice dress Di,' he said, just to break the tension.

'Yes, I got it from The Grange.'

'Oh. You aren't resisting any more then.'

'No, I didn't think I'd bother. Come and join us Maurice. Its going to be very lonely without all of them. Freddie and everyone. So you might as well stop fighting and be with people of your own kind.'

'No, Di,' he said sadly, shaking his head, 'I just can't,'

'That's a pity,' she replied flatly, dragging her finger across the snow on the wall between Maurice's and the next doors gate. She smiled, then covered the three steps to Maurice's next door neighbour's gate and started to walk up his path.

'What are you doing there?'

'Feeding on lovely, young, healthy flesh. Sounds good doesn't it? You don't even have far to go. I will start it off, help you out, like you helped me.'

He stared angrily at her.

'Come on Maurice,' she hissed angrily.

'No Diane, and please don't do that to my neighbour,' he said under his breath, not wanting his neighbour or anyone else normal in the street to hear.

'If it isn't him, it will be someone else. Maybe a child. They are so sweet and tasty, Maurice.' Maurice looked down at the snow for a moment in silence. She had put that thought in his mind and *by heck* it was tempting. He wished she hadn't said that, as he knew that they would be delicious to him. Diane thought he was going to change his mind after thinking about it. He couldn't let himself do it. But also felt impotent about tackling the larger group of vampires. Maurice looked at her and blinked slowly. He couldn't do anything about what she, The Master or any other vampire wanted to do. Maurice shut the door went and sat in his armchair, turned the television up and put his hands over his ears.

Just about the same time as Diane was having her evening meal, the gang finally reached the top of the lane and turned right, off the main road, to go across the top of the Pennines towards Lazy Farm and over into Yorkshire.

'We're well and truly in the Triangle now. Keep your eyes peeled.' Wee Renee said.

It had just started to snow and they were so thankful for the coverage it would give them. As Liz was facing backwards on the sledge, she was looking behind them down the lane at the junction between this and the road that led back down into Friarmere. Christine's house faced her, the other side of the junction, and The Grange further on.

They were about fifty feet from the junction, when all of a sudden the snow subsided as a snow cloud passed, and moonlight illuminated the lane. At the bottom, a man came out of the trees and started to wave at them. Liz screamed and they all turned around to see what was wrong. Their eyes followed her pointing finger and saw the man for themselves. It was Mark from their band who used to be a milkman a few days ago, now he was something else altogether. He waved at them and put his hands either side of his mouth to form a kind of megaphone.

'Cheerio!' he shouted and put his finger to his lips. He disappeared again.

'What was the meaning of that!' asked Freddie.

'He has seen us. Now the head vampire will know where we are. It isn't safe here. I want to go home, Andy.' Liz was panicking. Sue grabbed hold of Bob, feeling she had led him into terrible danger.

'Wait. Did anyone see him last night?' Wee Renee inquired.

'No, he definitely wasn't there. And if he knew we were here, why didn't he jump us? Why is he on his own, and not with the group?' asked Gary.

'He was doing a shush, with his finger on his lips... Do you know, I think he is on our side. Or has a soft spot for us at least,' Wee Renee said hopefully.

'Well, we will carry on. Time will tell whether he was a friend or foe. But I am inclined to agree with you, Wee Renee.'

'We can't do much else, now we are this far, can we? We're stuffed.' Pat grunted. Another cloud darkened the skies above them and the snow began to fall again.

When they got to the entrance to Lazy Farm where, just a couple of weeks ago, Michael Thompson had stood waiting for Stephen, they looked to the opposite side of the road from the farm. Where the public footpath, coming up from the village and through Lazy Farm, carried on.

'Up there,' said Bob. The group turned and began to file up the footpath. Gary went at the front. Liz got off her sledge, which now was quite light, just containing bedding and food. She pulled it behind her. The snow was not compacted at all, just like icing sugar, so Gary kicked it either way, although not long after this his legs were killing him. The footpath was only about four feet wide, so with the drifts of the snow from both walls, making a curve downwards, there was only room for them to walk single file. It was as quiet as the grave here and the trees were getting closer over the top of the path.

As they moved further up the path, the trees were getting thicker and soon they found themselves in a small wood. Soon the dark leafless trees met completely above them, which meant that there was less snow underneath, but also no starlight and moon to guide them. They carried on a little bit further, getting worried that soon they wouldn't be able to pull the sledges at all. Most of the snow here had just blown in and drifted, not fallen. Just as the covering had reduced so much that it was down to a only an inch in thickness, Bob pointed at the wall, a little further on.

'It's there!' he exclaimed. There was some white paint on the wall and indeed the dry stone walling had been removed a little, so you could step over into the moors on the left.

The trees were certainly very thick here, with a nearly complete roof above them of branches. There was patchy snow coverage, so they picked up the sledges and climbed over. Bob went ahead of them to show the way. Sue got worried when he got out of sight, then she heard him speak.

'Not far ahead, now. Come on everyone.' The rest of the group followed the path, his voice was very close. He waited until everyone was assembled. 'This is it. What do you think?'

Himself, Adam and a few of his friends had made this find. It had been here for many years with groups of kids discovering it every so often and thinking that they were the first.

'Welcome to my den.' It was completely snowless and covered with trees at the top in a canopy. It probably measured about twenty feet in a rough diameter and had a few stones, pebbles and grit on the floor, that kids had put there to make it less muddy over the years. It was sheltered, dry and much warmer, with only one way in or out.

'Wow!' beamed Gary, 'I used to come here and I had forgotten about it. I've probably not thought of this place for forty years,' he laughed, 'I remember bringing some of these rocks up. It's is a brilliant place, Bob!'

It had a strange feeling of home and safety about it. They just knew that everything would be fine here for the night. The first items to unpack were the tarpaulins, the hooks, the nails and the two washing lines. Tony, Gary and Danny lashed these quite high up to the corner trees and hung the tarpaulins over the ropes, so that they were sheltered once more. It had fashioned a kind of flat tent. They got a few tent pegs and fastened it down at the corners and another couple of areas. In other places the tent just flopped over. Bob found a few loose stones and anchored these down a bit. There was now one main entrance. With the trees behind them being so thick, there were only a few inches between them, they felt that only this entrance needed to be guarded.

Everything was dragged under the tarpaulin. The eleven of them got in and settled down inside. Bob had bought a wind up camping light. It was quite lovely in there. They got out their sandwiches and food. The only thing they would have loved was a hot drink, but the mood was light and hopeful. This is where they would stay until it got light. Hopefully out of the way and undiscovered. Gary peeked out, and could see near the path, a slight parting of the tree canopy, the odd feathery flake managed to flutter down. It was still snowing. Gary smiled, and hoped it would continue.

At about nine o'clock, The Master and the others gathered around the band room for the attack. The lights were off, which didn't mean anything as they could be hiding in the dark trying to trick them, but he could not smell anyone in there. He lifted his nose in the air, opened his mouth and stuck out his tongue slightly, his *children* doing the same. They were taking his lead, trying to learn from their master.

'What is this?' The Master turned full on towards Michael. His tone of voice and face was angry. 'You told me that they said they were coming back here.'

'That is what they told me. I am sorry Master. I can't help it if they are a bunch of liars.'

The Master stormed angrily over to the band room, out of their hiding place and sniffed the door and steps.

'They have not been here all day! Are you trying to double-cross me? Allowing them to escape!'

'No of course not, Master. They are somewhere, sneaking around in this village, hiding. I wouldn't be surprised if they are in the pub. Wherever they are, they are together, I know it.'

The vampires gazed at each other for explanation. This wasn't in their plans. All their excitement and the anticipation of lots of lovely food drained away from them. Their disappointment was obvious. The Master, still furious, but trying to keep a lid on it, regarded Michael, for a while. He was turned to one side of Michael, so he could only see one narrowed eye looking at him. Michael was breathing very fast, hoping that The Master would realise it wasn't his fault.

'We will check the pub,' The Master said, and instantly set off. He walked very quickly, with almost no effort. The other vampires easily kept up with him. This seemed to be their standard speed of walking. Michael however struggled to keep up. He would have to jog to keep up. However, in this snow, jogging was impossible. He kept falling and slipping and he was moving further and further away from the group.

'Stephen!' he shouted, 'Tell him, I'll be there as fast as I can.' Stephen heard him and grabbed his shoulder, pulling him along. Michael's feet made the odd connection with the ground but it really was Stephen pulling him to his destination. It really pinched on his shoulder as his jacket was twisted on his armpit, where Stephen had grabbed him, but he didn't complain.

The horde made their way to the pub. This gang totaled about fifty vampires. Because of their numbers and the fact that their Master was with them, they were not afraid of anyone and openly walked through the streets like an army. Who would stop them? The police? No, they were with them. A gang of musical vigilantes? Perhaps they would try. They were vastly outnumbered now. What could they do?

From a distance, The Master could see that the lights were off in the pub. The doors were locked and he could smell there had been no real fires in their chimney, for several hours. The Master did not feel hopeful but stuck out his tongue again, to sense what was there. 'There is no one in this building!' he seethed. Then he screamed loudly into the night and it was terrible.

'Find them!' he roared.

Luckily Michael was at the back of the group, with his head down. He was now in danger.

30 - Moors

It had been a calm and comfortable night for most of them. Whoever was on watch had Tony's gun, but it being so quiet, they only had to listen for the slightest twig to break to be alerted to danger. During Gary's watch, a long way away, he thought he heard a howl. Telling himself that it was probably the wind, when he didn't hear another one. He calmed back down. Then he heard another. And another. Within two minutes, there were constant howls.

Wee Renee looked up from her quilt at him. He stared at her. He held the gun tighter, swallowing hard. The only good thing was that they were so far away. She picked up her machete. They continued to fixate on each other until well after the howls stopped. The two of them didn't really sleep much for the rest of the night.

Pat and Wee Renee were on the last watch and woke the others at about 7.30am. It was still not light, but would be soon. Pat peeped out of the tarpaulin to see what the weather was holding for them and announced it was still lightly snowing. After a quick breakfast of sandwiches, they pulled their belongings back into their backpacks and sledges. Took down the tarpaulins and ropes, packing them carefully, before carrying all the paraphenalia out of the clearing. By this time it was light. They were warm and refreshed, but by the time they were over the stone wall and onto the path it was certainly colder.

They chattered as they ambled back down the public footpath. No need to be quiet in the daylight. At the bottom of the track, where it joined the road, Liz got back on the sledge. This was proving to be less of a hindrance, more of a necessity. It was very useful knowing she could constantly watch out from the rear of them.

They stood for a moment, admiring the snowy hills that they could see for miles either way. An ocean of white. The air was cool and tingly. Like sucking a mint.

'Shall we get off then?' asked Wee Renee. Without a word, the plodding began. After about ten minutes of walking in silence, Wee Renee said that they should sing Christmas Carols to keep their spirits up and pass the time. As all of them were music lovers or musicians they decided they would. Some of them were even putting some of the harmonies in.

Yesterday, they had done the majority of the walk upwards and now they were walking across the top of the Pennines. It was mainly flat over these ridges and soon they would actually be dropping down, and so most of the hard work was done. Andy was a little worried that when they were facing downwards that they would actually have to hold the sledges in front of them to stop them careering off down the bank. But they would have to cross that bridge when they came to it.

It was incredibly beautiful up here and peaceful, as if the rest of the world was perfect and there was nothing to worry about. They stopped for a small breather. As the snow was very light they looked down and behind them, over to the village of Friarmere, which was slightly behind them now and wondered when they would see it again. What kind of condition would it be in for them to go back to anyway? It was a sobering thought, that *they* were its last hope. The band was not going to let down the people who remained in Friarmere.

Gary thought that, if they kept their pace up, that they might be in Melden before dark. Freddie said that they could all go to *Our Doris's* house where Brenda was. Wherever anyone else decided to go, he was going there to find Brenda. He knew they would all be welcome there too. Laura's uncle was Chairman of Melden Band and she knew where he kept his key. If they needed somewhere to go in desperation she knew that they could get in there, at least. But Melden bandroom had nowhere near the comfort that Friarmere bandroom had. Plus, even their bandroom did not offer beds, a bathroom and a full kitchen, like *Our Doris's* house would. Not to mention a television, telephone and other methods of communication.

They walked on until Midday. The snow stopped again and they had a very good view. They sat on a wall and shared out the last of their food. Wee Renee took none as she said she knew she would get a *stitch* in her ribs, if she did.

'We could almost be in the Swiss Alps, couldn't we?' She said.

'It's very picturesque. I've never been this far up here in the snow.' Freddie stated.

'The Swiss Alps?' Liz said thoughtfully. 'I wonder if that is what attracted him to this area?'

'Maybe,' Freddie replied, 'or our isolation.'

'Or perhaps it was all the hot babes in Friarmere Band. I mean, he is still after Me and Rene.' Pat chuckled.

'I reckon he's a bit kinky then?' Freddie giggled, winking at Pat. She burst out laughing, whacking him on the back.

'I'll give you that one, Freddie, you bugger.'

The stone county marker was set into the wall, carved over a hundred years ago. A line dividing the red and the white rose counties. Bob sat above the marker, one foot either side, happily eating the last of the braun sandwiches. He looked to the right over to Lancashire and Friarmere and then left into Yorkshire and Melden. The future.

Gary only allowed fifteen minutes break. It would be dark in less than four hours. They gathered themselves together, took their positions and set off. After about half an hour they started to drop down. Every step was much easier and they could tell that, at this pace, they were going to make it before dark. They had escaped. Norman Morgan couldn't touch them again. They were home free.

What a strange bunch they looked. Dressed up for the weather with the three sledges being held at the front of them now, so they didn't do what sledges were actually designed for. Liz had gotten off hers, so they only had the diminished provisions and blankets on there.

Tony was wearing his cowboy hat. Freddie wore his tweed cap, with a red scarf tied over it, to keep his ears warm. Gary had his omnipresent baseball cap on, but with a pair of ear warmers that Sue had offered him, over the top. They were fluffy and pink, with the legend, *Girls Just Wanna Have Fun* embroidered on the band. He kept telling himself, he must remember to take them off as soon as they got to Melden. Sue herself, was wearing her sequined beret, which she loved. Laura had on a purple fleece snood. Danny had the plainest black hat woolen hat over his head.

Pat was the tallest, as she was wearing snow boots with very thick soles and a large Russian fur hat. Beside Pat, there was someone quite small, walking with a pink flowery continental quilt wrapped around her. Just the blue bobble from her hat could be seen popping out the top. She was singing *Deck The Halls* in an unbelievably loud, shrill voice.

They started seeing the odd house from a distance. They were getting closer. In the daytime, this place was eerie, bleak and beautiful. But it was still dangerous. There were miles of moorland, with nothing, no markers so they could easily get lost. There were sheer drops, underground pools and caves. They were very lucky to have each other. One or two people on their own up here would be very vulnerable.

They had another quick stop. They were getting tired now. Three of them were over sixty years old and not made for wild camp outs, hikes and adventures in the snow. As soon as they stopped, everyone started to get cold again. Liz was getting exhausted and Andy said she had to get back on the sledge. Wee Renee had some pear drops and they all had a couple and set off.

Liz got under about three quilts. Between herself and the sledge, was a sleeping bag. She was getting colder. Knowing that she was generating hardly any heat for the quilts to keep in, she had a decision to make. Should she, exhausted, get up and walk. Or stay and try and keep warm. The violent shivers and teeth chattering decided for her. She had been on there around her about half an hour. She said she was rested now, she got off and walked for a while to get warm. But she was far from it. After five minutes she was exhausted again, so had to sit back on the sledge. She would carry on this vicious circle for the rest of the journey. Liz wanted a hot drink to put heat inside her to help her generate it herself. She knew what she actually needed, what her body was screaming for, was meat. That was never going to happen.

They started to drop down further. It was just after two. Now, they thought that they might just make it after dark. It was further than they thought or they were taking longer than they had estimated. Tiredness was really setting in. Laura wondered how many calories she had burned over the last couple of days. The mood was getting more serious. They didn't sing anymore, or speak. Saving their breath and strength. They were thirsty and had finished all their sandwiches at the last stop. Fear looked at them from afar, it was in the distance but inched closer every minute as the day clicked on towards its close. They had to get there soon. Surely, now that they were well away from Friarmere, there was no danger.

The Master woke at three. An hour before everyone else. Again he sat in the dark. He had been trying to smell the group. He wanted, no needed to smell them, even faintly. To know that they were still in this village, hiding out, thinking that they could conquer him. He had made sure the roads were blocked off. The Master did not want outside interference with this battle at the moment. This war could be won quite easily and he did not want the odds stacked against him at the moment. The time would come when he was ready for the outside world but it wasn't yet.

When it was nearly dark he woke some of the others. Ones that would each have a group of less experienced vampires with them. He did not have to say what the primary objective was. They had tried several residences until just before daylight. He had stressed that he would not be giving up until he found them. Opening his front door, he sensed the first threads of night with his tongue. It took about five minutes for him to do this. Turning this way and that. The others waited, watching him.

'I cannot sense them. They must have done a really good job of hiding themselves. Go into every house in this village, if they are not there use your judgement on which to turn and which I would like to eat. They can be brought back here, I can hold them as I have made preparations. I also have a couple of other facilities elsewhere.'

When all the other vampires were awake he told them that they could not feed until the band were found. He put them in groups of ten, each had a leader, which they must obey as if it was The Master. He kept some of them to go with him. Some were with him in an advisory capacity.

The Master's group would be going to the houses of all the band that they had not already checked. Then the pub again and the bandroom just in case they had doubled back on them. Next, any other public buildings that the vampires could think of. The Master had not spoken to Michael since last night. Now he turned to him, his eyes bored right through him.

'What do you think they have done? You say you know them better than anyone.'

'I would say bandroom or pub again,' Michael shrugged, 'They are creatures of habit our Friarmere Band. All they like doing is banding and drinking and that is all they have in their life. If they have been going somewhere else, well, I have never heard of it.'

'Have you ever thought that maybe they didn't invite you because they didn't like you.'

'No, I have never thought of that, and I don't think it's a possibility. I do well in this village, I am well respected.'

'Hmmmmm....' interjected The Master. Michael could see what was starting to run through his mind and didn't like it. Michael was becoming a liability and was no longer useful to him. His palms were dripping with sweat. Michael thought fast.

'I know all the buildings, where public could gather. There is the garden centre, a couple of Churches, two schools and The Museum. I don't know of anywhere else, only a couple of other pubs and they never go in those ones, they don't like the beer. There's a few ideas for you Master. They have got to be in the village, somewhere haven't they. You can depend on me Master.'

The Master looked unconvinced but went with the plan anyway. He didn't have any better ideas.

'Right. I have another job for you later. Where you will be useful to me and my children.'

Michael let out a breath he hadn't realised he was holding. He would live another day. At least.

The vampire pack travelled as a whole from The Grange until they got to the main street. The Master signalled them to split into their groups and search Friarmere. They trickled outwards from this central point, spreading death and fear. Down the streets, they went, sniffing, tasting, looking for tracks. They covered the park, the canal, the public footpath, until it went onto the farmers land. They had never been here and the vampires could smell that.

The scourge went into each property, occasionally finding the odd person that was in a public building with some of their family. Sorting them. Again the pub was shut and locked and so was the bandroom. They could just about see their own tracks from last night and nothing else.

The Master had a fresh idea that they might be hiding out with someone who was supposed to be a spy for him, and that person was Maurice. There was only Maurice and Mark that had not joined his throng out of all the vampires.

The Master thought Maurice was a lonely old man that regretted his turning. He had a strong will to keep himself partly human and he was achieving this. The Master had to admit, he was impressive in his efforts.

As for Mark, he was just a maverick and seemed to like doing his own thing. A lone-hunter. He had made children before that acted like this, so he was not the first. Whereas The Master wasn't quite bothered about this, he also thought that Mark did not have his protection in the group. So for Mark's safety, the safety of one of his new children, it would be better if Mark ran with the pack, so to speak.

Needless to say, he would visit Maurice's and Mark's house, to check for the group. They came to Mark's first, who was not at home. *He must be out on the hunt*. The group had not been at Mark's. He suspected Mark might have been quite a loner before, as this house only smelled of Mark. The Master could only smell Wayne here on the entrance.

Maurice however, was at home quite clearly as the television was on loudly and the lights were on.

Maurice was watching a television documentary about whales. The Master walked up his path and with one swift movement on Maurice's door lock, opened his door. Maurice jumped up out of his chair, startled as to who it was, and became even more worried when he saw it was The Master. *I am in for it,* he thought.

'Have you seen them?' The Master asked sternly.

'Who?'

'Your friends. Your musical friends.'

'I haven't seen any of the others for a few days now. Have you lost them?' Maurice asked bemused.

'I seem to have done,' The Master replied sarcastically. Maurice looked down at his carpet for a few seconds. He didn't really know how to help.

'I am watching this documentary about whales. It's very good, but I had to dangle out of the window and knock the snow off my aerial with a yard brush,' he laughed. The Master didn't find it funny.

'Hmmmm…very interesting, Maurice. Enjoy it.' Maurice grinned at him, thinking he had successfully changed the subject. The Master moved from the door and stood in between Maurice and the television. He glowered hotly at Maurice. His nostrils flared and he bared his teeth. Maurice sunk lower in his armchair. He wished his good vision hadn't come back as he didn't want to see this. It wasn't the first time either in the last couple of days that he wished he was deaf too.

'Do not even think of harbouring one of them. I can smell there is no one here but this does not mean there won't be in the future. You know what will happen if you do.'

'I think I probably do,' said Maurice quietly, trying to focus on the carpet again, 'Do you want to stop for a drink or anything?'

'No, I have to find them tonight, and as I can't depend on you for any help, I can't waste time.'

'Right, okay I'll see you out then.' He smiled like The Master was his best friend in the world and walked him to the door, then shut it behind him.

He slumped against the back of the door. That had been terribly tense and had taken a lot out of him. One thing he knew for certain was that vampires could still feel fear. He hoped that they had got away. *Please let them be safe.* Deep in thought, he wandered back to his chair and sat down. *That could have gone a lot worse,* he thought, and carried on watching the documentary about whales. He was not worried at all about having to resist human flesh for the foreseeable future. Over the last few weeks he had emptied his freezer of everything else and it was full to the top with liver. He would manage all winter, if that is what it took.

The snow started to get thicker. The Master could no longer smell them, whatsoever and there were no footprints to follow. He did not know where they were and could not guess. He had a tiny niggling thought that his plan might come unstuck.

The Master would find them, and he could outlast them in their mortal bodies. Him and his children would be out looking again every night until he found them. They had got to surface at some point. He was furious.

To make him feel better tonight, he wanted to take his anger out on someone and unfortunately that someone was going to be Michael Thompson. It annoyed Norman that Michael was quite nonplussed about it all and thought losing them didn't matter because there are so many other souls in Friarmere. He beckoned him over and Michael strolled towards him, a cheerful smile on his face.

'You are no further help to me really, are you Michael?'

'At this stage, I have to be honest and say, I have no idea where they are. I cannot think of anywhere else and aren't prepared to bullshit you.' Norman was quite shocked at Michael's honesty. It diffused some of his anger. Micheal was so honest because he had been drinking whisky most of the night, out of his hip flask. He was trying to numb everything away and had done a pretty good job.

'What else can you do, Michael?' Norman looked down his nose at Michael who rubbed his chin and chuckled. He thought he would go for it.

'I thought it was about time that I become the same as you. I have been a good servant and served my time. Other people have been turned straightaway, whether they like it or not and I know I will like it. So, can we get on with it?'

The Master laughed loudly. It was not a good laugh.

'Turn you? I will never turn you. You will stay here in this mortal body and die tortured. You will grow old and see us stay young. Enjoy watching all this fun, when you can't take part. I can stop you being with Kate or anyone else.'

'Master, I have served my time. I have done everything for you. I have put myself in danger for you. I need you to do this,' Michael pleaded.

'To be honest Michael, you aren't any use to me as a human or a vampire. I would keep your mouth shut or else you will end up neither one, very quickly. For the moment I will keep you as a human. I do not have one of those to walk in the daytime at the moment. Whilst you still can do that, you are of the smallest use to me.'

Norman was imperious, condescending and really going for the jugular, for once with words.

'I also find you and your brother slightly amusing, if managed carefully. We all laugh about you, behind your backs. The way you mess everything up, however hard you try, it can be a tonic here as it can get quite solomn in this house, so that is good. We all love a bit of gossip. At least that is something that is going to keep you alive you tiresome little man.'

Michael certainly had sobered up a lot. Never had he felt so worthless and there were plenty of times that he had, thoughout his life. Norman observed the others over Michael's shoulder, and to them he said,

'Keep looking. You can now feed if you would like to go and find yourself some tasty morsels. I know I will be.'

Just like that, he walked away from Michael who stood alone in the middle of the village. He felt alone and was alone. This was the moment he knew that he had picked the wrong side. But it was, what it was. It was okay. He would find someone else in time. A friend, or group of friends or a lover. He knew that now he was a man far stronger than he had been before. With a sigh he made his way alone back up to The Grange. Where he would cook his own meal, and eat it in solitude.

31 - Hairy

They had just seen the first road sign for Melden, as darkness hit them. Hoping that, even with all of them out in the dark, The Master would have to come a long way to get them. By the time he had worked out where they were, they should have arrived somewhere safe by then, perhaps already starting to get help from the police. It was the elephant in the room. No one spoke but their pace quickened, even though they were exhausted.

Yorkshire stretched before the friends. Its enormity relaxed them as they got closer to their destination step by step. They would find help here, lots of help. No more fighting and struggling for them. Then they could go home and everything would be fine by Christmas.

Freddie knew the way to his sister-in-law's house even with his eyes closed, so they were taking his lead. The first street light they got to signaled the end of the moors and they were so glad for it. Gary and Wee Renee still couldn't forget those howls. They wouldn't for a long time.

The snow was just as bad here. It didn't look like any cars or public transport were running. Which was a little concerning, as a fleet of policeman would still take many hours to walk over the moors to Friarmere. There were quite a few abandoned cars, and an empty council truck, left willy nilly across, what used to be the road. As the snow came high up their boots, knee-deep in many places, they guessed that over here was worse. It was different snow. Less powdery and drifting, perfect snowman-snow. Luckily, the depth and the fact it stuck fast to their trousers, did not trouble them so much as they were walking downbank.

They stomped through it - crossing the threshold into Melden felt like frantic steps to salvation. The outskirts behind them they were making good time. Just before five o'clock they were walking through the main street of the village. The shops were closed. The night was fine and they could see down the length of the village. Not a single person was about, apart from them. Laura remarked that a lot of people would not be using the chip shop or anything like that in this kind of weather, plus some people would not have been able to get to work. Lies we tell ourselves to feel better.

Bob felt it was good to be out of Friarmere and here in comforting safety. They all relaxed a little, Gary reminding them to make sure that all their weapons were hidden. Sue said that if they were seen they would look very odd anyway. People in quilts, strange hats and dragging three sledges, one that held a woman. Freddie said she had a point. Even in Yorkshire, they probably looked weird.

Wee Renee had the idea that they could pretend that they were carol singers. Cries of *oh no please, not more carols* came back to her. They were so sick of singing that they thought they could not muster up even a small rendition of *Jingle Bells*. But never put off, Wee Renee sang on her own loudly, to make up for the others.

Doris lived through the other side of the Melden unfortunately, so it was probably the longest trek that they could have had from Friarmere. She lived in a cul-de-sac of very nice detached houses. All the gardens were beautifully manicured even in the winter. Her husband, a successful solicitor had sadly passed away about ten years ago. Since then Doris's companion had been a fluffy westie dog and no one else.

She had two other sisters in Melden alongside Brenda, who was only over the hill with Freddie. Doris hadn't ever had children, Freddie didn't know why, and didn't like to ask. He had liked Ken, Doris' husband. Himself and Brenda had socialised a lot with the two of them. Often taking their holidays with them. He didn't have as much to do with Brenda's younger sisters. He thought one was boring and one was stuck-up. They both had daughter's who were grown up now and lived in the village.

As they turned into Doris' street, they saw that the lights were on but the curtains were shut, a good sign. Filing up the street, looking either way, as they had become accustomed to do, checking whether they were being watched. They knocked on the door and instantly heard a dog barking. Next, a thin wavering voice.

'Who is it?'

'Brenda, is that you?' Freddie boomed out happily. The door opened immediately and Brenda stood the other side, grabbing hold of Freddie, giving him the most enormous hug. Over his shoulder she noticed the other ten people, what a ragtag group they were.

'Come in, you are welcome. Everyone, come in, quickly, quickly, out of the cold.' As they started up the steps and she said, 'Wait a sec!' and laid down a newspaper all over the carpet. They happily stepped into Doris's living room as, counting Brenda, there were twelve people, which was way too many for Doris' hallway.

'Don't tell me you have walked all the way over here?' Brenda asked. They nodded back at her. She took a moment to appreciate the full state of the group. Of course, she knew each one from the band, and they knew her. She had never seen them look so thin, tired and scared. Each one looked older. Their eyes

had changed. She could see hardness and also melancholy in them. Their tale would come. But first she needed to look after this group.

'Thank you for looking after my Freddie. I have been so worried.'

'We all looked after each other, Brenda,' Freddie replied wearily.

'Right, take your coats off, you're in now,' she wafted her hand towards them, as if to hurry them along.

'I will put the kettle on and get some dinner on the stove and then you can tell me what in hell's name has gone on.'

She started on her way to the kitchen. Used to only dealing with Freddie and him always obeying her word on asking.

'Friarmere isn't safe,' Pat said exhaling, 'That's the sum of it.' Brenda turned around slowly to face them all.

'Neither is Melden.' They looked at her in astonishment. Liz gently started to shake her head, she could hear a whining noise in her ear. 'It's like something out of your nightmares, isn't it?' Brenda said knowingly.

'Yes, Brenda. Wee vampires. Who would have thought it in our lifetime?' said Wee Renee

Brenda looked at her and cocked her head.

'If it is, they are very hairy ones!' The group stared in silence, they couldn't understand what she was saying. What was she getting at?

'What do you mean?' asked Gary.

'We have monsters roaming the streets. Wolves. They *are* covered in hair, aren't they?' The group went silent. The wolves were here. They must have come to get the sheep over the moors, but they were roaming the streets of Melden! Brenda had just said it.

'Yes they only come out at night so they are definitely nocturnal. But they howl, it goes right through me. My sisters have seen them too. They have just about been able to come back and forth in the daytime to bring shopping.'

'At least there are ways we can cope with them,' said Gary happily.

'Yes, they're not wee supernatural creatures. Just flesh and blood, like us,' reassured Wee Renee.

'Why haven't you called the police about them, or the council?' asked Sue.

'There is no phone service of any kind. And they have some people with them who, I don't know... are walking them I suppose, but they have no leads. The people look a bit threatening actually. So we are just hoping it stops.'

'How is Our Doris?' Freddie asked, concerned.

'She is not well, and very weak. Anyway, I have still not given you anything to eat or drink.' She bustled off into the kitchen. When she was out of earshot, Liz beckoned them all towards her.

'I think it is something to do with the vampires in Friarmere. I can feel it in my bones. I can't explain, but something isn't right,' Liz whispered.

'By the way, everyone calls Doris, *Our Doris*. They have since she was little. I thought I would tell you. She will expect you to do it as well. You'll get used to it,' Freddie advised.

'How weird,' said Wee Renee.

Tony gestured at Wee Renee with his thumb and laughed. Pat looked at him, gimlet eyed.

The clattering in the kitchen stopped and Brenda popped her head out of the doorway.

'Aren't you all sitting down? Get comfy.' They started to settle in various seats. Bob, flopping down onto the floor. Then Brenda started shouting from the kitchen.

'I suppose, from what Our Doris told me, that it started the night of this party.' They all started to tense up and regarded each other. Brenda carried on shouting through. 'It was a new lady in the village that hosted it and Our Doris got invited. Melden Brass Band were there. Our Doris said she had a lovely time, with the food and dancing, but afterwards everyone had a weird case of food poisoning. In fact this lady, is the one with the wolves, some of the band hang around with her now, but she looks mad to me. Crackers. I mean, who keeps wolves as pets?'

They all caught their breath in their throats, their mouths went dry and Liz felt a pounding in her temples.

'Oh bloody hell Brenda!' shouted Freddie.

THE END

Until Book 2

19206665R00230

Printed in Poland
by Amazon Fulfillment
Poland Sp. z o.o., Wrocław